Books by Rita Mae Brown

THE HAND THAT CRADLES THE ROCK
SONGS TO A HANDSOME WOMAN
THE PLAIN BROWN RAPPER
RUBYFRUIT JUNGLE
IN HER DAY
SIX OF ONE
SOUTHERN DISCOMFORT
SUDDEN DEATH
HIGH HEARTS
STARTING FROM SCRATCH: A DIFFERENT KIND
OF WRITERS' MANUAL
BINGO
VENUS ENVY
DOLLEY: A NOVEL OF DOLLEY MADISON IN LOVE
AND IN WAR
RIDING SHOTGUN
RITA WILL: A MEMOIR OF A LITERARY
RABBLE-ROUSER
LOOSE LIPS
ALMA MATER
HOTSPUR
FULL CRY
OUTFOXED
THE HUNT BALL
THE HOUNDS AND THE FURY
THE TELL-TALE HORSE
THE SAND CASTLE
HOUNDED TO DEATH
ANIMAL MAGNETISM: MY LIFE WITH CREATURES
GREAT AND SMALL

Cat of the Century

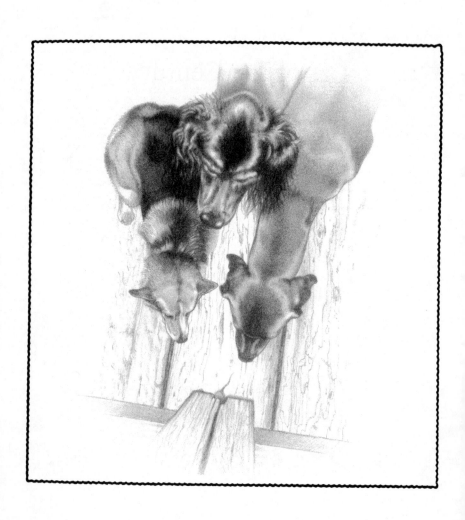

Cat *of the* Century

A MRS. MURPHY MYSTERY

RITA MAE BROWN

& SNEAKY PIE BROWN

ILLUSTRATIONS BY MICHAEL GELLATLY

DOUBLEDAY LARGE PRINT HOME LIBRARY EDITION

BANTAM BOOKS•NEW YORK

This Large Print Edition, prepared especially for Doubleday Large Print Home Library, contains the complete, unabridged text of the original Publisher's Edition.

Cat of the Century is a work of fiction. Names, characters, places, and incidents either are the product of the author's imagination or are used fictitiously. Any resemblance to actual persons, living or dead, events, or locales is entirely coincidental.

Published in the United States by Bantam Books, an imprint of The Random House Publishing Group, a division of Random House, Inc., New York.

Bantam Books and the rooster colophon are registered trademarks of Random House, Inc.

ISBN 978-1-61664-329-4

Printed in the United States of America

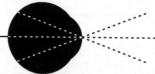

This Large Print Book carries the Seal of Approval of N.A.V.H.

*With gratitude and fond memory
to
Irwyn Applebaum and Barb Burg*

Author's Note

I would like to thank Dr. Jahnae Barnett, Kenda Shindler, Gayle Lampe, D. Scott Miniea, and Brenda Foster, all of William Woods University, for being such good sports and allowing Sneaky Pie and me to set this mystery at the university. I especially thank Dr. Barnett, Mrs. Shindler, and Miss Lampe for letting me use their names in this novel. Obviously, this is a work of fiction so while I use their names, the events are made up. As with any such work, the events, characters, and incidents depicted are products of the feline imagination as well as my own. Any resemblance to actual events, or persons, living or dead, is entirely coincidental. There are XVIII Wheelers Truck Washes and they are owned by Eddie Barnett. Go on, pull in one.

Author's Note

Cast of Characters

Mary Minor Haristeen—"Harry" is hardworking, watchful, and usually good-natured. Having just tipped over into her early forties, she's lived long enough to know life rarely turns out as one expects it will turn out. However, that's not necessarily a bad thing.

Pharamond Haristeen, D.V.M.—"Fair" is a tall, powerfully built man. He's more sensitive than his wife, often better able to read people's emotions.

Aunt Tally Urquhart—She is about to turn one hundred and she's ready for her next hundred. The old girl knows the emperor wears no clothes. In fact, she takes delight in this wisdom.

Inez Carpenter, D.V.M.—Inez met Tally at William Woods University. She is

now ninety-eight. She has shepherded
Fair's career, taking pride in his
success in equine veterinary
medicine. She, herself, is one of the
most respected vets in the country, a
pioneer for women's progress in this
field.

Marilyn Sanburne, Sr.—"Big Mim" is
Tally's niece. Born to privilege, she can
sometimes be a snob but is basically a
good person. Now in her seventies she
tries hard to see other people's points
of view.

Marilyn Sanburne, Jr.—"Little Mim"
knows she will never be the force in the
community her powerful mother is. Her
response to this was to get elected
vice mayor of Crozet. She'll be
powerful in a different way as the years
roll on.

Mariah D'Angelo—She graduated from
William Woods University in 1974. A
successful businesswoman, she owns
a high-end jewelry store in Kansas City
where she is the head of their WWU

Alumnae Association. She loathes Flo
Langston.

Flo Langston—Flo returns the favor.
She couldn't stand Mariah when they
were freshmen together and she can't
stand her now. Flo has made pots of
money as a stockbroker and she is the
head of St. Louis's WWU Alumnae
Association. St. Louis and Kansas City
are as different as chalk and cheese;
perhaps the animosity of Flo and
Mariah reflects that.

Liz Filmore—She is in her late thirties,
and heads the WWU Alumnae
Association chapter in Richmond,
Virginia. She considers herself Flo's
protégée. Flo remains silent on that
subject but the two are in constant
contact. Liz manages Inez Carpenter's
portfolio.

Terri Kincaid—She is a few years
younger than Liz and a close friend
who is also a WWU graduate. She
chairs the small alumnae chapter in
Charlottesville, Virginia, while owning

and running a store on the north side of Barracks Road Shopping Center. Terri specializes in expensive French and Italian ceramics, dishware, etc. She's a bit of a nervous Nellie.

Garvey Watson—Garvey owns Thompson and Watson, an exclusive men's clothing store located next to Terri Kincaid's store. In his early seventies, he's a kind man, a community favorite. He's also African American. Garvey's many white friends don't really see him as a black man, which can be both good and bad. He's just Garvey Watson but he sees all the shades of gray in most issues whereas his white friends often do not.

William Woods University,
Fulton, Missouri

Dr. Jahnae Barnett—President of the university, she spills over with energy, ideas, and a passion for education. She's one of those people who can pull the best out of others.

Miss Gayle Lampe—weighted down with titles, awards, and ribbons from the show ring, is oblivious to all that. Her focus is always on those beautiful Saddlebred horses and the young humans who ride them at William Woods. Like the above mentioned president of this unique institution, an institution focusing on developing the total individual, she is warm and approachable.

Kenda Shindler—Dr. Barnett's assistant has the perfect personality for the job. She's positive, good with detail, and not one to walk away from a problem.

Trudy Sweetwater—A fictional Fulton girl who graduated from William Woods in 1996, she heads the alumnae association in the town that is home to the university. She possesses common sense, which when you think of it, isn't common at all.

The Really Important Characters

Mrs. Murphy—She's a tiger cat of high intelligence. She's sleek, loves her humans as well as the dog with whom she shares this life. The other cat she also loves, but finds it more difficult than loving the dog.

Pewter—The other cat is rotund, gray, and appallingly self-centered. As my Southern mother would say about Pewter, "She's as fat as a tick and wrapped up in self-regard, bless her heart." Still, Pewter comes through in a pinch.

Tee Tucker—She is a Pembroke corgi, full of enthusiasm and bright spirit. She is devoted to Harry and Fair and adores Mrs. Murphy and Pewter, too, although there can be pronounced differences of opinion. Wonderful as she and all corgis are, it's best not to invite her to your cocktail party. She'll try to herd the guests.

Simon—He is an oppossum who lives in the loft of the Haristeens' barn. He's a sweet fellow if a trifle simple.

Doodles—This young Gordon setter belongs to Aunt Tally. He knows his human is old, tough though she is, and he is vigilant.

Erno—He is a gorgeous vizsla owned by Inez Carpenter. He's also young, versatile in his abilities, and learning about life from the others. He loves Inez.

Cat of the Century

1

A lone figure walked along a shoveled-off bricklaid path. The dormant gardens glimmered with frost. The skies seemed low enough to touch.

Aunt Tally, two weeks away from her one-hundredth birthday, called her Gordon setter, Doodles.

As the young dog joyfully returned to his master, Aunt Tally leaned on her silver-headed cane, the head being in the graceful shape of a hound. Apart from having to use that cane—thanks to the usual involuntary dismounts all horsewomen take—she betrayed few signs of her advanced years. Had you seen her peering at the ground as she walked along, you would have pegged her at eighty, perhaps.

"More snow coming." She squinted at the sky this March 11, Wednesday.

Doodles, who had sharper senses, replied, *"Before sundown."*

Aunt Tally stroked the dog's head upon hearing the little yodel.

Tightening her cashmere scarf, she continued on.

A deep rumble alerted Doodles, who recognized the motor's signature sound as well as the sound of the tires. Identifying a vehicle by its tire sound and motor is easy for dogs. Humans can't do it.

Doodles wagged her tail as she bounded up to the front of the house, where Marilyn "Big Mim" Sanburne, Tally's niece, had parked her brand-new Dodge half-ton.

The two walked to the back of the house to join Tally.

Big Mim, teasingly called "The Queen of Crozet," was a formidable woman. However, even Big Mim could be backed off by the small, lean Tally.

"What are you doing out here? It's 24°F."

"Checking for my crocus. A shoot here

and a shoot there and I get to thinking about the redbuds."

Big Mim put one gloved hand on her hip. "Redbuds aren't going to be in full flower until about April fifteenth. You know that."

"Of course I do. That doesn't mean I can't check them." She tapped her cane on the old brick. "I'm longing for spring. By this time of the year I've had enough."

"You really will have enough if you don't come in out of the cold. You'll catch your death."

"It's not a baseball," the old woman replied.

"You know what I mean," Big Mim said, sounding tolerant. "Are you ready to go, or do you need anything from the house?"

"Just need to put up the dog." Aunt Tally walked to the back door, opened it, and Doodles scooted in, happy for the warmth.

"Purse?" Big Mim raised an eyebrow.

"My wallet's in my coat pocket. Purses are a pain. Even if I find one that slings just right over my shoulder, sooner or later it drops down. Hard to carry a purse with a cane."

"Guess it is." Big Mim walked to the passenger side of her blue truck and opened the door for Tally, who climbed in unassisted.

Once out on the road, the two chattered as only two people who have known each other all their lives can. Aunt Tally had been pushing thirty when Big Mim was born. It was a day of celebration. Aunt Tally, thanks to a disastrous love affair when young, shied away from marriage but not affairs. She treated Big Mim as her own daughter, which had occasioned some arguments with Tally's late, loved sister. A brother to Big Mim followed later, but he died on the hideous Bataan Death March. Apart from rage and grief, the result was that no Urquhart of any succeeding generation would buy a Japanese car or any product if they could help it. As with all old Virginia families, regardless of generations of marriages on both the male and female sides, they generally referred to themselves by the surname of the first European to settle on Virginia soil. In this case, the Urquharts.

"Speech?"

Aunt Tally, staring straight ahead, raised her voice a bit. "Oh, Mimsy, I make notes. I read them. I throw them out. I can't bear the thought of standing up there spouting bromides and sentimental mush. I haven't found what I want to say."

"That's a first."

Aunt Tally ignored this, instead concentrating on an upcoming T-cross. Her farm, Rose Hill, reposed about four miles west of Harry Haristeen's farm. They'd passed Harry's place on the way to Crozet, reaching the intersection of a dirt road and the two-lane paved highway on which they traveled.

"Can never drive over this without thinking about Ralston Peavey." Aunt Tally repositioned her cane to her left side. "Never found his murderer."

"Someone really wanted him out of this world." Big Mim remembered it, as well. "Fall, wasn't it?"

Aunt Tally nodded in affirmation. "A light frost, patchy fog."

"1964. The year sticks in my head because that was the first year Jim was elected mayor."

Jim Sanburne, her husband, remained mayor, and their daughter, Little Mim, was now vice mayor. The joke was, father and daughter came from two different political parties. Being a small town, Crozet never bothered with term limits. Jim, a good mayor, would most likely retain his office until such day as he died.

"Jim picked up the call from Dinny Myers; wish we had him back. There was a sheriff with sense," Aunt Tally mumbled.

"Oh, the one we have now has sense. You just think everything was better when you were younger."

"'Twas." Aunt Tally raised her voice. "This country is going to hell in a handbasket. Well, I'm not going off on that; it'll ruin my day. But even you have to admit that Ralston Peavey was the best blacksmith you ever saw."

"He was. He was."

Pleased with her little victory, Aunt Tally recalled the details as they rolled over the spot. "Found Ralston right here, spread-eagled in the middle of the road, facedown. Run over one way and then backed over. To make sure he was dead, I reckon."

"Jim saw him before Dinny removed the corpse. Said the tire tracks were clear. They hoped to find the killer from the tire treads. Never happened, of course."

"Dinny and the department really did check every set of tires in the area. He couldn't do all of Albemarle County, but he did check Crozet. Nothing. Not one thing. Some folks thought whoever did it was not from these parts. Not me. I think it was one of us."

Big Mim slowed for a curve. "Well, Ralston could drink. He was pretty loaded."

"He didn't lie down in the middle of the road because he was drunk."

"His truck was by the side of the road." Big Mim, who enjoyed driving her new truck, picked up speed. "I still think he'd been fooling around, and the husband found out and killed him."

"Maybe, but we all knew who was

weak that way. He'd never done it before. Two kids—what, eight and ten—
and he seemed to get along with them. I
wonder if it wasn't something else.
Couldn't be drugs. That hadn't taken off
yet."

"Can't imagine Ralston a dealer. Although, being a blacksmith, he had the
perfect job for distributing."

"No." Aunt Tally shook her head.
"Something else."

Big Mim paused. "Let's just say not a
stone was left unturned."

"One was, or we'd have the killer."
Tally frowned.

"After all this time, maybe he's dead
himself."

"Mimsy, I've seen a lot. One of these
days, might be 2050, the truth will wrig-
gle out. Always does."

"Talk to Inez?" Big Mim mentioned
Aunt Tally's best friend, who had
graduated from William Woods University—then known as William Woods College—two years behind Aunt Tally. The
lovely school, located in Fulton, Missouri, had provided Aunt Tally with her
first taste of life outside Virginia.

"She's flying in two days before, because of the alumnae board meeting."

"Good. Harry's driving."

Mary Minor "Harry" Haristeen was not a William Woods graduate. She had graduated from Smith College. Age forty, best described as an attractive tomboy, she now put all her attentions to farming, her true love, as she'd quit her job at the post office two years earlier. Harry would be going to the celebration at Aunt Tally's alma mater because she loved the old lady and knew the event was not to be missed, especially since the salty woman would give a speech. "Be good for Harry to get away," Aunt Tally said.

At that moment, Harry had her hands full with a William Woods alumna, no less.

2

"That pot was made in Italy. Of course you'll replace it." Terri Kincaid, barricaded behind the counter, leveled a harsh gaze at Harry.

Only three years apart in age, Terri being thirty-seven, the women had known each other for a long time. Harry, a country girl with natural good looks, couldn't be bothered with the accoutrements of femininity. Terri lived for them. These two were oil and water.

Observing Harry's predicament was Liz Filmore from Richmond, a friend of Terri's and another William Woods alumna.

Also present, his arms crossed over his chest with lips pursed, was Garvey Watson. A tall, elegant African American, he owned the successful men's clothing store next door. Garvey had a gift for retail.

Harry thought his pursed lips might be because he was upset the pot was broken.

Tucker, Harry's corgi, sat mournfully at her feet. The dog, jostled by a customer leaving, had knocked over the pot, which was sitting on a low wrought-iron table. It wasn't Tucker's fault, but what could Harry say?

The shards of pottery, picked up by Harry, rested on the counter, the deep layers of green and yellow glaze quite pretty.

"How much?" Harry, tight with the buck, winced.

"Two hundred forty-nine dollars, plus five percent sales tax," Terri announced.

Harry fetched her checkbook and a pen from the inside of her Carhartt Detroit jacket.

As Harry wrote the check, Terri nattered on, "I'm so excited. We've already raised twenty thousand dollars from local alumnae, and I haven't even started yet. Liz is going to video the entire speech to

use for future fund-raisers." Liz and Terri were thick as thieves. "I really wish I could be there, but we'll throw another birthday party as a fund-raiser back here. I can't afford to leave the store, especially if good weather comes in. People spend more if they have spring fever."

"Let's hope so," Garvey said. "Bad economy. People are pulling back."

Liz spoke up. "Garvey, people always need clothes. Terri's business might be down, but she'll weather the storm. So will you, unless men want to go naked— a scary thought. Eljo's is your only competition."

She cited a lovely men's clothing store on Elliewood Avenue by the University of Virginia.

"I certainly hope you're right," Garvey murmured, not sounding at all convinced.

Terri smiled broadly as she took Harry's check. "I won't ask for ID," she joked.

"Good." Harry put a good face on it, but she always thought Terri was a pain in the neck, her screech over the broken pot further confirming that opinion.

"Do you know that all the alumnae over eighty will attend? There are forty of them. Isn't that wonderful? Our alumnae fund is paying for those who can't afford the airfare, and the motels in and around Fulton are giving us a special rate."

"Wonderful," Harry replied tensely.

Forking over two hundred fifty dollars plus tax was eating at her.

Terri, not one to keep her woes to herself, would fan the flames of any discontent if Harry had balked at payment. Harry loathed that in a man or woman. But she hadn't just fallen off the turnip truck. She'd learned to keep her opinion to herself unless speaking with her husband or best friends. Keep it level, keep it smooth. She tried.

Terri, young for such a task, headed Charlottesville's William Woods Alumnae Association. Once men were admitted to William Woods in 1996, an argument arose over the word "alumnae." Should they change it to "alumni"? The Old Girls fought that one. For most of their lives they had lived under male honorifics or terms. Let the men grapple with "alumnae." Surely their parts wouldn't shrivel.

So alumnae it was, at least in the eyes of the female graduates.

Such battles never interested Harry, but she did understand one great fundamental of life: Men had to prove they were men. Women did not have to prove they were women. This anxiety could make weak men either silly or downright dangerous. Strong men sailed right through.

Harry focused on the basics: animal behavior, food, clothing, shelter. She zeroed right to the core of an issue, which made people who couldn't accept brute reality nervous. Harry knew the human animal had set the natural order on its head, that among humans the weak devoured the strong. As her mother used to put it, "The squeakiest wheel gets the oil."

No reason to burden Terri with reality, for Terri was one of those benighted souls who believed laws were the answer. You have a problem? Pass another law.

Liz lightened the moment. "Harry, your corgi has good taste. That was a beautiful vase."

Harry smiled. "Tucker has better taste than I do."

"Thank you," the dog replied.

Garvey joked, "Bring her in my store. If she tears up an item or chews shoes, I'll know to order more."

"Garvey, you crack me up." Harry laughed at him.

Terri, a clotheshorse, asked Harry, "Do you know what you're going to wear?"

"Uh, well, it will probably be cold. That long wraparound wool skirt, the one I wear with the big gold pin on the front. I thought that."

"But what about the dinner, and, of course, there will be the choral groups. Aunt Tally will be serenaded. You need some variety in your wardrobe."

"I don't know. I'll think of something."

"No jeans and cowboy boots," Terri smugly decreed.

"Tell her to shut up," Tucker grumbled.

"We'll go in a minute." Harry smiled down at her constant companion. "Terri, hope business is good." With that, she vacated the shop, Garvey on her heels.

"Sorry your little dog broke the pot." He shivered, for the wind was cold; he wore only a sweater. "This sweater would look great on Fair." He poked his own chest.

"Would." Harry nodded. "He's a bit of a peacock."

"I'd go out of business without peacocks. See you soon, I hope."

He ducked into his store.

"Jeez." She looked down at Tucker. "It's picked up. Wind's got teeth in it."

Within a minute they reached the truck. Harry unlocked the door. It was a 1978 Ford F-150. Ran like a top. She lifted the corgi up, then slid in herself, quickly closing the door.

"So?" Pewter, the fat gray cat, looked at the dog.

Mrs. Murphy, the slender tabby, said nothing but was grateful when Harry started the engine. As the truck hadn't been parked long, the heat came on.

All four creatures sat for a moment, just enjoying the warmth.

Harry always left an old blanket on the

seat for the animals to snuggle in and keep warm.

As Harry turned out of Barracks Road Shopping Center onto Barracks Road, Tucker filled in the two cats on the broken pot.

Harry rarely traveled without her friends. With few exceptions, their friendship meant the most to her in the world. For one thing, they never lied to her. For another thing, they didn't care if she wore jeans and cowboy boots, earrings and mascara—two nods to girly things. Fussing over her face and attire was just too much work for Harry. She had more important things to do.

The old truck lacked cup holders, but Harry had installed one. She plopped her cell phone into it. The phone rang. She wouldn't use her phone when driving, because she didn't trust herself not to lose concentration.

Already she'd put in a full day. At 5:30 A.M. she'd fed her husband, Fair, and herself. He'd then left for his practice—equine veterinary medicine. She fed the horses, mucked their stalls, turned them out with their blankets on. She'd called

Southern States, a regional agricultural supply chain, and put in her seed and fertilizer order. This way she reaped a small discount for ordering early. Boy, it cost, too.

Thanks to some traffic, she turned down the mile-long dirt driveway to her farm thirty-five minutes after leaving the shopping center. She parked the truck by the barn, making use of the over-hang. It felt like snow. If the weather turned nasty, the overhang would keep some of the snow off the windshield.

She flipped open the cell phone to see the missed call. Big Mim.

She hurried into the old farmhouse to use the landline.

Upon hearing the familiar voice, Big Mim ordered without formalities, "Harry, you need to call Inez Carpenter in Richmond."

"Of course."

Harry did as she was told.

Although Tally's best friend was ninety-eight, her voice was strong.

They chatted for a few moments, then Inez got to the point. "Harry, as you know, I'm head of the William Woods Alumnae

Association chapter here in Richmond—well, I'm emeritus. The board wants to present Tally with something from ourselves. I know better than to ask Mim. She'll wave me off. Any ideas?"

"She'd like a purple-martin house."

Harry mentioned a beautiful insect-eating bird with specific housing tastes. Purple martins returned to Virginia in the spring and liked to live in colonies. Multiple gourds hanging on cross rails or large birdhouses with many apartments appealed to them. One had to carefully clean out their quarters when they left for the fall and winter. A scout, flying ahead of the flock, would arrive in February to inspect the furnishings. If dirty, the purple martin wouldn't return to nest there.

"Oh." Inez's voice raised a notch. "What a good suggestion." A pause followed. "You have a mind for puzzles. If we have a little time when we're in Fulton, I have one for you. Let's keep it between us."

"Sounds interesting."

A very long pause followed this, and the nonagenarian lowered her voice. "Perhaps too interesting."

3

"Wonder what it's about." Harry had just finished telling Fair about her conversation with Inez.

"Inez isn't given to overstatement." He speared the last piece of rib eye on his plate, having carefully pared off the fat.

Tucker, Mrs. Murphy, and Pewter, alert, sat at his feet. They'd already worked over Harry.

"Guess I'll find out. She didn't want to tell me over the phone."

"Then it involves someone's reputation or something dicey." Fair felt the glow that attends a full stomach.

"You're probably right. Inez wouldn't want to besmirch someone. She may have doubts, but she'll hold her fire until she has everything locked up tight. I've learned a lot from her."

"Me, too." He smiled.

Inez had wanted to be a librarian while at William Woods but, upon graduation, decided she really wanted to be an equine vet. She went back to the college, took organic chemistry and other science courses, then applied to Cornell. She was accepted as the only woman in her class, and when she moved back to Virginia, she was the only woman equine vet in the state. The gods gave her a great gift. She could see what other vets who lacked a feeling for horses couldn't. There were those who thought Inez could read a horse's mind. Within ten years, she was envied by some while others felt only pure jealousy. Many, however, admired her. She was considered one of the best equine vets in Virginia. By the time she was fifty, she was thought to be one of the best in the nation.

When Fair did his residency, he was accepted by Inez. Her practice included the counties just west of Richmond. She specialized in equine reproduction. Fair was her understudy. She always bragged about him, saying he wasn't only her handsomest understudy but her best. He, too, had a feeling for horses, learning to trust his instincts as much as if not more than technology.

When his term of residency ended, Fair established a clinic in Crozet, Virginia, his hometown, thereby diving into vats of debt. Inez threw him as much business as she could from Louisa County, her westernmost territory. She began dragging him along to conferences. Her luster rubbed off on him. He was damned good, too.

"Surely you have a scrap of fat on that plate?" Pewter stood on her hind legs to pat Fair's thigh with her front paw.

Fair cast his blue eyes down at the rotund kitty. "I'd be ashamed to be that fat."

Nonetheless, he tossed her a fat scrap, along with one each to Mrs. Murphy and Tucker.

Pewter let the insult pass. The tidbit was too good.

"I'm glad you could make it home for supper."

"Feels like it's been weeks." He sighed, leaning back in his chair.

"It has."

Foaling season started in January, especially for the Thoroughbreds, but it continued for other breeds into April. Occasionally, a late foal would even be born in June. Like humans, foals arrived on their own timetable, which always seemed to be in the middle of the night. Fair had learned to snatch sleep when he could. He could even sleep standing up.

Ninety-nine percent of the time, the baby entered this world healthy. Occasionally, there would be birth defects. Some could be corrected with surgery, but others were hopeless and the animal had to be humanely destroyed. Sometimes the problem was with the mother. Fortunately, this foaling season had been very good, with few miseries, and tonight Fair had made it home early. With luck, he might even sleep for seven hours.

"Thought I'd take the dually to Fulton. Sucks gas, but I think that long a trip might be asking too much of the '78."

"How long is it?" He smiled as Pewter, happy, flopped at Harry's side.

"Sixteen hours. I can do it in less if I'm vigilant. But I think I'll take two days and stop in Kentucky to see Joan and Larry." She mentioned two dear friends. Joan Hamilton owned Kalarama Farm, where she bred Saddlebreds; Larry Hodge, her husband, trained them and other people's horses for showing. He owned a separate place, Simmstown, which he rented out. He was also an auctioneer, having a real flair for it. They were one of those great teams like Abbott and Costello or Fred and Ginger.

"Bring pictures of Shortro."

Harry nodded. Shortro had been given to her by a client of Joan's. He was a gray Saddlebred and was just turning four. He was smart, kind, and eager to learn, and Harry had fallen in love with the fellow.

Fair reached for his beer, glancing out the kitchen window. "Winter won't give up."

"Don't I know it. But the snowdrops are showing their little heads. Soon my crocus shoots will pop up. Sooner or later, winter will release his grip."

"I love a good snow, but by March I'm

ready for the change, as is everyone."
He paused. "The dually. No, honey, don't
take it. It's a great truck, mind you, but
you don't want to drive sixteen hours
with those double wheels. I mean, the
turning radius alone will get you when
you snake through St. Louis. What a
goddamned bottleneck that is."

"'Tis. I adore St. Louis. Just wish
they'd build more bridges over the Mississippi and a new bypass."

"Given that our bridges are falling
down, they might have to. The Mississippi is treacherous. That reminds me to
reread *Life on the Mississippi*."

"Well, what can I drive? I'm not flying.
For one thing, I wouldn't be able to take
the kids. For another, it's crowded,
planes are late or canceled, you don't
even get a sandwich, you pay for your
bag to be checked, and an airplane pol-
lutes eight times as much as a train. As
far as I'm concerned, air travel needs to
be a thing of the past if we're really going green."

"Don't count on it. Those special-
interest lobbies couldn't give a damn
about what's good for the environment,

much less the country." He drained his glass. "And the public deluded itself into thinking that long-life electric bulbs and electric cars will solve the problem. Until we phase out polluting industries like air travel, we're sunk." He paused. "It's complicated. I know that. If we end those industries without creating new ones and retraining people to work in the new ones, we're creating tremendous hardship for sectors of our population. There's no easy answer, but there *are* answers." Fair cared passionately about environmental issues.

"You're right. The public doesn't care about the greed, corruption, or rape of the environment as long as they get what they need. At least that's what I think."

"Not need but want," Fair remarked shrewdly, while patting Pewter's head.

She stood on her hind legs again. Fair had cleaned his plate, but he did drop a little piece of piecrust.

"*Pig.*" Mrs. Murphy swept her whiskers forward. She wasn't one for sweets or piecrusts.

Pewter liked dough, any kind of bread.

"You're no cripple. If you want more, ask for it."

"Don't." The tiger turned, sauntering out of the kitchen.

"You're right. Back to my problem."

"Let me think on it. I could rent a car. We don't have one, and for a trip like this, you really need a car."

"I don't need one here. The old '78 does the job."

"It's not long on comfort."

"I sit on a cushion." She smiled, then looked out the window. She rose, walking over for a better look. "Flurries."

"Damn."

"Good thing I kept the fire going."

"What about the bedroom?" Their bedroom was cold.

"Stoked that, too. But I can keep you warm."

He laughed. "I'm a lucky man." Then he said with feeling, "I am. I'm married to the woman I love. I love my work. I have wonderful friends—human and animal. And I live in one of the most beautiful places in the world. If I ever forget to be grateful, smack me."

"Will do." Harry finished her hot tea. "I

hope this do for Aunt Tally doesn't do her in."

"Tally? Christ, she'll probably outlive us all."

"Probably, but I have a funny feeling about this."

Fair had learned not to discount Harry's feelings, just as he'd learned through experience not to discount when Inez said a horse was unhappy, even with no apparent physical cause. "You mean she'll get sick or something?"

"No." Harry placed the cup on the saucer. "I can't put my finger on it. This is going to be a huge fund-raiser. Times are tough, so it's especially important. Then that smarmy little social climber Terri Kincaid—who plucks my last nerve, by the way—wants to have another fund-raiser here. They're working Tally too hard, I think. I know Inez put her foot down with the Richmond chapter about having a special fund-raiser tied to Tally turning one hundred."

"They can wait until Inez turns a hundred. Two more years. You know she was in her early eighties when I did my residency? Apart from a bad back—and what vet or horseman doesn't have one—she looked about fifty."

"Some people just have it. Others die of lung cancer at thirty without ever smoking." Harry had accepted in her teens that there was no rhyme or reason to these things.

But being a fearful species, humans want reasons, so they invent them. That's what the cats had decided. They'd also concluded other things about the human animal, few of their conclusions complimentary. But Mrs. Murphy staunchly defended Harry and Fair by saying they possessed catlike qualities.

Tucker loved her humans. She didn't care if they were turned around backward.

"Back to your premonition."

"Did I say premonition?" Fair shook his head no, so Harry continued. "Well, I guess it is. Maybe it's because of the financial pressure. I'm making too much of it. But," she searched for the right words, "I feel this may backfire."

"I hope not."

"I hope not, too, because the college—well, it's a university now—is doing everything right about the big blowout. According to Inez and Tally, it's one of the best-run higher-education institutions in the country."

"You know Inez and I can still argue about our alma maters. She thinks Cornell is the best, and I think it's Auburn." He rose and cleared the table. "Let's hope all goes well. If it doesn't, you're far away from me. I don't much like that."

"It's not about me. It's a feeling."

"Harry, if anything does run amiss, you'll soon be in the middle of it. You can't help yourself."

"*True,*" Tucker piped up.

"That's enough, Tucker," Harry reprimanded the corgi.

"*She understood,*" Tucker announced.

"*No, she didn't. She wanted you to stop barking,*" Mrs. Murphy replied.

"*I only barked once.*"

The cat brushed against the mighty little dog, for she did love her. Pewter, who had moved to her cozy fleece bed, opened one eye. She closed her eye again.

Harry did not say anything about her

husband's assessment of her landing in the middle of a mess, because it was true.

Fair filled the sink. They didn't use a microwave or dishwasher. They turned on the electric lights only in the room where they were eating, reading, or watching TV. Fair was setting aside money to build a good old farmer's windmill. That would help with energy costs. "Honey, give me a couple of days on the car thing. I really don't want you driving all that way in anything but a safe vehicle."

"Renting will be really expensive."

"Let me worry about that." He scrubbed a dish, then turned to smile at her. "Actually, I don't want to deny you the pleasure of worrying about money."

"Go on." She rose, grabbed a dish towel to wipe off the plates and glasses. "Boy, it's coming down now."

"I'll say. And that's another reason I want you in a safe car. There are no barriers between Missouri and Canada. The weather sweeps down. Here, we have the Alleghenies first and then the Blue Ridge. It's one of the reasons our weather is so glorious." He paused. "Most of the time."

She tossed the towel over her shoulder. "Still is. It's pretty. We're just ready for spring."

4

"Additional revenue." Liz Filmore, the head of the William Woods Alumnae Association of Richmond, concluded her push.

Listening on the other end of the phone was Flo Langston, head of the St. Louis chapter.

Flo had a seat on the stock exchange and was the head of her own successful firm, while Liz, with her husband, Tim, owned a small investment firm.

Liz had been a rising star at an old Richmond brokerage house. She'd learned a great deal. She met Tim, who worked at a rival firm. They hit it off, married, and started their own company, more or less boutique investing. They focused on emerging technologies, small start-up companies. Liz considered Flo a mentor. Flo considered Liz a pest.

"It might." Flo responded to the idea that special T-shirts might bring more money into William Woods. Perhaps with one of Tally's famous—or infamous—quips. "However, I sense T-shirt fatigue out there. Perhaps we could come up with something a little more useful."

"What about those pink cases with tools that have pink handles? I saw them on display at . . . maybe it was the Cincinnati airport. I can't remember. I'm on the road so much."

"Yes, I've seen those. For Aunt Tally we should have blood red." Flo laughed. "But they're expensive, depending on how many tools one purchases. Let's keep that idea in reserve. Perhaps we could negotiate with the firm to actually make a set in William Woods colors and sell them in the Logo store. The Logo store makes a valuable contribution to the budget."

"Yes, it does." Liz had pored over the alumnae fund accounting returns to double-check them. The Fulton accounting firm did a good job. She'd never found anything to send up a red flag.

All members of alumnae and alumni associations in universities took their fiduciary responsibilities seriously, which began with understanding the income, cash flow, and running costs of the university. They all faced the age-old problem of when debt was useful and when it was not. In one sense, debt was a multiplier of wealth. In another it could break you in two. Debt, if acquired wisely, could allow a college or business to purchase equipment, which would save man-hours and build new, energy-efficient buildings. The truth was in figuring out debt-to-asset ratios and when the debt could successfully be repaid. The alumnae board's recommendations to the administration were held in high regard. One reason was that Flo had proved prescient about the economy over the decades.

"I want to encourage you." Flo's melodic voice was soothing. "I just don't think T-shirts are the answer. Many of the alums being brought in will be eighty or older, some of them on a fixed income. Fortunately, that's a small number. Most are solvent. Still, I don't think we should tempt them. The money can come from younger alumnae who will also be attending—the strong economic base. They, too, want more than a T-shirt."

"Aunt Tally loves horses."

"And horses are a big part of William Woods, but not every graduate avails herself or himself of the program. 'Course, the over-eighties are all women. Some actually majored in history." Flo laughed.

"She likes to garden."

"Hmm. Even a lady of advanced years can pot a plant. I think you've got it. Gloves in one of our colors, with perhaps Tally's birthdate imprinted: March twenty-fifth, 1909. I'll pay for the over-eighty crowd. Each of those women should have a gift."

"That's wonderful. I'll get right on it." Liz paused. "Would you like me to clear it with Mariah?"

"Certainly not. I'll call her."

Flo and Mariah D'Angelo had graduated in 1974 and both majored in economics. They cordially loathed each other; always had. Mariah headed the Kansas City chapter, St. Louis's great Missouri urban rival. Both women displayed brilliance and a certain cunning allied with good looks. Both married well in money terms, but in emotional terms it was anybody's guess. But as their husbands were fifty-eight and sixty, respectively, whatever straying they may have done in the past would have been curtailed by the usual lessening of ability in that crucial area of male anatomy.

In their junior years, both Flo and Mariah fell in love with a student, Dick Langston, at Westminster College, the then all-male school across town. Flo married him. Mariah eventually retaliated by marrying the head of a huge construction firm, a man much richer than Dick Langston. He was on the road a great deal, visiting sites. That suited Mariah just fine.

Flo, in one of her typical farsighted moves, bought a ton of stock in the company that would eventually manufacture Viagra. Despite the New Depression, sales kept growing. Plus, her husband benefited from it, so she did, too. She kept this to herself.

"She is our treasurer." Liz dug the hole deeper, reminding Flo of why she considered Liz a pest, albeit a brilliant one.

"She's very competent at that." Flo gave credit where credit was due.

"I keep meaning to tell you, you were right all along about complex derivatives. I should have listened."

"Liz, if I couldn't fully understand complex derivatives, then no one could. I know that sounds arrogant, but there isn't a financial instrument I don't understand. It was all smoke and mirrors. You have got to realize—and I don't know when you will—that the market is not driven by intelligence. In a sense it isn't even driven by greed. It's driven by the male ego. And they're sheep. Being a woman is a tremendous advantage, because we know when the emperor has no clothes."

A long, mournful pause followed. "I know it now."

"Are you and Tim in danger?" She mentioned Liz's husband.

"Things are bad all over, but we're hanging in there."

"All over," Flo said flatly. "Indeed they are."

"When do you think it will end? You know, when will the market come back up?"

Flo sucked air in through her teeth. "I don't know, but it won't be back up when the government predicts it will. I think two more years."

"Gawd," Liz moaned. "Two years."

"Give or take." Flo didn't feel like hearing Liz weep and wail, if she was headed that way. "You've come up with some good products. You'll be fine."

Liz replied, "I'm learning a lot. Guess we all are. I've learned a lot from you. Tim, too. We see things for the first time. You've seen it all before. Helps me put things in perspective."

What Liz never mentioned to Flo or anyone was that one reason their company grew so rapidly was Tim's selling skills. He'd learned by selling lemonade as a little kid, then graduated to a newspaper route. In college he sold marijuana and cocaine, investing the proceeds.

Like Liz, he worked for a large brokerage firm and soaked up everything. The investments from his college business funded the start of their own brokerage company. Tim's selling skills were complemented by Liz's keen judgment on rising and falling companies. Her management abilities completed the picture.

Flo, after thanking Liz for the compliment, then changed the subject. "You know, I think of this often. Our alma mater is better managed than most government agencies. And we should thank our lucky stars that Kenneth Lay was not a graduate."

At this they both laughed, for Kenneth Lay, the now deceased head of Enron, had graduated from the University of Missouri, a wonderful state university. Unfortunately for Mizzou, he promised them millions. They based their budget on it and then he bellied up. Mizzou would pull through. But the crisis caused pain that would continue for some years.

"When are you arriving?" Liz asked.

"In time for our first meeting. It's not that far a drive—two hours from where we live—but I think I'll come the night before. I hate worrying about time. Gayle Lampe lives on campus, and I'll bunk with her."

Gayle Lampe had been head of Equestrian Studies and had written a book that was the successor to Helen Crabtree's text about Saddle Seat. As Miss Crabtree was the leading light of this type of riding, this was no mean feat.

"You'll have a good time. I'm coming in a day early, too. Tim wants to be there. We'll stay at the bed-and-breakfast."

"Be good to see him."

"Tim wants to celebrate Tally's big day, and we aren't far from her orbit."

"Honey, none of us is."

With that, Flo signed off, then dialed Mariah. Flo operated on the theory that if you kiss a toad first thing in the morning, nothing after that kiss will be as offensive. Although it was midday, she considered any contact with Mariah contact with a toad. She laughed to herself that comparing Mariah to a toad was an insult to the toad.

"Mariah, Flo here."

The sandpaper voice, deepened with years of assistance from Lucky Strikes and good bourbon, responded, "Yes, Flo, what can I do for you?"

"Liz Filmore has come up with the idea of getting garden gloves imprinted with Tally Urquhart's birthday."

A little snort followed. "For God's sake, why?"

"Listen, Mariah, it's better than a T-shirt, and Liz is determined to do it. She'll use her own funds." Flo had not discussed this, but she would call Liz immediately and tell her this was the deal.

"In that case, we have nothing to lose."

"Indeed."

"I'm looking forward to the celebration. I'll see you there."

"Yes, you will." Icy bitch, Flo thought to herself, then hung up and dialed Liz.

Flo figured if she had one dollar for every call she'd made for her alma mater over the years, she'd have enough to own five thousand shares of Coca-Cola.

"Liz, Flo."

"Yes. Did Mariah pitch a fit and fall in it? It wasn't her idea."

Flo let out a whoop. "No. But she does insist you pay for the gloves yourself. Of course, you'll retrieve your money from the sales, so we'll have to keystone the price. And as I said, I'll pay for the over-eighties and special mementos."

Keystoning meant doubling the wholesale cost of an item. So if the gloves cost eleven dollars, they would be sold for twenty-two. It was standard retail practice. Therefore, even if items were discounted thirty percent, there would still be a profit.

"I intended to pay for the gloves. Should have said so up front. Thanks again for your generosity. About keystoning, let me find out about the cost. I might have to drop it back a bit, but there will be profit."

"'Net profit'—the two most beautiful words in the English language," Flo purred.

"Was she . . . herself?"

"She was, but in check. She's sharp, sharp, sharp when it comes to money, and she watches our treasury like a hawk." She paused, "A hawk who wears far too much gaudy jewelry from her expensive store."

Flo thought retail was quite difficult and admired anyone who succeeded, whether it be a huge corporation or a small neighborhood nursery.

Again, the two women signed off.

Flo truly did look forward to March 25, but she knew the meeting of the alumnae board would be tense. Money was tight everywhere. If people were going to fight, they were going to fight over sex or money. As far as she knew, there was no sex among the board members. Then the thought of Mariah in bed with Andrea, a rotund board member from Omaha, sent her into a fit of laughter.

5

Halfway across the country, the administration of William Woods University prepared for the centennial.

President Jahnae H. Barnett, Ph.D., possessed that marvelous ability of finding the right person for the right job. While someone in the administration needed to oversee the gala, it would best serve the university if the actual centennial chair happened to be an alumna, someone not on the payroll. Given the economic crash and the subsequent hiring freeze, President Barnett's people labored with overload. Dedicated and efficient, everyone in the administration pulled their weight and then some. So, too, did the department chairs. Putting another responsibility on them wasn't fair when an alumna volunteer might be available.

Academics, notoriously naïve where money was concerned, tried the patience of most university presidents. Issues became moral arguments. Tedious, unnecessary, counterproductive, the venom one academic reserved for another was exceeded only by the venom poured on people who were successful outside the ivory tower. Again, President Barnett had sidestepped this emotional snake pit during her long tenure as leader. She worked closely with personnel, pinpointing people who excelled in their field, keeping a positive outlook, and rarely giving in to intellectual snobbery. One of the reasons William Woods was such a happy place could be traced to fastidious hiring at all levels. Mistakes had been made—impossible not to make a few—but those individuals were let go without fanfare and in such a way as not to obliterate their fragile egos.

Ego. Sometimes President Barnett wondered what life would be like without it. She had weekly conversations with Flo Langston as well as Mariah

D'Angelo. Neither Flo nor Mariah, so shrewd in all other respects, could recognize that their own hostility toward each other stemmed from ego. President Barnett managed to harness them to pull together for William Woods University. It wasn't easy.

Trudy Sweetwater, the local alumna in charge of Tally's blowout, sat in the comfortable chair in President Barnett's office. She worked for a small irrigation-equipment company in Fulton. She was far from rich, but she loved her alma mater and was a good organizer—something her employer had long ago recognized, too.

Named Gertrude for her paternal grandmother, thirty-one-year-old Trudy hated the name. "Trudy" wasn't so bad.

"I've arranged a caravan to Callaway Hills. They've graciously offered to serve a light lunch."

The vivacious and quite pretty president beamed and said, "Wonderful."

Callaway Hills Stables, one of the great Saddlebred establishments in America, was guided for years by Mrs. Weldon, breeder of the great Will Shriver. She passed away in 2007 and her daughter, Tony, had taken over. Those incredible Callaway horses continued to be born, trained, and shown.

"You know Tony; she'll have every horse in the stables gleaming." Trudy smiled.

"She does anyway." Jahnae Barnett had ridden in the Concert of Champions at the American Royal in Kansas City, one of the big-five old shows in the Saddlebred world: the Junior League, Mercer County Fair, Shelbyville, the Kentucky State Fair, and the Kansas City Royal. She had a keen appreciation of what it took to excel, and was thrilled when Marjorie Townsend, a fifteen-year-old who was like a daughter to her, also rode at the Royal.

These days she was lucky to ride a bicycle. Time. Just no time.

"Inez will be paired with Tally, of course."

"She's one of our most successful graduates." President Barnett checked her notes. "The Jameson Singers?"

"Ready."

"Gin?" Said with a slow smile.

"Bombay Sapphire and Tanqueray. Inez said that Tally likes to switch off from time to time. She starts when the sun goes down, but Inez says she has rarely seen Tally drunk. The woman has an amazing capacity for alcohol."

"So I hear. You know if you need anything, Kenda Shindler"—she referred to her assistant—"or Gayle Lampe will help. I don't remember when I've seen Gayle so excited. She's dying to spend time with Inez."

"She gets that excited over a box of Rogers' Chocolates." Trudy laughed, naming the candy company in Canada.

President Barnett laughed, too. "Point taken. Anything else?"

"Mariah called. Her computer crashed. She's afraid she won't have the alumnae treasury figures in time for the meeting. But she says she'll have a techie on it, pronto."

President Barnett raised her eyebrows. "Okay."

Trudy added some crucial information. "It appears she didn't keep a backup."

The eyebrows shot straight upward. "Oh, no."

"She says not to worry."

"I don't suppose she kept a regular accounting record just in case?"

Trudy shook her head. "People are forgetting how to keep written records on their own."

"All we need is one huge electrical disaster or other form of disaster and there goes everything. I still keep my logbook, and I carry it with me."

"I do, too. My mother pounded that into me." Trudy nodded her head.

"Remind me to tell your mother she's right." President Barnett leaned back in her chair. "Well, everything seems to be on track, except for the computer crash."

Money arouses passions. If President Barnett had only known how high, she might have canceled the whole damned thing.

On that same day Harry finished the end-of-day chores, her cats and dog helping.

Tucker barked, *"Fair and intruders!"*

The vet truck rolled down the drive, still a little muddy after the light snow last week plus the freezing and thawing. In Fair's wake was Fred Willard, driving a new Volvo XC70, and someone behind him in a Volvo SUV.

Harry wondered why the caravan.

Fair hopped out of his truck and put his arm around his wife's waist, getting straw on himself and propelling her toward the XC70, a lovely silver station wagon. Fred emerged and handed Harry the key.

"Six cylinders." Fred, a Volvo salesman, smiled.

"You rented a Volvo?" Harry was incredulous.

"I bought a Volvo."

"Fair, we're in a depression!"

"Recession," Fair replied.

"Bullpucky," Harry shot back.

"I have enough, recession or depression, and you're driving to Fulton, Missouri, in something safe."

He was one hundred percent correct. Besides, they really needed a vehicle that wasn't a truck.

Harry, stunned, finally spoke. "It's beautiful. And I will be safe."

She couldn't have been more wrong.

6

"I resent that." Mariah D'Angelo's cheeks burned with indignation.

"You can resent it all you like, Mariah. You fell down on the job." Flo stated this calmly—too calmly.

"The techie is working on the problem. In the meantime, I've made notes from memory." Mariah slapped the table.

"How do we know you didn't make up the figures to cover yourself?" Flo went for the throat.

Inez lightly tapped the table with her gavel. "Ladies, this solves nothing. If we compare last year's income and expenditures to what we have so far, based on Mariah's memory, we'll get some idea of where we stand. Why you all trust computers is beyond me. You should keep the books by hand as well as on your computer. I'm not saying, Mariah, that you didn't need to file everything on your computer. I know it makes it easy to print copies, but it's always a good idea to keep vital information in a form not dependent upon electricity."

Mariah stammered. Nothing coherent came out.

Flo leaned back in her chair with her hands folded.

Liz Filmore, ever eager to put the Richmond chapter in a good light, said, "We do that."

"How wonderful for you." Mariah's voice could cut ice.

"Let's take a break. A fifteen-minute break. When we return, I expect to see an attitude adjustment." Inez rapped the gavel on the table again, her disgust apparent.

She rose, steadying herself for a moment on the table's edge. Her knees throbbed. Bad weather was coming. She stepped into the hallway. Although the alumnae chair emeritus, Inez had to take over the actual chair's duties because Mariah and Flo had made it impossible for Liz. Too young, cowed by the rich St. Louis and Kansas City alumnae, Liz couldn't keep order. Neither Mariah nor Flo paid the least bit of attention to her, but they respected Inez, even feared her a little. She was the only person on the twelve-woman alumnae board who could keep order. As St. Louis and Kansas City were vitally important to the economic health of Missouri, so they were to William Woods. Having a representative from each city was important. Seattle, large as it was, had not fielded as many alumnae over the years as had the two great and completely different Missouri cities.

Small knots of women chatted in the halls, lobbying for pet projects or gossiping about Mariah's computer crash. Some found it suspicious. Others felt that those things just happened.

Flo fanned the suspicious people. "Until we have an accurate accounting, I must assume all is not well with our funds."

"Are you suggesting Mariah misused them?" DeeDee Halstead, head of the L.A. chapter, leveled her gaze at Flo.

Flo hesitated just enough to intimate perhaps that was the case, but she said, "Mariah has enough money; she doesn't have to steal ours."

Flo left this group, satisfied she'd stirred the pot. She passed a few other members on her way to the ladies' room. As she opened the door to enter, Mariah pushed it to exit. They knocked each other off balance. Regaining that balance, they stared at each other for a moment.

"I should have known it was you." Mariah brushed back a straying lock of expensively colored hair.

"All you had to do was get your fat butt out of the way," Flo sniffed.

"Diva that you are, Flo, your butt—which surely harbors more cellulite than you care to admit—is no smaller than mine. But, you know, I've always respected your success. That's why I know you're trying to ruin me."

"What?" Flo was puzzled and irritated.

"Whenever we've been forced to talk to each other about school projects, you've mentioned a company or two. I researched them and sometimes even invested in them. Much as I hate your guts, I know you are a financial wizard."

"What's your point?"

"You set me up for a fall. I made money—until now."

"You're not my client. I have nothing to do with whatever it is you're talking about."

Mariah spat, "Liz is your protégée. I'm her client and I've lost a lot. You're behind it, and I know it!"

"I did no such thing. You're out of your mind." Flo raised her voice.

"I'm going to take you down, and you won't get up again." Mariah shook her finger in Flo's carefully made-up face.

"You'll go down with me." Flo brushed by her furious enemy.

While Flo and Mariah displayed their mutual antipathy, Inez, alone, walked to a window that faced north. Tree branches denuded of leaves waved in the wind. A front was on the way. She hadn't watched the weather today, but her body proved

more reliable than newscasters. Whatever was behind the front made her
bones ache.

Kenda Shindler, a cheerful soul—
which was helpful in her role as assistant to the president—was walking
down the hall and stopped to chat with
Inez. "Have you heard the weather report?"

"No," Inez replied.

"Unfortunately, a big snowstorm is
heading our way. The weatherman predicts it will last at least two days." She
paused. "How's it going?"

"I'd like to take Flo and Mariah and
knock their heads together. It's only ten
o'clock. By lunch I may be ready to kill
them."

"Ah." Kenda knew well their conflicts.

Inez shrugged. "Ever notice how
some people are energized by an enemy?" Kenda nodded, so Inez continued, "That's what we've got here. Tons
of energy but to no good purpose."

"Well, if anyone can straighten them
out, it's you."

"Thank you." Inez had her doubts.
"Tally in yet?"

"Yes, that's why I came by the meeting. They arrived an hour ago. Big Mim, Little Mim, and Tally. Good thing they flew in a day early. Oh, yes—Harry is here, too. With two cats and a dog." Kenda lowered her voice. "Is the dog properly housebroken?"

"Tucker? Oh, my, yes. And knowing Harry, she probably brought kitty litter and a box. She's good that way. I'll be glad to see all of them. It will be like old times, Tally and I rooming together."

"I wish I'd known William Woods when you were a student here." Kenda smiled.

"Smaller then. William Woods fosters lifelong friendships. That's certainly consistent. One becomes educated and grounded in our culture and uplifted by friendships."

Down the hallway, Mariah had raised her voice, and both women turned to look in her direction.

"I don't think they got the message about friendship." Kenda half-giggled.

"Oil and water, chalk and cheese."

"Board meeting tomorrow?" Kenda asked.

"Yes. Everything is taking twice as

long as it should." Inez grimaced. "Yet another meeting."

"Maybe Aunt Tally would like to sit in."

Inez laughed. "Kenda, I love Tally like a sister, but she has no patience with people. Never has. She'd take her cane and lambaste both Mariah and Flo."

Kenda said conspiratorially, "That might be just what they need."

"You've got a point there." Inez glanced at her watch, which sported a big round dial, making it easy to read, then called out, "Ladies, let's get back to it."

Kenda whispered, "Good luck."

"The thing is, they both want what's best for William Woods. I try to bear that in mind. And you know, Kenda, you work with the tools you're given. Does no good to complain."

"Right." Kenda admired Inez's outlook.

Two hours later, an exhausted Inez approached Fairchild Alumni House. She noticed the new Volvo station wagon parked by the curb.

Tally flung open the front door of the house as Inez neared. She'd been watching from the front window.

"Chickpea!" Tally threw open her arms, cane in one hand.

"Blossom!" Inez embraced her old friend. "We are going to have the best time ever."

"Always do. Step in. Nasty cold."

"Yes, it is." Inez closed the front door behind her as Tucker raced to meet her, sliding halfway down the short hall.

"Inez!" The corgi rejoiced at the older woman's presence.

"Tucker." Inez, with difficulty, knelt down to pet the dog.

"We can all get down. The trick is getting up." Tally grinned.

"Give me your cane and I'll make it look easy."

Tally handed over the cane with the silver hound's head for a grip. "Need another one?"

"I do not." Inez put both hands on the hound's head, steadied on the cane, and then rose without a wobble.

Tally slipped her arm through Inez's. "We're still upright."

Harry emerged from the kitchen. "Inez. I'm fixing tea. Like a cup?"

"Indeed. I took a chill walking back from the administration building."

Mrs. Murphy and Pewter shot out of the kitchen.

"*Inez!*" Mrs. Murphy rubbed against Inez's leg.

"Aren't you the pretty kitty." Inez liked Mrs. Murphy. She then spoke to Pewter. "Off your diet, I see."

"*I'm not fat. I have large bones.*"

"*Oh la,*" Mrs. Murphy sassed.

Pewter reached over to box her ears, but Mrs. Murphy easily eluded that paw.

Tally steered Inez toward the living room. No sooner had they settled down than Harry reappeared with a tray full of sandwiches. She placed it on the coffee table, then returned with the teapot and two cups. She called upstairs to Big Mim and her daughter, Little Mim, but they called back that they were unpacking.

Trudy Sweetwater had filled the fridge with all the necessities.

"Aren't you joining us?" Inez asked.

"Thank you, no," Harry politely declined. "You two need to catch up."

By their second cup they'd done just that.

Tally leaned back in the comfortable wing chair. "What do you think?" She meant about the hostility between Mariah and Flo.

"I don't think Mariah is stealing, but, Tally, my fear is those two will again divide the board into two camps. Happened five years ago, and we finally solved that problem when some of the more partisan people rotated off the board, while others, more open, came on to serve. Nothing will get done as each side jockeys for power."

"I fear that, too, Inez."

Inez nodded. "You see where gridlock brought Congress and the country. I don't want it to happen to us. There's got to be a way to stop it."

"What was it Professor Chuck Jones used to say?"

They both said in unison, "Trust your instincts and don't expect life to be logical."

7

Farmer that she was, Harry checked the Weather Channel. She could read the radar accurately for a layperson. A mighty clump of green with a yellow center and red spot bore down on Fulton, Missouri. From the speed with which it moved across middle America, Harry surmised it would arrive in central Missouri's lovely Callaway County by late tomorrow afternoon or early evening. If she wanted to explore the campus and visit the barns, this would be the time.

Big Mim and Little Mim were meeting with tomorrow's event organizers. Inez and Tally chattered gaily in the living room, having emptied their pot of tea.

Tally was also emptying her flask of gin. Happiness followed.

Harry wrapped a cashmere scarf around her neck; lined gloves and a non-bulky down jacket provided warmth. Cold though it was, the wind was what cut to the bone. She stepped outside, her three companions with her.

Pewter stopped, then wailed, *"It's too cold."*

Harry looked down at the rotund kitty, fluffed up, hunched down. "Pewter."

"Wimp." Mrs. Murphy delivered her judgment.

"I don't care what you think." Pewter narrowed her eyes.

"All right." Harry scooped up Pewter, opened the front door, and placed her inside. "Aunt Tally," she called out, "I've got Mrs. Murphy and Tucker with me. Pewter's in the house."

"Okay." Aunt Tally called back as Pewter hastened toward the sound of her voice.

Pewter remembered that Harry had put crackers on the tea tray. Perhaps she could snag a few.

Closing the door once more, Harry

headed off to her left toward the Rowland Applied Riding Arena, which was behind Tucker Dining Hall and other buildings. A pleasant walk on a pleasant day, it wasn't a bad walk on an unpleasant day.

The first stable at the Bancroft Equestrian Center came into view after seven minutes of leisurely walking. Once inside, both Harry and her friends were happy to be out of the wind. A few students performed chores in the clean, tidy building. The large UPHA arena was under the roof behind the main entrance area. Harry walked back to it, leaning over the side of arena boards. Three students worked Saddlebreds.

"Hello." A bright voice caused her to turn from the horses.

A petite, lean woman with an enormous smile held out her hand. "Gayle Lampe."

That smile was infectious. Harry smiled back. "Mrs. Fair Haristeen. Everyone calls me Harry."

"And?" Gayle indicated the four-footed contingent.

"Tucker."

At the sound of her name Tucker sat and raised her paw, which Gayle solemnly shook.

"Mrs. Murphy."

The tiger cat looked up as Gayle petted their heads.

"Used to horses, I can see."

"I have Thoroughbreds and one Saddlebred, Shortro, given to me by Renata DeCarlo."

At the mention of the movie star's name, Gayle replied, "Joan Hamilton of Kalarama. You must know her, because Renata is a client."

"I do."

"Kalarama, Callaway—both help us with horses. We don't buy any horses, and you know we teach all four disciplines. Horses are donated, some of them very good. We're indebted to people for their help. We've never sold a horse for meat price, and we don't put them down if they have injuries that render them nonserviceable. We find them homes and, more to the point, we check up on them when we can."

"That's an enviable record."

"That's William Woods." Gayle couldn't

refrain from boasting, but as the university was her life and she'd won many awards for both teaching and competing, she had good cause.

"What a glorious legacy."

Gayle noticed one of the students losing energy. "Keep your leg on, Tori. She's going to break gait."

"Yes, Professor Lampe." Tori pressed more firmly. Sure enough, the chestnut stepped up her pace.

"You must be here for Tally Urquhart."

"Yes, Miss Lampe," Harry answered with a slow smile.

"Call me Gayle. You may call me worse when you know me. Come on into my office."

Her office, a rectangular space with a window so she could look into the arena, was a perfect location for the premier Saddle Seat instructor in America.

"I read your book," Harry spilled.

"You did?" Gayle seemed astonished as she offered Harry a chair.

Mrs. Murphy jumped into Harry's lap. "Joan Hamilton suggested it. I learned a lot. Saddlebreds are all in front of you.

You need really good hands. Thank you for your work."

"Are you showing?"

"No, I foxhunt and trail ride."

"I wish we had foxhunting here. We have to go to St. Louis or Kansas City. It teaches balance over terrain, something we don't really get here. And, of course, the other professors and I have to tell the kids the fox isn't harmed."

"Good for environmental studies. You see things and get to places many people don't get to even with ATVs." Harry noticed the framed photos on the wall. "Quite a gallery. Saddlebreds are so beautiful, no wonder movie stars like William Shatner and Renata DeCarlo show them."

"Beautiful they are. I wish more people realized how versatile they are."

"Yes," Harry replied simply. "Will you be giving a speech tomorrow night?"

"Me? No." Gayle smiled with relief. "Jahnae Barnett, our president, will. Have you met her?"

"No, I just got in about three hours ago."

"I'll make a point of introducing you.

She's extraordinary: a good administrator, someone who loves the classroom, a wonderful fund-raiser, but most of all, a true visionary. When people do what they love, everyone benefits."

"I believe that. Your career testifies to that. I'm sorry I won't hear you speak."

"Come back. Actually do come back. We keep riding in the ring in winter, but when the show season starts, we do take the students outside. Do you know most of our equestrian science graduates are working in the horse world?"

"I didn't know that."

Gayle glanced down at Tucker, who had come around to sit by her. "What an expressive face. Corgis are tough dogs." She paused. "We are very grateful to Aunt Tally and to her family for allowing us to celebrate her centennial and raise funds. I don't need to tell you how tight things are."

"Doesn't seem to be an end in sight."

"Her niece, Mrs. Sanburne, whom I'm sure you know, has pledged $250,000. Callaway Hills Stables has also pledged a nice sum, because the late Mrs. Weldon," Gayle paused, "adored Tally.

Tally stood up to her, but she was funny about it. Mrs. Weldon respected her because Tally never told her anything that wasn't so."

"That's Aunt Tally." Harry nodded.

"We are hoping to raise half a million. I don't know where we are now, but perhaps after Tally's speech, which should be memorable, more will be forthcoming."

"A half a million." Harry pursed her lips. "That's an ambitious sum."

Gayle pushed back a stray lock of hair. "Yes, it is. Then I think about those mega-universities with portfolios worth billions. It's overwhelming." She smiled broadly. "We aren't a mega-university for which I am grateful. What we have, though, is our Ivy League Society. Did Tally mention it to you?"

"No."

"Many of our alumnae and alumni and friends, as well as people who did not attend here but who are attracted to our ethic and our commitment to the student, make William Woods University a beneficiary of a will, insurance policy, or trust. Tally is a member of the Ivy League

Society, but she warns us that she intends to live forever."

Harry laughed. "She's making a run for it."

"I so look forward to seeing her tomorrow and to hearing her speech on the very day she hits the century mark."

At that moment, feeling a Tanqueray glow, Tally was discussing her speech.

"And . . . ?" She had given Inez the gist of it.

"Blossom, reality is always in order. From what you've told me, that's what you're doing: telling the truth. Odd, isn't it? We try to tell the truth throughout our lives, but for some reason people don't begin to listen until we're old."

"Idiots!" Aunt Tally waved a dismissive hand.

"More by the minute, too." Inez settled back in the comfortable chair. "People believe what they see on TV. Astonishes me. Or what beeps up from their hand-held BlackBerries and whatever."

"All of that controlled by large corporations. Well, not blogging and messages, but I am always suspicious where large profits are in order. I mean, Chickpea, there's not big money to be made from a tablet and a pen. Electrify it and . . . well."

"Profits, yes, but I don't think the power companies are perverting messages. However, all these devices draw power and give off heat. And think about it: You can't just throw out a computer. There are chips and things in there that apparently become dangerous when disintegrating, so they must be properly disposed of. If that is the case—and according to our refuse rules in Virginia, it is—then why aren't they dangerous to use? Isn't heat coming off the screen? Aren't those little semiconductors and wires emitting fumes or something unhealthy?" Inez, trained in the scientific method, was highly suspicious.

"Of course. Call attention to it with proof, and everyone and everything tied to computers will deny it. Remember when the tobacco industry fought the truth? How blindly stupid of them. Am I against smoking? No. But it damages the lungs. End of story. Am I against computers? No. But they damage the eyes and God knows what else."

"Truth is ever and always in short supply." Inez smiled ruefully.

Aunt Tally raised her voice. "You know what, I don't give a damn. I care about my people. If other people want to be sheep, let them march off to be sheared or, worse, to the slaughterhouse. You can't save people who won't save themselves."

"I suppose the truth is, you don't want them to take you down with them." Inez drew a deep breath. "To change the subject, this alumnae committee is making an old woman older."

Slyly, Aunt Tally purred, "Is that possible?"

Inez laughed. "You're older than I."

Aunt Tally laughed, too. "Touché. What's troubling you?"

Inez scrunched down deeper in the chair. Pewter had artfully placed herself on the padded area so Inez stroked her, which pleased the little egotist.

Aunt Tally raised her eyebrows.

"Before I answer your question, let me ask you one. Do you feel old?"

"Oh," a pause followed, "when I get out of bed it takes me fifteen minutes to straighten up. And I never feel old when I take my medicine." She held up her martini glass. "Truthfully, no. I look in the mirror. I know I'm old, but inside I don't feel it."

"I didn't. I do now."

"Why, you look the same to me. You have boundless energy. And you take no prisoners. You haven't changed."

"I realize I don't relish solving problems like I once did. I thank Mariah D'Angelo and Flo Langston for that."

"Really?" Aunt Tally's eyebrows shot upward quickly.

"Yes. There was a time when I would have felt such accomplishment in harnessing those two to pull together. Now I think I can do it but I'm tired, tired of people's petty damned egos. If I didn't love our alma mater so much, I'd have chucked the whole bag of beans."

Aunt Tally rubbed her tennis elbow, which ached from the increasing low pressure. "Can't Liz resume being chair-woman?"

"Hell, no. That's why Jahnae asked me to again chair the committee. Liz bounced between Mariah and Flo like a shuttlecock."

"I thought our broker was Flo's crea-ture." Then Aunt Tally corrected herself. "I'm talking about only a small portion of my discretionary funds when I call Liz my broker; you know that Scott and Stringfellow manages the bulk of my family funds." She cited a prestigious Virginia firm whose performance record and care of clients spanned most of the twentieth century.

"Yes and no. The board itself elected Liz their chair last year. She's still young—well, young to us; she's barely forty, if that."

"Darling, these days they get face-lifts, boob jobs, fanny-lifts, tummy tucks at thirty."

Inez wrinkled her nose. "All that vio-lence done to young bodies. Well, back to your question, more or less. Liz pays great attention to Flo; after all, they are in the same business. But Mariah has pots of money. Liz tried to walk a middle course as chair, but they both over-whelmed her."

"Hmm. I never perceived her as weak."

"She isn't. But those two are stronger, and she can't please both."

"She's done a good job with your portfolio since Victor died, hasn't she?" Aunt Tally mentioned Inez's late financial adviser.

"She has, but she's not really chair-man or chairwoman material. I'm an in-terim, but we need to elect a new chair. Of course, first I have to convince Liz to resign."

"Easy. Tell her we'll both pull our ac-counts."

"Blossom!"

"Inez, that's the way the world works."

"I'm not doing that. You know me bet-ter than that."

"*Meow.*" Pewter wanted Inez to con-tinue petting her, as she'd stopped.

"Yes, I do, but that doesn't prevent me from telling you the fastest way to achieve the desired result."

"*Me. Me. Me!*" Pewter raised her voice.

Inez looked at the cat, smiled, and resumed petting her. "The trick is to make Liz think this is her own idea."

"Well, if anyone can do it, you can."

"Yes, I think I can, but it gets back to my feeling old. Once I would have seen this as a game. I'd make up little goals and tick them off until I reached the final goal. Oh, you know, stuff like, first ten yards, introduce the concept in an off-hand way. Second ten yards, mention the time this wrangling takes away from her true calling. You get the idea."

"Clever."

"Clever it may be, but I resent it. I *am* getting old."

"Chickpea, people can feel management fatigue at forty-two. You just need a break."

"Perhaps." Inez felt better after listening to her dear friend. "There is one other little item, and this gets to the benefits of old age: One has many contacts, friends. When Mariah said at the meeting today that her computer crashed—"

Aunt Tally interrupted, "Wait a minute, I don't know about this."

"No one does, although I did have to tell Jahnae, who, being herself, remained calm and suggested a few paths to clarity. And you'd better be quiet. This is board business."

"Oh, balls! I'm your best friend, your second skin and, furthermore, I will be one hundred years old tomorrow. I'm entitled to secrets!" She grinned, and in that grin, Inez saw her friend again as she was at twenty.

"I know it, but I had to say it. Okay, here's the rub. Mariah is our treasurer. We open every meeting with the secretary's report, followed by the treasurer's report. Mariah said her computer crashed. She didn't keep a written record."

"Idiot. Young people really are stupid to trust machines."

"Well, Blossom, we were idiots in our own way. We believed the War to End All Wars had done so."

"All right." Aunt Tally grimaced but held up her martini glass in a silent toast to Inez's insight.

"I called Billy Bonito, who is president of the Big River Bank, where our account smolders." She smiled.

"Billy Bonito who drove fine harness horses?"

"Still does, although he hasn't the time to compete as he once did. You weren't there in '77. Sugarcane collapsed in a workout at the Kentucky State Fair. I was there as the guest of Paul Hamilton."

"I miss him." Aunt Tally recalled Joan's late father, who had purchased Kalarama Farm after World War II. "Frances, too." She mentioned his wife, Frances Paralee who passed in 2005 at age eighty-five.

"We were standing at the workout chute that led into the grand arena when she just dropped in the traces. I ran over, as there wasn't time to find Billy's regular vet. To make a long story a little shorter, I managed to save her. She retired to become a foundation broodmare for Billy."

"Wonder if he's still so handsome?"

"'Spect he is. Anyway, I flatly told him our problem and knew I was asking him to do something improper. He understood. For one thing, if something is amiss in that account, we've got to catch it right away."

"And?" Aunt Tally was keen on this now.

"The account is in good order. However, Mariah did withdraw twenty-five
thousand dollars, in cash, which she replaced today at 2:12 P.M. She transferred
money from a joint account—personal—
at Big River."

Sitting bolt upright, Aunt Tally whispered, "That's not right."

"I know it. I suspect that is why the
computer crashed, and I put 'crash' in
quotation marks."

"Does she have the right to issue
checks?"

"She does, but the twenty-five thousand was cash.

A silence followed. "Get rid of her. We
can't make a big deal out of it, but this
must never happen again. No officer
can write a check to herself." Another
pause. "Mariah doesn't strike me as
dumb enough to pull a stunt like this."

"Me, neither. That's what really worries me. The incongruity of it."

"Any withdrawal, check or cash, is on
a computer file."

"Right." Inez paused. "She then con-
tributed twenty-five thousand to your
fund with a personal check."

"Oh, dear."

Inez sighed. "This just doesn't compute, forgive the pun."

"Still, she has to go."

"I know. I know. While I was at it, I did a little snooping around through friends. Her business—Fletcher, Maitland, and D'Angelo—is losing money. People aren't buying much jewelry these days. Her husband's construction business is down. He's laid off thirty percent of his workers, but he does have large projects rolling, one of which is the new hospital near Independence, Missouri."

A very long silence followed this. "Can you remove her without fanfare? But I'm not sure we should right at this moment. It would be easier to get the board to pass an amendment saying all checks need to be countersigned by the secretary. In fact, we should have done that years ago." Aunt Tally nodded. "Andrea from Omaha is the secretary, and that one is sharp as a tack."

"She is. I need to speak to her first, then build a consensus in a nonthreatening way. Even if I don't specifically mention the twenty-five thousand dollars, if I float this issue it means Flo will take the warpath. She'll sense Mariah has dropped the ball, and she'll be relentless until she finds out. Even if she doesn't, she'll create more problems. I doubt Mariah will take this calmly, even though she'll know I know."

"Why?"

"I'll tell her."

"What a pickle."

"Exactly."

8

Looking out the window of the class-room, Liz saw Gayle giving Harry, Mrs. Murphy, and Tucker the garden tour of the Bancroft Center, the new Rowland Applied Riding Arena, and fenced areas.

She returned her blue-eyed gaze to the two women standing before her, neither one in good humor this afternoon. It was as though she'd overheard Inez and Aunt Tally discussing her lack of leadership. Had she known being chair of the alumnae board would prove so onerous, she'd never have accepted. Seeing Inez forcefully maintain order and keep the group on track only underscored her failings. She wanted to get herself back on course, not least because some of the women were her clients. Mostly it was due to ego. She'd resign soon enough, because this was a real pain in the rear end, but she wanted to do it on her own terms and after some small success.

She didn't hustle the board for business any more than any of the other women did. Flo was a broker, as was she. Mariah owned and operated a high-end jewelry store in Kansas City. Andrea, along with her husband, owned a large trucking operation based just west of Omaha. DeeDee, from L.A., was one of the most successful real estate brokers in the vast easy-money city— well, easy one day, hard the next. Another member ran a large paving-stone company; one was a boutique grocer. The range of activities was impressive. A physician and a lawyer were also on the board. Trudy Sweetwater worked for an irrigation company and Mo Avola bred Red Angus cattle.

Interestingly, no academics served. Liz once asked Inez why, and the thin old lady quipped, "They don't know how to make real money."

Liz wondered if John Maynard Keynes

qualified as an academic and decided it was best not to counter Inez.

"Will you get to the point?" Mariah plopped behind a school desk.

Flo also decided to sit.

The classroom, which would be empty for another two hours, proved pleasantly warm. Liz sat between the two, moving her light desk so they'd be in a semicircle.

"Well, I'd like to iron out some difficulties. I feel guilty that Inez has had to step in for me and it's because I can't get you two to cooperate."

Flo, eyes narrowed, said through compressed lips, "I will do anything for William Woods. Just what the hell is it you wish me to cooperate about?"

Measuring her words, Liz replied, "It seems to me that whatever Mariah suggests, you counter, and"—she looked at Mariah—"whatever Flo says or suggests, you take issue with."

"Is it my fault Flo's ego is in an ever-expanding state—gaseous, you might say." Mariah smiled wickedly through her violet-tinged lipstick.

"Ego! Mariah, you still haven't forgiven me for stealing, as you put it, Dick Langston."

"I confess. When he chose you, I was upset, but as time has passed, I'm ever so glad." She waited a beat. "He's aged terribly since losing the Democratic nomination for governor eight years ago." She looked at her nails, looked up again. "And, really, darling, couldn't you two find a better plastic surgeon? He looks . . . well, Asian."

"You leave my husband out of this," Flo spat.

"Look, you two, this is exactly what I'm talking about. I don't know all that has transpired in the past. Can't you table it for the good of the school?"

"I'll be convinced it's for the good of the school when she doesn't put forward Pete"—Flo named Mariah's husband—"to construct any new buildings on campus."

"I have never, never put forward my husband. He makes a bid like any other contractor in this state."

"And you're an important member of the alumnae board. I say that gives Pete the inside track."

"It does not. He's above reproach."

"Better than I can say for you." Flo fluffed her streaked hair with her right hand.

Mariah, face flushed, half-rose out of the wooden seat. "Just what does that mean?" She caught herself, sat down, then calmly switched subjects. "Were we to have a dishonesty contest, I do think I'd trail you, darling."

"That's enough." Liz slammed her hand on the table.

Flo, coolly assessing the attractive younger woman, spoke in a dark alto, "Just who do you think you're talking to?"

"You, Flo. You . . . you should be above this."

Mariah, arms crossed over her hunter-green sweater and a gold pashmina draped over her shoulders, laughed. "You two could win Oscars. What a performance. I'm actually impressed."

Flo snapped her head in Mariah's direction. "What in the hell are you talking about?"

"This is just too orchestrated, you know—pupil chides mentor, mentor retaliates. You're in collusion. And you both want to destroy me."

"Why would I want to destroy you?" Liz was incredulous. "I do business with you."

"Yes, you do. And you've been good up until now. I think Flo used you to get back at me. 'Make her a lot of money,' she probably said, 'Then pull the plug.'"

"You're out of your mind." Flo was slack jawed.

"Clever. I'll give it to you. Of course, I knew Liz would follow your lead, but the profits were impressive, and I—stupidly, I freely admit—thought perhaps she could put business before your personal relationship. Too late, I realized your relationship was more complicated than that. You had to have been feeding Liz information."

"I did not! For one thing, Mariah, you know nothing about my business except that I'm a broker. I stick to the basics: food, shelter, energy, and agriculture. I don't even suggest investing in clothing. Ever present in my mind is the flameout of Halston. I'm extremely cautious about emerging technologies. Yes,

I could have made my clients much more money in the dot-com explosion, but that was more than a decade ago. I was just beginning to hit my stride. I deliver slow, sustained growth. Liz goes after the high-risk stuff, and if you've been part of that, so be it. I, too, have bought into some packages she's put together—non-technology, if you care. But it's not my area of expertise."

"Brava," Mariah said drily.

It was Liz's turn to speak. "Mariah, the market is down thirty-five percent. Chrysler and GM have collapsed. The government spent our money bailing them, plus they've thrown billions at failing banks. Lehman Brothers died a painful death, and AIG has been a holy horror. I didn't create those conditions, but Tim and I are doing better than average. Our customer portfolios have lost— of course they have—but less than the market average. Furthermore, I don't think I should discuss the particulars of your portfolio with Flo in the room."

"You don't have to; she already knows them."

"I do not." Flo took a breath, composed herself. Once again her hand fluttered to her hair. "I have, however, considered your business. On Dick's 57th birthday, I bought him a gold Jaeger-LeCoultre Reverso. At that time, it cost $16,700. It's an understated, fabulous watch, wouldn't you agree?"

"Fabulous." Mariah nodded.

"Along the way, I did price the gold Rolex Oyster, which ran for about thirty thousand. The platinum was out of sight. I was just curious. Curious about pearls, too, as I've always wanted another strand. I so love pearls." She paused, a large smile animating her face. "Yet Fletcher, Maitland, and D'Angelo routinely sell these brands for about thirty percent less. Only Tourneau does that," she named a firm specializing in watches, "and at those prices they sell rebuilt ones, although they do sell new ones for a bit less than other companies. But no one delivers the deals you do."

"We're quite proud of that. We're efficiently run. Always have been. Cut the fat."

"You liar. You're selling fakes."

"How dare you! How dare you accuse me of such a thing!"

"I dare because it's true, and I will prove it."

Mariah stood up, threw her shawl more tightly around her throat, and picked up her alpaca coat. She headed for the door, then turned. "Liz, Flo, I will expose you two if it's the last thing I do." She slammed the door behind her.

Flo rose and picked up her jacket—a lined waxed Filson, since she'd planned for the weather. "Liz, I'd say your attempt to get us working together was a spectacular failure. Or, to use your word, a 'flameout.'"

Liz, shaky, rose to her feet, also. "Flo, is it true about Mariah?"

"I will prove it. In my own good time." She turned a steely gaze on her understudy. "I always get to the bottom of things, Liz. Never forget that."

9

Pewter flopped on her side on the parlor rug and opened one eye when Harry, Mrs. Murphy, and Tucker gratefully came in from the cold.

Tucker hurried over. *"You missed seeing all the horses."*

"We have horses at home." Pewter rolled onto her other side.

"Lazy. Fat, lazy cat."

"Am not."

Tucker, a twinkle in her eye, said, *"Biggest manure pile I've ever seen."*

Irritated, Pewter lifted her head. *"Why would I care about a manure pile?"*

"Oh, you know, in case you had to throw up a hairball."

Mrs. Murphy's laughter further enraged Pewter, who shot up and swatted at the corgi, who ducked. *"Death to tail-less dogs!"*

"Sourpuss." The corgi bounded to the kitchen.

Harry, already in the kitchen, heard the fuss. "What's going on out there?"

"Oh, nothing." All three animals were now in the kitchen and responded in unison.

Given that it was late March, the sun set later. However, the low, billowing gray clouds, emitting a soft glow, moved quickly overhead and blotted out the sun.

"Someone's coming," Tucker barked.

Many someones. The Jameson Singers gathered outside the front door. Their first song, "Charleston," brought back Tally's youth.

Big Mim, upon hearing the lively song, opened the door. "Come on in. It's bitter cold out there."

The young women filed in to the parlor, formed a triple row semicircle, and began to sing the songs that Tally and Inez would know. Soon the two old ladies sang along with them.

"I Wonder Who's Kissing Her Now"

led into "Black Bottom." Song after song recalled a past, at once near yet far. Tears rolled down Tally's cheeks, then Inez's, and soon everyone was crying.

Harry's grandfather had had an affair with Tally. This had all come to light a few years ago, but Harry was reminded of it now, reminded of how bittersweet Aunt Tally's life had been.

After the songs ended, Aunt Tally laughed and said, "We're all a bunch of big babies."

Everyone laughed with her.

Big Mim and Little Mim had known of the serenade, so they brought back from town a smorgasbord of food to augment what Trudy Sweetwater had supplied. The students dove in. William Woods's cafeteria food was good, but students did get bored with it. Champagne was uncorked, and Aunt Tally as well as the more rigid Big Mim chose not to ask anyone's age. Surely one glass of champagne to toast a grand old gal was not out of order.

Finally, by eight, all had left. The Albemarle County contingent and Inez recapped today, and Tally and Inez reminisced about their wonderful, funny experiences when they were students in the late twenties and early thirties of the twentieth century. A sharp wind rattled one of the front windows.

"That packed a punch." Harry rose to see. "Oh, my God, it's snowing. Really snowing. I didn't think it would get here until tomorrow afternoon."

Aunt Tally, Inez, Big Mim, and Little Mim came to the windows. The cats jumped on the back of the stuffed chair to get a better look.

"Sweeps over the prairie like wildfire. Nothing to stop it," Inez remarked.

"I had no idea." Harry wished she could see the prairie, which she figured started in Kansas. Harry had never seen the west and longed to do so.

"This old house is in good shape, but it isn't insulated the way newer ones are. Better put an extra blanket on the bed, girls." Aunt Tally remembered her first year adjusting to Missouri weather.

Harry looked down at Tucker. "Oh, little one, we'd better get our evening constitutional in right now."

"I'm not going out in that," Pewter quickly spoke up. *"I'm using the dirt box."*

Harry had put the dirt box in the basement and left the door ajar. She cleaned the box about every hour on the hour.

Outside, the snow, coming down in large flakes, was beautiful. Tucker, in her blue collar and blue leash, looked smart as she, Mrs. Murphy, and Harry took a brisk walk.

Harry figured that walking behind the stables was the best idea. Just in case Tucker couldn't make it that far, she had a yellow plastic bag unwrapped over her arm. Her winter coat somewhat got in the way.

Fortunately, Tucker waited until behind the stables. When the corgi was finished, they walked by the manure pile.

The last stall-mucking had been completed, and steam rose off the piled-up mixture of bedding and manure.

"Blood." Tucker sniffed, pulling Harry to the pile.

"So it is." Mrs. Murphy put her nose at the bottom of the large manure pile.

"Come on, Tucker, you've smelled horse poop before." Harry tugged at the leash.

"Mom, blood. Fresh blood. If I can smell it through all this, there's a lot of it!"

To no avail, Harry chirped to her friend, "Come on, Tucker. It really is cold, and it's snowing harder."

Reluctantly, Tucker gave up. She knew that when the pile froze, no scent would lift off.

Later, as everyone retired to their quarters, Inez rapped on Aunt Tally's bedroom door. "Awake?"

"Come on in."

The two sat there, wrapped in heavy robes. Across her lap, Inez had a long, wrapped gift.

"I brought you a present."

"Let's celebrate it with a dash of gin and a cigarette. I'm dying for a cig."

"Thought you gave them up," Inez remarked, who smoked three cigarettes a day, no more, no less.

"Did. But being back at college reminds me of when I smoked like a chimney."

Inez laughed. "We thought we were so daring."

"Modern." Aunt Tally got up, retrieved her gin from the chest of drawers along with a bottle of vermouth.

"Glasses?"

"Brought two up."

She mixed a martini, sans olive, and handed the stiff drink to Inez.

"Potent." Inez smiled broadly.

"I'm not a wimp. Neither are you. None of these designer drinks. Gimme the real stuff. May I open my gift?"

"Please." Inez placed her glass on the nightstand and gave Tally the present topped off with a colorful burgundy-and-forest-green bow, school colors.

Like an eager child, Aunt Tally removed the bow and tore off the paper. "It's a cane, just like my silver one but with a gold head! Oh, Inez, gold is frightfully expensive."

"Pull the head."

As Tally did so, a long, straight sword slid out with a quiet swish from the ebony cane, which was a scabbard. "Glory be."

"Sharp, sharp, sharp."

"What an extravagant present."

"You're worth it. Keep it close, Blossom. These are crazy times, what with young people hooked on meth, some on PCP. Makes marijuana and cocaine look benign. Drugs mystify me. I can't understand why anyone would do them."

"Me, either. Gin is much better." Aunt Tally laughed. "What a beautiful, beautiful gift. You're a sweetie to worry about me. No crackhead will get me, Chickpea. I'm too mean."

"You've got a point there." Inez savored her martini.

"It is a crazy world, isn't it? I never thought I'd live to see my country topsy-turvy, the lunatics running the asylum. Drugs, a fence at the border with Mexico, religious nuts. Crazy."

Though not particularly nostalgic, Inez did think things were better in her youth, with the exception of entrenched sexism and racism; even then, in most situations people behaved with good manners in daily discourse, regardless of hardships. Inez took another sip. "You asked earlier if I feel old. When I look at the world now, I don't feel old but I don't understand, and the loss of civility truly upsets me."

"Me, too. And the language. Vulgar. Shows a pathetic lack of imagination. If you're going to insult someone, be creative. The 'F' word is so . . . well, non-creative."

" 'Tis." Inez inhaled the smoke Tally exhaled. "Oh, give me a cigarette."

Tally lit one for Inez off hers and handed it over. "Another nail in your coffin."

Inez laughed. "You do bring out the worst in me."

"I hope so. What are friends for?" Aunt Tally glanced at the small electric clock by the bedstead. "Another four hours and I will be one hundred. I was born at 2:02 A.M." She leaned forward, placing her hand over her friend's. "I wish I could do it all over again."

"Me, too."

"You know, Inez, I really don't want to die."

"I don't, either. I know many of our classmates suffered so at the end that they wanted to die. We're still healthy. It's a game of chance. We drew lucky cards."

"So we did, but if it's my time, then I hope it's fast. No lingering."

"I feel the same way." Inez's eyes misted. "Oh, Tally, where, where did the time go? Like you, I'd do it all over again, even those times when my heart was barbecued on a spit. I love this life."

Aunt Tally finished her gin. "Me, too. And one of the reasons I love it is because I have you for a friend."

"Oh—" Inez couldn't finish her sentence.

They cried, then laughed, finished their martinis and cigarettes, and went to bed, as the world outside transformed into a cold but extraordinary winter kingdom.

10

Given that it was going to be a long day, Inez started the meeting at nine. A foot of snow already covered the ground. Still, it kept coming down.

She looked around the room. "Let's wait five minutes."

Flo wiggled in her seat but said nothing. She conspicuously checked her watch.

Five minutes passed.

"Does anyone have any idea where Mariah is?" Inez asked.

"We can go on without her," Liz stated.

"Yes."

The meeting went smoothly without Flo and Mariah sniping at each other.

Inez wrapped it up in an hour, to her

great surprise. Then she walked through the hall to Kenda Shindler's office.

"Hello."

"Kenda, did Mariah call you to say she wouldn't be attending the meeting?"

"No."

"That's not like her."

Inez left after a pleasant exchange. She walked along the shoveled paths back to the Fairchild Alumni House. Once there, she pulled out her cell and called Pete, Mariah's husband. Not wishing to worry him, she asked if he knew where Mariah had stayed last night. He cited a very nice B&B. Then Inez told him that Mariah hadn't attended the board meeting. This surprised him, but he didn't seem alarmed.

Next Inez called Gayle Lampe, because Gayle knew Mariah's habits fairly well; they often traveled to the summer Saddlebred shows together. But Gayle hadn't heard from Mariah after a quick coffee in Gayle's office at about 6:00 P.M., the previous evening.

Inez fought a sinking feeling in her stomach. She didn't want to spoil Tally's big day with her worry over Mariah. First she called Jahnae Barnett. Jahnae suggested they should leave a message with the proprietor of the B&B. If Mariah didn't show up by 2:00 P.M., Jahnae would call the police.

11

Deputy Knute Sorenson arrived at Jahnae Barnett's office at 3:00 P.M. in a hard snow. Residents of Callaway County might be accustomed to driving in the snow, but there was always a slick spot here or there or the one fool who flew along at sixty miles an hour, only to spin out of control. It had taken the deputy longer to get to the campus than he would have liked.

Inez, tired, waited with Jahnae. The president had also called her husband, Eddie Barnett, a calm figure in a crisis and one not given to flights of fancy. Cognizant of news that the storm would worsen, he was heading home from one of his XVIII Wheelers Truck Washes out on Route 70. While Eddie might not carry an official title at the school, his common sense was appreciated by his wife, who was facing a troublesome, perhaps deeply upsetting situation.

Inez explained to Deputy Sorenson, a competent fellow of about thirty-four, who was missing and why she thought it highly unusual.

"Any reasons you can think of concerning her absence?" He was a pleasant, respectful young man.

"No," Inez replied patiently. "She did borrow from the alumnae accounts without clearing it with the board, but she replaced the money quickly. Twenty-five thousand dollars."

"Did anyone else know but you?"

"The president, Dr. Barnett, was informed yesterday."

"Did Mrs. D'Angelo have enemies that you knew about?"

"Flo Langston. Perhaps 'rival' is a better term than 'enemy.' They graduated in the same class in 1974. Never did get along."

"Did Mrs. Langston know about the twenty-five thousand dollars?"

"No," Inez crisply replied. "Had she

known, she would have used it against her. The two have been fighting for control of the board for the last year. It reached a nadir recently. The standing chair had to step down, which is why I'm acting chair despite my advanced age."

"Which is?" He'd been scribbling in his notebook.

"Ninety-eight."

He looked up quickly from his notebook, his brown eyes wide. "Ninety-eight."

"Ninety-eight." Inez smiled, and old though she was, a hint of flirtation infused that smile.

"If you don't mind me asking, ma'am, how have you kept so, uh, fit?"

"I'm an equine vet. Still go out on a case as a consultant. Lots of physical labor and using one's mind. And I'm an alumna of William Woods. I like to think I've kept going because I want to know what's happening at my alma mater."

Jahnae said evenly, "I called the bed-and-breakfast where Mariah was staying; she never came back last night. Her car is parked by the barns. She often parks there when visiting here. She's a passionate horsewoman. We are beginning to worry, obviously."

Inez spoke up, "No one has touched the car, for what that's worth."

"Might be helpful." He then asked, "Did she ever threaten anyone physically?"

"Well," Inez temporized, "not exactly. Two board meetings back, she threatened to tear off Flo Langston's face."

"Was Mrs. Langston frightened or angry?" He scribbled again.

"Angry. She said if she were to tear off Mariah's face, she wouldn't know where to start since she always saw two."

It took the deputy a moment to grasp the insult.

Jahnae said, "Officer, is there any way to keep this low-key? We're celebrating the one hundredth birthday of one of our alumna this evening. The weather is already causing some distress. We don't need"—she thought for a moment—"another problem. We've assembled the alumnae board so that you might question them as soon as possible. They're sworn to secrecy until after the event."

"Think they'll keep their promise?" He'd seen enough of human behavior to know that most people couldn't resist being the bearer of bad news; the greater the disaster, the happier they were to report it.

"I believe they will." Inez smiled. "If not, they answer to me."

He studied her for a moment, then smiled slightly. "I see."

Before questioning the board, Deputy Sorenson called for a backup. "Gina, I'm at William Woods. Will you go to the stables on campus and—" He glanced at Inez.

"New Range Rover Sport, black." She supplied the information.

"Find a new black Range Rover Sport parked back at the barns. The owner is missing. I've got some people to question. If there's anything there, I don't want it to walk."

Gina readily agreed. As everyone knew the university, she needed no directions. Deputy Sorenson then walked into the conference room.

Jahnae touched Inez on the shoulder. "Would you like me to attend?"

"No, you have enough to do. If there's any further development, I'll call you on your cell." Inez breathed deeply. "She's dead, Jahnae. I feel it in my bones."

Her face registering not shock but sad agreement, Jahnae nodded. "Let's pray she's not."

By 4:00 P.M., nothing new had turned up, and Inez walked through the snow to clear her head, then returned to the Fairchild Alumni House. Tally, Big Mim, and Little Mim were upstairs, getting ready for this evening's festivities. Harry was ironing her skirt in the kitchen. She hated ironing but had dutifully found the ironing board in a hallway closet. Inez told Harry everything, because she trusted Harry's keen mind.

"Tally won't find out until after the celebration, hopefully." Harry set the iron on its haunches. "Could Mariah have been involved in something more scandalous than a money problem?"

"Possible. These days anything is possible. Actually, it was probably always that way. It's just now we're badgered by news around the clock. It only makes things worse, I think." Inez sank into a kitchen chair.

"Maybe she had something on someone on the board. Blackmail. If business is on the skids, human behavior can always be relied upon for misdeeds. Or sex. Never run out of problems there."

"The D'Angelos are successful people; they contribute heavily to political campaigns. It's crossed my mind that she might have gotten involved in something unsavory, as you have said, gotten the goods on a prominent public figure. Mariah is too smart to try blackmail. It would have been disguised as something else." Inez tipped her head back, her silver curls catching what little light there was. She'd lit a cigarette, one of the three she smoked every day. "God, that tastes good."

"Cooper loves Dunhills, too. Terribly expensive. She can't afford them, but I know when she treats herself, it's the red pack. She doesn't like menthol."

"Haven't seen Cooper in a while. Remind me to bum a cig off of her. I love it.

Clears out my sinuses. I shouldn't be smoking, but . . ."

"Inez, at your age, you can do as you damned well please."

A big grin crossed Inez's symmetrical face. "I need to be reminded of that more often. I don't know how long I have to live, but less than you."

"I hope not." Harry smiled.

"If only I could live forever," Inez said wistfully. "I find this earth fascinating. I don't want to leave." She took another deep drag. "You'll never know how I struggled to give up this habit. Used to smoke a pack a day when I was practicing. At this point, why bother? Your sentiments." She nodded to Harry.

Harry returned to the subject at hand. "Do you know the candidates or elected officials that Mariah backed?"

"No. I'll ask Flo. They're at loggerheads about that, too. Flo's Democrat. Mariah, Republican."

"Have they ever agreed on anything? Charity, perhaps?"

Inez's head perked upward slightly. "Why do you say that?"

"They're community leaders; leaders

are always involved in some kind of charity. It's easy to steal from charities. For instance, you create a special need, like funding wheelchairs for indigent children. And when money comes in for your wheels-for-kids, you do supply wheelchairs. With lots of publicity. You then run all your expenses through the 501(c)3 corporation, a charitable nonprofit. You can live like a king. You can also create another corporation, and the wheels-for-kids makes gifts and loans to it."

"How do you know about this?"

"Had some dealings with the Brothers of Love on the mountain."

"Up next to Swannanoa." Inez cited a place just to the south of Route 250, below the Skyline Drive on- and off-ramp. "It may well be one of the most interesting places in Virginia, as it was founded, in a sense, to study religions without judgment, perhaps a century ago."

"Right."

"The Brothers of Love are crooked?" Inez was shocked.

"Some were. It's been straightened out."

"I'm happy to hear that. I—well, I don't want to get off track here. You think Mariah might have set up a charity?"

"Just a thought."

"I'll investigate. If she had, I'd think I'd know about it. Board members are merciless in pressing other board members about some special project."

Harry excused herself for a moment to go upstairs to the bathroom. She'd imbibed far too much tea.

Mrs. Murphy jumped onto Inez's lap. *"There's blood mixed into the manure. Tucker said so."*

Tucker, on the floor, said, *"If only you could learn what we're saying."*

"I still think you're making it up." Pewter rolled over to her left side. *"You just want me to be jealous because I didn't come along."*

"Pewter, I've read astronomy books over Harry's shoulder. I don't remember learning that you are the center of the universe." Mrs. Murphy flashed her Cheshire cat smile.

"Hateful fleabag," Pewter insulted her friend.

"Oh la," Mrs. Murphy sassed, which further inflamed Pewter.

Harry returned to the kitchen.

Inez was enjoying her nicotine hit as the cigarette burned down. "Both Flo and Mariah are totally devoted to William Woods and both were in Kansas City at the American Royal horse show in 1984, when Skywalk and Imperator went head to head in the five-gaited class. They were often at important events, not together, but there."

"I don't know much about Saddlebreds, but I really loved the Shelbyville show, and that Shortro is a dream."

"Good minds. Good mouths. Well, Skywalk, trained and ridden by Mitch Clark, and Imperator with Don Harris in the irons, were like the Yankees versus the Dodgers in the old days. Electricity. I was there, too. That is the extent of Flo and Mariah's confluence in the horse world. As to fund-raising—for, say, rebuilding a historic place or something like that—they were often involved."

"I see. Inez, if Mariah did have a special charity, would Flo have supported it?"

"Depends on the charity. That's why I think Mariah's disappearance is related to something else. Politics—as I mentioned, politics usually brings out the worst in people."

"I'm beginning to think politics is a platform for extreme egotism," Harry mused. "One stokes greed, the other fuels ego—the desire for power over others."

"Got that right, Snookums." Inez used the old term from Fanny Brice's radio show, then realized Harry had never heard of it. *"The Baby Snooks Show."*

"Pardon?"

"Baby Snooks was Fanny Brice's radio show. Screamingly funny. You saw *Funny Girl,* I'm sure."

"A revival. Wish I could have seen it with Barbra Streisand."

"Barbra Streisand started out singing at the Bon Soir on West Eighth Street in the Village."

"Inez, is there anything you don't know?"

Inez laughed. "When you're ninety-eight, you've lived a lot, plus I'm blessed with a sharp memory. . . . I have so many interests. Is there anything I don't know? Lots. I don't know why the human animal so likes to destroy things—living things—and I don't know where Mariah is." Her voice lowered.

"I'm so sorry, Inez. As chairman of the alumnae board, this lands in your lap."

"I'm worried, Harry." She paused and half-whispered, "Deeply worried."

"I'll help in any way I can."

"I know you will. I wanted to talk to you about the problems on the board before we got here. You often have unconventional solutions. Little did I know when I made that phone call that it would be something big when we got here. You have a good mind, and you aren't misled by sentiment. That's uncommon, really. You don't let emotion cloud your thinking."

"Thank you, Inez. Do you think Aunt Tally is in danger?"

A long pause followed. "It's possible. She has an unerring ability to stir a hornet's nest."

The animals had been listening.

"The blood in the manure pile," Tucker

said. *"Let's get out of here and go back there."*

Mrs. Murphy replied sensibly, *"Tucker, a blizzard is developing. There's more than a foot of snow on the ground already. The manure pile is covered and frozen. You know that. We couldn't dig into it if we had to."*

Pewter, finally drawn into this, said, *"I didn't see the manure pile, but it sounds as though it's in plain view."*

"In the back, but it's not hard to find," Mrs. Murphy answered. *"A manure pile is not a likely place to actually kill someone, though. For one thing, if the killer and Mariah made noise, a student might have heard it; the horses certainly would have. I bet Mariah was killed—if indeed she was—somewhere else. As the manure pile was fresh on the top, it would have been pretty easy to dump her there, pull the fresh manure over the body. Or the attack could have started there if the attacker was able to silence her in some fashion. I don't know; right now it makes no sense."*

"You don't know if the blood you smelled was hers, Tucker." Pewter was

now sorry she hadn't gone to the barns. *"And your idea means whoever put the body there would have to be lucky that the pile wasn't frozen."*

"Or they knew the maintenance routine." Tucker sat still. *"If only we could get Mom back there."*

"That's not going to be anytime soon." Mrs. Murphy looked toward the window.

Whiteout.

12

The wind whipped the heavy snows sideways at times. The mercury hung at twenty-two degrees but threatened to go lower as the night of March 25 deepened. By six, the time of the celebration, the auditorium held the students who lived on campus and most of the faculty and staff. The over-eighty alumnae had been bused in. All the alumnae board, except for Mariah, sat in the front row on the right of the center aisle. The elderly graduates sat on the left. The auditorium was half-full. There was no way those living far away could fight the storm. As it was, the students would be walking back to their residence halls holding hands in a chain. Losing one's way in a whiteout was easy, far easier than one would suspect. All people in cold climates knew stories of farmers frozen to death not ten yards from the barn door.

Harry left her three animal companions in the house. None of them had minded. She sat toward the front. Big Mim and Little Mim sat directly below the podium. Inez sat next to Jahnae Barnett and Aunt Tally on the stage.

Jahnae spoke, lovingly sketching the university's history. It was founded in 1870, five years after the end of The War Between the States, in response to the needs of female children orphaned by the conflict. Sixty-one years later, Tally Urquhart graduated. The Great Depression was two years old; Germany was rearming. Dismal though things might be, sound entered movies, and people flocked to theaters to forget their troubles. Professional sports provided another bright spot. It might have been the Great Depression, but the young were ever hopeful. This applied to the class of 1931 and to Inez's class, 1933.

Then as now, one of the hallmarks of William Woods was the lifelong friendships forged during the students' two years. William Woods became a four-year institution years after Tally and then Inez had graduated. At this, Jahnae introduced Inez, providing a bit of her history.

Inez could always command an audience. "I first met Tally Urquhart in 1931, my freshman year, in the stable. She said, 'Put your hands down.'

"I was riding a hunter but with Saddle Seat hands. From that day to this, my oldest and dearest friend has spoken her mind, usually without honey-coating her thoughts. She was right. My hands needed to come down.

"As you can imagine, we've lived through a great deal. We're still here. I will always be grateful to William Woods for the superior education I received at a time when not many women managed to achieve a higher education nor were encouraged to do so. Most of our classmates are gone now, but we have maintained vibrant friendships. I hope this one lasts another eighty years and then some, but failing that, we'll make the most of what time we have left.

"Without further ado, Tally Urquhart."

To thunderous applause, Inez took her seat next to Jahnae, who leaned over to congratulate her.

Using her gold-headed cane from Inez, Tally reached the podium without hobbling. Given Tally's short stature, Jahnae had arranged for a low podium. Tally wanted to stand. No chair for her.

Aunt Tally's eyes, still quite good, swept the audience, lingering on her niece and grand-niece; then she cast her eyes at Harry. Taking a deep breath, she addressed the assembled.

"Thank you for braving a Missouri spring to be here." She paused for the ripple of laughter, then continued, "You know how old I am. A woman who will tell her age will tell anything. I intend to do just that.

"I applaud your good sense in attending William Woods. I look back on my time here with untrammeled joy. I know I speak for Inez, too, for all the Grande Dames. The rest of our classmates have gone on. I miss them. This will happen to you many decades from now, the good-byes to those who sustained you in life. You go on. You retain their wisdom. You try to incorporate their best qualities into your behavior.

"One professor stands out in my mind—a wonderful, wonderful history professor, Chuck Jones. He used to tell us over and over again—to the point where Inez and I could look at each other, wink, and then repeat—'Trust your instincts and don't expect life to be logical.' He told us the truth.

"I will now try to live up to what I learned here, to what life has taught me, and to my own instincts. I will tell you the truth as best I know it.

"The first truth really is to trust your instincts. How easy that sounds. How difficult in practice. Why? Because all religion and government want to do is take you away from you. This isn't to say that organized religion is bad, only that it has strayed far away from spirit and is now part and parcel of the political structure. I guess the leaders of the various churches have forgotten Christ's words, 'Render therefore to Caesar the things that are Caesar's and to God the things that are God's.'

"As to the United States government, at the federal level it is a disaster. At the state level it can be intrusive. At the local level it often works very well. The further a politician is removed from those who are governed, the more mistakes he or she makes. And we have no statesmen, only politicians, hence the disasters that will accumulate and intensify until you become involved, which is to say fight back. Remember—in fact, tattoo this on the inside of your eyelids—Jefferson's quote that every American should hold sacred: 'That government is best which governs least.'

"Never ever believe that laws will solve a problem. The law allows what honor forbids. A problem will be solved only by people, not by a piece of paper."

She caught her breath, smiled, then continued, "So much for the so-called big issues. Now to life.

"Never hope more than you work.

"Animals never make a virtue out of boredom, best you don't, either.

"Don't get addicted to the struggle. If that statement doesn't make sense now, it will over time.

"There are some people you can't satisfy even if you blow a fan on them in hell. Ditch 'em. If that person is your boss, start looking for another job.

"Corruption is like a lily—brush against it, however lightly, and some of the pollen smears on you. Therefore choose your friends and your employers wisely. When the day comes that some of you start your own businesses and hire employees, concern yourself more with that person's character than their résumé. This gets back to the first thing I said: Trust your instincts.

"No dog would pay for sex. Humans, mostly men, worldwide, do. And people call dogs dumb animals.

"For God's sake, don't try to be perfect. It's impossible and you will become impossibly tedious.

"I have always believed a window into a person's true nature is how they treat animals, children, and the elderly. A person who mistreats animals isn't worth knowing. A person who mistreats children—especially those who abuse and kill them—should be shot without wasting any taxpayer money for a trial and for feeding them in prison. When a perpetrator of heinous crimes can live in a climate-controlled environment and eat three meals a day while good people go hungry, something is very wrong. Americans are paying for serial killers, rapists, and child abusers to live better than they do."

She paused for a moment, again swept the room with her eyes, and moved on to less troubling subjects. "Fall in love with open eyes. Easier said than done, so should you find yourself in a situation where you love someone who lacks the good taste to return the compliment, move on. You're better off without him or her.

"If your cat or dog doesn't like someone, trust your cat or dog.

"Obey the Ten Commandments. And they are the Ten Commandments not the Ten Suggestions.

"Having memorized them, I don't recall any exhortation not to smoke, drink, or overeat. Now if you stop smoking and drinking, you may not live longer but it will seem longer.

"Any offer too good to be true, is.

"Well, I've rattled on, hopped around, I'm not much of a speech giver. I still have goals, old as I am, and hope you do, too. I've pretty much given up on self-improvement, but there are things I'd like to know, such as the fact that cats were worshipped for milennia in ancient Egypt. When did that practice stop? And why don't our cats notice?

"Another thing, and this is just something from our community: In 1964 a young blacksmith was found dead in the road. No one ever caught the killer, and I've always wanted to know who did it. It's our county's Black Dahlia case.

"I'd like to see one of my horses or one of my niece's horses win the Maryland Cup, which is a steeplechase race." She smiled broadly. "Small goals, they won't set the world on fire, but if you have a goal, you'll push on.

"I wish each of you a long life if you have the will to live it, and life takes will. Perhaps someday something in my ramblings will pop into your head and you'll think, 'She knew her beans.'

"As for aging, don't fear it. Aging is a

return to your true self. The mind under-
stands time, the heart does not. My
heart is here at William Woods: the century is irrelevant."

She lifted her right hand, palm open,
and gestured to the assembled. "On-
ward and upward."

With that, she came out from behind
the podium and bowed, balancing on
her cane. The gesture was not lost on
her, for in more primitive times, one lowered one's head to the hetman or leader.
If your performance displeased, off with
your head.

Aunt Tally's remained securely on her
shoulders, for the audience cheered.
The young people in the audience liked
that she spoke to them without a whiff
of bullshit. That alone was worth applause.

Inez rose, as did Jahnae. Inez, having
lived almost to one hundred herself,
agreed with every word Tally had ut-
tered. She'd lived long enough to know
that Americans were like Gulliver in Lil-
liput: tied down by cords of government
regulation. And like Gulliver, we must
free ourselves, she thought to herself.

One willowy girl in the audience wiped away a tear. Even if she had to stand in line for an hour at the reception to talk to Tally, she would do it.

They filed out of the auditorium to the reception room, where dinner was waiting. Few students could have paid for this special dinner, nor could some of the over-eighty alumnae. Big Mim, asking for anonymity, had paid for the entire feast.

The Ivy Room, decorated in green and burgundy, smelled of roast beef, which was being served buffet style. As freshmen, sophomores, and most juniors were underage, no alcohol was served. However, Jahnae, being a wonderful hostess, had ordered a pitcher with Tanqueray and nestled it in a champagne bucket stuffed with shaved ice. The bucket sported burgundy-and-dark-green ribbons with an enormous bow. A place card reading "Tally Urquhart" in italics signified Tally's seat at the table. The vermouth was in a silver teapot, and the olives were on a small silver plate, toothpicks spearing them.

Jahnae had arranged for waitstaff to

bring filled dishes to the three tables of over-eighty alumnae. Some of the women would not have been able to get the food and carry it. A student waiter was in charge of alcoholic drinks at those special tables. He was amazed at how much those old girls could knock back.

The members of the alumnae board were seated at a table adjacent to Tally's.

Once the room was filled, Jahnae briefly welcomed everyone and encouraged them to enjoy the food. After dessert and coffee, students and friends could speak with their celebrated guest.

At the head table, Jahnae whispered to Tally that the vermouth was in the silver teapot.

"You've thought of everything," Aunt Tally praised her, as she fixed herself a liberal martini, then mixed a second one for Inez and a third for Little Mim. Big Mim rarely drank any form of alcohol and Harry drank only beer.

"But the weather," Jahnae laughed.

Aunt Tally offered to mix a martini for Jahnae. "The bartender's hand makes a mean martini," she said. In the South, the bartender's hand is the secret ingredient to a perfect drink. Jahnae understood and whispered, "On duty." That was easier than saying no, since Tally liked to share. Jahnae wasn't much of a drinker.

Harry held up her drink as Jahnae stood.

"To Tally Urquhart, an example to us all, a woman of high intelligence and keen observation and a born hell-raiser." Jahnae laughed again.

Big Mim, looking nothing like her seventy-some years, her jewelry understated but major, held up her iced tea. "To my aunt, who so resembles my mother and my brother, Myron, who died on the Bataan Death March: Here's to one hundred more years. Jahnae, might I add that if you had to live with her, the hell-raising might wear on you a bit." Big Mim laughed. "Aunt Tally, you really are one in a million."

Another toast and more laughter.

Next, Inez proposed a toast. "Here we are in 2009. Seventy-eight years of friendship with rarely a cross word but gales of laughter. May each of you have a friend so dear."

While toasts continued at table one, the alumnae board at table two put on a good face, but they were reeling over Mariah's disappearance as well as at the questioning by the police.

Liz Filmore, whose husband, Tim, sat next to her, moaned, "It seems so odd not to have Mariah here."

No one mentioned Pete, since he rarely accompanied Mariah. They usually went their separate ways.

"For one thing, it's quieter." Flo rose and made her way to the buffet table, which was already jammed with students.

The students gave way to Flo. They would have in most instances, but Gayle Lampe had impressed upon them to honor the alumnae board. As most of the assembled knew Gayle from the riding program, she'd been able to talk to them at the stables. This made her appeal—her order, really—more powerful. She had also impressed upon them the need to converse with the over-eighty crowd. She'd quipped, "You might learn something."

At the alumnae board table Andrea Rolf, an energetic member from the class of 1989, was nobody's fool. "Liz, drop it. We don't want Tally to get wind of it. Not during her time of triumph, anyway."

Liz halfway listened, then asked, "Did you like her?"

"Tally or Mariah?" Andrea couldn't help but tease her.

"Mariah, of course." Liz had knocked back two well-made daiquiris, and on a blizzard night, no less. Her husband kept a watchful eye without being too noticeable about it. She'd managed to guzzle more drinks when he'd been pulled away in conversation. He knew she was unsteady just as he knew no matter how hard he tried, she'd knock back the booze.

"Yes, I liked her. Her endless drawing of attention to her accomplishments was wearing thin, but I got along with her just fine."

"I'll go with." Liz used the Midwestern shorthand for "I'll go with you" as she rose to accompany her husband to the buffet. A bit of the Midwest had rubbed off on her during her four years in Fulton, as it had on all the graduates.

He put his hands under her elbows, all but lifting her up.

As the Filmores left for the buffet table, DeeDee Halstead, the alumnae member from Los Angeles, class of 1978, picked up her whiskey sour. "To Tally."

They stood, holding their glasses, and boomed out, "To Tally."

Liz, now at the buffet table, moaned, "How could they do that without me?"

Tim, hoping to keep her level, said, "You can make as many toasts as you want back at the table."

She leaned against him for a moment. "You're right, I can."

By now Flo had returned to their table and was enjoying her food. She encouraged the others to get to the buffet line.

But Trudy Sweetwater, who was tired and worried, had lost her appetite.

Andrea noticed and said, "Trudy, at least eat some salad. You'll pick up, and it's so healthy."

"I know." Trudy sighed.

Flo, with a strong voice, advised, "I understand. But there's nothing you can do. This really is Tally's big day. Let's put Mariah aside. I know that's easy coming from me, since I truly could not stand the woman, but Tally comes first." She looked up to see Tim and Liz approaching. "Try."

"You're right." Trudy got up; Andrea went with her.

Liz, once seated beside her husband, tested a piece of roast beef. "Delicious."

Tim did likewise. "Good beef out here."

Flo liked Tim well enough. "People still run big herds. When land prices hit the roof, some folks sold out and we suffered the rash of overdevelopment that many parts of the country did, but, Tim, real Missouri is still cattle, farming, and a little fishing to do you good." She beamed, for she loved her state.

Liz, oblivious to the discussion, piped up. "You know, I've come up with a package that focuses on computer-chip nanotechnology. It's the future."

"Liz, this isn't the time to discuss business," DeeDee chided her.

"Oh." Liz looked crestfallen.

"Eat your supper, honey. We may not get hot food for a day or two," Tim cajoled her.

"Why?"

He replied, "I expect whole swaths of Missouri will be without power. This storm is getting stronger and stronger."

Flo looked out the long windows of the banquet room. The outdoor lights glowed as best they could through the thick snow. "Yes, it is."

By the time everyone had dessert and coffee, the wind was shaking the building. Jahnae, forgoing dessert, spoke to each woman at the over-eighty tables. She then stopped by all the other tables to remind the students to go back to the residence halls in human chains.

The minute the dessert dishes were picked up, people descended on Tally. Big Mim stood with her aunt to assist her. Inez rose, too, since students wished to talk to her, as well.

For an hour, Aunt Tally signed programs and chatted. The line had dwindled and she was about to take a step toward the over-eighty tables when a willowy, attractive girl held out her hand.

"Miss Urquhart, I'm Aileen Tinsdale. I was named for my maternal grand-mother, Aileen Peavey."

"For heaven's sake!" Aunt Tally held the girl's hand. "You're Ralston's grand-daughter."

"I am."

Big Mim, Little Mim, Inez, and Harry all stared at the young woman. Her blue eyes, blonde hair, and regular features made her very attractive. Her manner made her more so.

"I remember when your grandmother left. Too many memories. We heard she moved to St. Louis because she found a good job there. Ralston had made some money, but not enough."

"Grandma passed away from colon cancer last year." Tears came into Aileen's eyes. "If only she could have seen you again."

Aunt Tally, touched, said, "I would have liked that. She was a good woman who faced a terrible situation. I'm so sorry to hear she's on the other side. Are you George's daughter or Linda's?"

Aileen added, "Linda's. My mother is doing fine."

"How's George? He was ten when I last saw him."

"Uncle George is great. Grandma said he looked just like Ralston."

"Is George happy?"

"Yes. He has three sons, and he and his wife, Judy, are so funny together. He owns a pharmacy in St. Joseph."

"Why St. Joseph?"

"St. Louis overwhelmed Grandma, but she had a really good job as an executive secretary. She met Clyde Waverly, a cattleman from St. Joe. He told her if she married him she'd never have to work outside the house again. She did and moved to St. Joe. It's a really nice place. I miss it. I love college, but I guess you always miss home. I miss my horse. Mom and Dad said next year they'd pay to board him here."

"That would be ideal." Aunt Tally liked this young woman. She didn't let go of her hand. "Any brothers and sisters?"

"One each. Hannah's two years behind me. John is four."

"I never heard from your grandmother after she left. Then I lost track," Tally said wistfully.

"Grandma didn't keep up with people back in Virginia. She couldn't take the reminders. She said she wanted to forget, and then she thought everyone had forgotten her and Ralston. She never really forgot."

"Neither did we," Aunt Tally said. "Honey, if you give me your address, I will keep in touch."

Aileen had been hoping for this. She pulled out a pink slip of paper on which she'd written her school address and phone number, her email address, and her home address in St. Joseph.

Aileen then noticed students lining up.

"Dr. Barnett told us we have to walk back to the residence halls in lines. The weather's so bad. I've never seen it this bad." She squeezed Aunt Tally's hand. "I'm so excited to meet you." She turned to Inez. "And you, too, Dr. Carpenter. Grandma told me you paved the way in Virginia."

"Your grandmother was very kind." Inez hugged the young woman, as did Aunt Tally.

After Aileen left, Aunt Tally said sotto voce to Inez, "All this hugging. I think every student hugged me. I'm not one for intemperate embrace, but I was glad to hug that child. I so hope the killer is found before I die!"

The alumnae board, waiting to say their good-byes, stepped forward after Aileen had walked away.

Liz overheard the last part of the conversation, as had Flo.

"You know." Liz began to wail.

"Know what?" Aunt Tally was puzzled.

"About Mariah."

Flo said sharply, "Liz, shut up."

"What's going on?" Aunt Tally was more than curious. She knew something was being kept from her.

At that moment Inez would have gladly killed Liz. The thought was occurring to Jahnae, as well.

Smoothly, Inez told her dear friend, "Blossom, one of our board members appears to be in trouble. We don't know any more than that."

"She's dead! I know she's dead." Liz, being a somewhat inebriated twit, made it worse.

"For Christ's sake, Tim. Get her out of here," Flo commanded Liz's husband.

He did as he was told, but Liz did not go quietly. She'd snuck in a third drink, which was all too apparent to her husband.

"You all are trying to shut me up!"

"That's right." Tim moved her faster and faster to the door.

He didn't stop for her coat but hauled her out in the high wind and snow, all but dragging her to the rental car.

"My coat."

"I'll get it later." He slammed the door and hoped the cheap piece of metal would start.

Nothing like a rental car to make one appreciate a good vehicle.

Back in the building, Aunt Tally squared off at the alumnae board. "Is she dead?"

Andrea replied honestly, "We don't know, but she's missing, and it's not like Mariah to miss a board meeting or your party."

"Why would Mariah . . . Well, let me put it this way: Who would wish her harm?"

Flo, to her credit, said, "Apart from me, I can't think of anyone."

Inez noticed the lines of students moving out and whispered to Harry, "Will you fetch our coats?"

"Of course." Harry left with Little Mim, who wanted to pick up her mother's and her own.

Back at the group, Aunt Tally thanked the alumnae board for their efforts and made them feel better. "I know you all didn't want to disturb me. I'm sure Mariah's vanishing was a strain on everyone. Thank you for considering my feelings on my special day."

Flo nodded. "Sooner or later we'll get to the bottom of this. You have a special present from the board. It's waiting for you at Rose Hill."

This certainly lifted Aunt Tally's spirits. "I can't wait."

She bid everyone good-bye, then she, Big Mim, Little Mim, Inez, and Harry donned their coats. Jahnae walked them to the door. A driver with a school vehicle waited for them. He first ferried Aunt Tally to the passenger seat. Although they were only a short distance from the door, the winds almost blew the tiny old lady away.

13

Once back at Fairchild Alumni House, the humans were greeted by the animals. Everyone sat in the living room as the lights flickered.

"If the power goes, no heat. No hot anything. The stove is electric," Big Mim announced.

"This won't be the first time William Woods has lost power. Let me rummage around. I bet there's a propane heater somewhere." Harry got up, with Mrs. Murphy, Tucker, and Pewter right behind her.

She checked the kitchen closets. Then she went into the basement. Sure enough, there was a propane heater, and it was full.

She brought it upstairs and placed it in the living room. "Just in case."

"Better look for candles or flashlights," Mrs. Murphy suggested.

Although Harry didn't understand what her cat was saying, she began searching for those very items. If you live in the country, you tend to think ahead. She found candles on the shelves of the broom closet and one flashlight. She brought these back to the living room.

"Detective work." Little Mim reached for a candle.

Inez and Tally had been discussing Mariah's no-show.

Aunt Tally turned a sharp eye on Inez. "What do you think?"

"Something has happened to her."

"Like foul play," Little Mim whispered.

"Don't jump the gun." Aunt Tally's voice rose. "She could have had a heart attack or a stroke. For all we know, she's in the hospital. Or having an affair, slipping off before a big storm. That would give her an excuse. Power goes out. No cell phone service or landlines. It's a possibility."

"Kenda Shindler called the hospitals.

In Columbia. In Jefferson City. In Kansas City. In St. Louis," Inez said. "No Mariah."

"She could have had a stroke and lost some memory. Maybe she doesn't know who she is." Aunt Tally then smiled. "Or she could know exactly who she is—people in love are resourceful. Like I said, the storm is a great opportunity."

"You know, we're all probably overreacting, thanks in part to Liz Filmore. Silly and drunk." Inez folded her hands across her chest. "Liz rubs some people the wrong way. I get along with her, but she's a social climber—at least, that's how I read her. But that tawdry ambition makes her work hard to make money. Good for me."

"Liz was loaded. Tim should have stuck a wine-soaked tennis ball in her mouth. Would have shut her up and pacified her at the same time." Aunt Tally laughed.

"Low-pressure systems don't help," Little Mim said. Then she explained, "People feel tired, some get edgy. Maybe it's not so bad."

"This is awful to say, but we're family." Inez winked. "The meeting really was easier without Mariah. Of course, if the situation had been reversed—if Flo didn't show up and Mariah did—it would have been just as easy."

As Inez spoke, the lights flickered again but remained on. "I'm sorry for the blizzard and I'm sorry for the worry. Casts a shadow over your big day." She turned to Aunt Tally. "I hope it was wonderful."

"It really was. The biggest surprise was meeting Ralston Peavey's granddaughter. I still can't believe it."

"Me, neither," Big Mim agreed, and this was echoed by her daughter.

Tucker, Mrs. Murphy, and Pewter could feel the barometer drop more acutely than the humans could. Tucker wanted to go back to the manure pile, even if it was freezing over and covered with snow. On the other hand, she was happy to be inside. Really, she was getting as bad as Harry: She hated not knowing something.

Flo, plaid wool throw around her legs, was stretched out on Gayle's sofa in the living room. Each woman would occasionally glance out the windows. Each time, they marveled at the volume of snow. They, too, were discussing Mariah.

"You must have some idea?" Gayle was worried.

"None. Look, Gayle, I couldn't stand her. Didn't even want to be in the same room with her. If she was up to no good, she certainly wasn't going to tell me."

"Apart from your college clashes, did she do something recently that offended you?"

"*She* offends me. Her very person. I've felt that way since I first met her. Haven't you ever met someone and disliked them instantly?"

"Once. I avoided him."

"Well, I couldn't very well avoid Mariah. I swear, she spent more time at William Woods now than when she was a student, just to torment me. God knows, she never missed a chance to drive in from Kansas City. And her being on the alumnae board means I have to deal with her a lot. She's just so . . . pushy." She'd searched for that word.

"She is. But it's in the service of the school."

"Oh, bollocks. The alumnae board is a way for her to get attention. She's raised a lot of money already. She craves attention. Always has."

"I suppose she does," Gayle reluctantly agreed. "It would appear that Liz Filmore suffers from attention-deficit syndrome, too." She grinned mischievously. "Neither woman gets enough."

"Give credit where credit is due." Flo wrinkled her nose. "Mariah does raise money, and she wants attention for that. Liz wants attention for herself."

"Looks like it," Gayle agreed again.

"Mariah would not miss a meeting. Hell, she'd go just to irritate me." Flo crossed one foot over the other. "She's done something terrible. She's on the lam. I guarantee it."

"Flo," Gayle took a deep breath, "what an awful thought."

Flo thought for a moment, pulled the blanket more tightly around her. "Mariah inspires awful thoughts."

Neither Flo nor Gayle knew of the twenty-five thousand dollars that had been drawn from the Kansas City account. Although it had been repaid, both women would have been outraged.

Gayle shifted on her chair. "It will all come out in the wash." She paused. "Certainly was a lovely dinner. Can you imagine reaching one hundred?"

"You know, I never thought about it." A deep sigh followed. "The only way, really, would be to marry a plastic surgeon. Maybe then you'd look seventy."

"Maybe then your navel would be between your eyes." Gayle giggled.

"The third eye of prophecy," Flo shot back, and they laughed uproariously.

14

As a precaution, four of the maintenance workers bunked up at the university. Like the alumnae, people who
worked at William Woods eventually fell
under its spell. Hardworking, straight-
forward Missouri men, not one of them
could bear the thought of "their kids"
shivering in their rooms or not being
able to get hot food.

While Aunt Tally had celebrated, the
four men divided up the campus, each
protecting his quadrant. Every residence hall was hooked up to a series of
generators, and the maintenance men
showed the CA, often a graduate student, how to cut off the circuit breakers,
then turn on the generator. A few of the
students, not country folk, knew how to

check a circuit breaker but didn't understand why they needed to cut the power when it was out. Patiently, they were informed that if the power came back on and the generator was running, they'd blow out everything.

The final carrying out of manure to the big snow-covered pile was done. The horses would be in superclean stalls in case they couldn't be thoroughly mucked out tomorrow. The students had put down extra bedding. Water usually didn't freeze inside the barns, but they knew that would happen tonight. Generators were hooked up in the barn so the pumps would still work. The frozen buckets could be dumped, then refilled with fresh water in the morning. Horses drank as much as sixteen gallons of water on a hot day; on a cold one, they still needed a lot of water.

When Fuji Wertland knocked on the door of the alumni house, Harry and Tucker greeted him. The power had gone out an hour ago. The ladies sat around the propane heater.

"Come on in. I'm surprised you could get through," Harry said.

"Snow's supposed to end sometime tomorrow." He shrugged. "Who knows? A weatherman can be wrong half the time and still keep his job." He stepped inside.

At fifty-four, Fuji kept in shape. Small of build and a quick thinker, he headed maintenance, an important position on any campus and one that faculty and students rarely considered.

"We can offer you some cookies but no stove." She smiled.

"I'm here to hook up the generator. You know to cut the circuit breakers and—"

"We're country people," Aunt Tally called out from the living room. "We know the drill."

He nodded as he passed the living room.

"All I found was the propane heater. If I'd known there was a generator, I would have hooked it up," Harry said.

"We keep it locked up. Things that expensive can walk." He fished his flashlight out of his jacket and opened the door to the dark basement. "Let me show you where the circuit breakers are."

"Found them." Harry nonetheless fell in behind Fuji, as Tucker trailed behind her.

Mrs. Murphy and Pewter stayed in the parlor.

"Seen one basement, seen 'em all," Pewter announced.

Down in the basement, Fuji popped open the metal cover of the box and flipped off the main breaker, which was a bright-blue longer switch at the bottom of the two rows of small black switches.

"Flip it on when the power returns," he told Harry, as he walked to a closet in the back.

Harry remained near the breaker. As Fuji opened the closet with his key, she called, "Need help carrying the generator?"

"No, thanks. Ten gallons of gas are here in two five-gallon cans. This closet has ventilation toward the back." He shined his flashlight at the long, narrow louvers at the top of the ceiling.

He carried the generator, placed it under the circuit breakers, and hooked it up. "Someone will need to get up in the middle of the night and top it off." Fuji set both cans in front of the closet but not next to the generator. At least Harry wouldn't have far to carry one.

"I'll do it." Harry followed Fuji back up the stairs.

The refrigerator hummed again.

"Inez, they're playing our song," Aunt Tally quipped.

Little Mim walked into the kitchen. "How about some soup? Won't take long to heat it up." She smiled at Fuji.

Although the ladies were full, they were more than happy to make something hot for Fuji.

"No, thank you, ma'am." He walked to the front door. "There's a lot left to do. This storm is brutal."

Harry said, "Thank you. Do you have a cell?"

"Do. 'Course, it's not working now. No satellite TV. We'll sleep in a trailer back behind the stables. It's there for times like this or for graduation, when we work around the clock. The boys and I hoped to watch some basketball. We'll play cards instead." He grinned. "I'll clean those dogs out."

"Hey, remind me never to play cards with you." She opened the door. "Thank you, Mr. Wertland."

He touched his finger to his lad's cap. Harry noticed that the truck windshield was already thickly covered with snow. He couldn't have been in the house longer than fifteen minutes.

She closed the door against the frigid air.

Big Mim had turned off the propane heater. The distinct, not exactly pleasant odor of propane filled the house.

Everyone was in the kitchen, including the two cats.

The teapot whistled. Little Mim poured the hot water into a Brown Betty snug in a knitted tea cozy. Whoever outfitted the alumni house understood tea and possibly had spent time in England.

"Hooray." Harry eagerly put out teacups.

Aunt Tally and Big Mim perched on the chairs at the table.

"I'm going to sit here and be waited

on." Aunt Tally heard the radiator gurgle, as she waited for her tea.

"Me, too," Pewter said.

Little Mim, eager to return to her husband, Blair, lamented, "Even if the snow stops sometime tomorrow, we won't get a flight out for days."

"It will probably take at least one day to open the interstates. Longer than that for the other roads."

"All we need is the interstate. Blair will be having fits. Phones are out and the cell isn't working." Little Mim daintily placed two brown sugar cubes in her tea.

"Once the snow stops, the cell will eventually work. Need to call my husband, too." Harry knew Fair would be fretting. "I can squeeze everyone into that new station wagon he bought me."

"I'll hire a private jet." Big Mim poured tea for everyone. "What's the point of having money if you don't use it, especially at a time like this?" She got up to bring tea to Inez. "I'll take you home, too, of course."

"I've never been in a private jet." Inez was excited about the prospect.

"Narrow. Comfortable but narrow." Little Mim, having grown up with privilege, had flown in many a private jet.

"I'm not flying," Tucker told everyone, even though she hadn't been asked. *"Hurts my ears."*

"Hurts mine, too, because I'd have to hear about it." Mrs. Murphy poked fun.

As they enjoyed the warmth creeping back into the house, they forgot about alumnae meetings, Mariah, the depressing state of the economy.

Quiet, close times free of ringing phones, radio noise, and flickering TV screens were rare these days. They'd all lived long enough to know such peacefulness would eventually give way to overwork, anxiety, life's troubles. Just how much trouble not one of them could have imagined.

15

On Sunday, March 29, Harry finally pulled into the long, crushed-stone driveway to the farm. She'd left Fulton on Saturday morning, after the main roads had been plowed. She drove carefully for two days, usually in snow, because the remnants of the storm moved east as she did. As she went through West Virginia, the snow had thickened. Once home, she figured that in about four hours, heavier snow would be at their doorstep. In the last four days she'd seen more snow than she had in the previous decade.

Fair ran out to greet her, forgetting to put on a coat. "Honey, I thought you'd never get home."

"Me, neither." She kissed him. "This

station wagon is terrific. You know, I averaged twenty-two miles per gallon."

"Pay attention to me," Pewter wailed, as she didn't want to jump down into the snow.

Fair scooped her up under one arm and Mrs. Murphy with the other.

Harry and Tucker followed inside, glad to be upright. Driving that long gave Harry kinks in her back.

Fair ran out to collect Harry's bag. Back inside, he carried it straight to the upstairs bedroom.

"I'm the last to return home. Inez went back to Rose Hill with Aunt Tally. I actually like long drives. I can think. Didn't make sense to squeeze into that little jet, then have to spend the money to fly back on a big one to retrieve the car. Too much money and too much time," Harry said.

"I'm sure glad you're home. I hated the thought of you driving through all that snow."

"Wasn't so bad. I mean, after what I saw in Fulton, Missouri." She ran water in the teapot. "A cup of tea my way."

Her kitchen had never looked so good

to her—nor to Pewter, who made a bee-line for the food bowls, which Fair had filled. Soon, all three animals' faces had disappeared in ceramic dog and cat dishes.

"We have them well trained," Pewter giggled.

Every now and then on the road, Harry had called Fair on her cell. Not one for talking much while driving, she needed to do it to keep awake. She'd told him about Mariah's disappearance, Aunt Tally's speech, and meeting Aileen Tinsdale.

"Doesn't bode well," was her terse comment now. "When Inez got to Tally's, she called me. Isn't she amazing—Aunt Tally, too? They get around; their minds are sharp."

"I guess if you don't use it you lose it. Applies to other parts, as well." He smiled. "Oh, Terri Kincaid called. At least she's not charging you for a pot someone else broke. I wouldn't put it past her. She'd heard about the lady who 'disappeared'—her word. Bad news travels fast."

"He just figure that out?" Pewter taunted.

"Keep eating," Tucker said.

"You don't need to encourage her." Mrs. Murphy lifted her head from the bowl. "I'm glad we're home. We were lucky there was a blizzard."

"Why?" Pewter asked.

"Because the blizzard pinned down the killer," the tiger replied.

"You don't know that the killer was on campus," Pewter replied.

"No, I don't. Time will tell." Mrs. Murphy bit the kibble piece in the shape of a fish in half.

Tired though she was from the travel and commotion, Inez checked her notebook, in which she kept an abbreviated record of proceedings. The full minutes from the last two years' worth of meetings were at home. She pored over the various chapters' financial reports, which she always stapled to the back of her notebook. Nothing in those documents hinted at wrongdoing. After four hours of review, she still wasn't satisfied.

"Flo." Inez's voice was strong over the phone line, as she called from Aunt Tally's. "Did you make it home all right?"

"Did. My sweet son dug out the walkway. Otherwise I would have needed snowshoes to get to the door. You know, I think this was one of the worst blizzards I've ever seen. I hope it didn't spoil Tally's big day too much."

"No. Gives her one more thing to talk about." Inez laughed. "Flo, I'm calling you because I checked my notes from the last two years. I also went over all the financial reports. Everything looks okay, but we both know how easy it is to make something appear strong on paper."

"Funny, I did the same thing. In a situation like this, when a treasurer misses a meeting and can't be found, my first thought is that he or she has absconded with the funds. I assume you checked our account once phones and computers were up."

"Did. Fine. You know, Flo, people who steal, if they're very smart, plan far ahead. When the time is right, they clean everything out and disappear. If I were doing such a thing, I'd go to Uruguay."

"Good Lord, why?"

"Well, it's beautiful in many places, has some sophistication, and the local authorities aren't looking to arrest you for something you've committed in another country. Plus, contributions, so to speak, go a long way. I'd feel quite safe there."

"I can't imagine Mariah in Uruguay."

"Neither can I. But I can't find the hole, know what I mean? And I really don't think Mariah is a thief."

"I do. I just hope this has nothing to do with the board."

Flo was and wasn't right.

16

Sitting in her luxurious office near the St. Louis Ritz-Carlton, Flo looked outside at the snow piled high along the street sides. One needed a pole vault to get over it, but then, not that many people walked in this part of town. Slushing along in an expensive vehicle was the transportation of choice. People did walk in this gracious city, though, especially through huge Forest Park or down at the reclaimed, tidied-up area by the muddy Mississippi itself. She'd lived long enough to see St. Louis, a city she loved, shed old clothes and try on new ones. That's how she thought of renewal projects. After William Woods, she'd done two years of graduate work at Washington University. Mariah attended the Darden School of Business at the University of Virginia after graduating from William Woods—a fact Mariah swiftly inflicted on anyone she'd just met. As far as Flo was concerned—and Dick, too—Washington University was one of the greatest universities in the United States. Then again, how could Charlottesville, Virginia, home to UVA, hold a candle to St. Louis? For one thing, St. Louis had the Cardinals.

Beat that, Flo thought to herself, reviewing what she thought of Mariah's postgraduate work.

Flo could have warned Gayle of her findings, but the malicious delight in telling Jahnae Barnett first overcame her loyalty to a woman she truly admired. Not that she wanted to distress Jahnae, who had transformed William Woods and continued to do so, turning a small, lovely, all-women's college into a small coed university powerhouse. Recently, two graduates had signed Major League Baseball contracts. Nick Wooley went to the Kansas City Royals, and Josh Goodin joined the Baltimore Orioles. Flo just gloated over that, as did alumnae who didn't give a jot for base-ball.

She twirled a pencil around her fingers, then punched in the numbers.

"Kenda," Flo said as she heard the familiar voice, "let me talk to the chief. I know why Mariah has vanished."

"She's in her office, but let me check if anyone is in there."

"Fine." Flo hummed to herself as she was on hold.

A click, then Kenda's voice said, "Put you right through."

"Hello, Flo. How are you?" Jahnae braced herself for what she suspected would be another blast against Mariah D'Angelo.

"I know why Mariah hotfooted it."

"Yes." Not a hint of nervousness.

"I've long wondered how my classmate could offer such spectacular deals through Fletcher, Maitland, and D'Angelo. For the last year I have investigated, at my own expense, the watches, diamonds, and pearls she carries. Well, the pearls—Mikimotos—and the diamonds are genuine. The discounts on diamonds and pearls are much less than those on watches— Baume and Mercier, Piaget, Rolex, and Jaeger-LeCoultre, to name a few. Naturally, I know many people, including many of our alumnae, who have patronized Mariah's store. I hired a jeweler with impeccable credentials—one from Charlottesville, actually, Keller and George, as I knew that store was the one that inspired Big Mouth to go into jewelry. I was able to gather a group of alumnae here in St. Louis and ones in Louisville, Lexington, and Cincinnati. You'll notice I didn't reach out to anyone in Kansas City. Too close to home. Someone might tip her off."

Jahnae interjected, "You told these people that their watches might be fakes to get them to meet with you?"

"No. Not exactly. I said there was a growing market for reconditioned secondhand watches and asked if they would want an appraisal. A bit of a cheat, but they were getting the appraisal free. I paid for it. They didn't."

"And?" Jahnae didn't like what she was hearing, but she was also unhappily amazed that Flo would go to such lengths.

"Most were not genuine. A few were." A deeply satisfied silence followed this. "But I also paid the appraiser to lie about the value. I wanted to accuse her face-to-face. Petty, I know, but quite thrilling to see her turn puce!"

"I see."

"I have all the documentation."

"When did you confront Mariah?"

"I accused her to her face after our second board meeting. She hotly denied it, of course. Mariah knows, as I said, that the high-end watch brands jealously guard their reputations, not just for stellar work but for authenticity. The companies know there are fakes out there. They're right to be vigilant. They would sue her ass into next week, excuse the French, and so would the customers she bilked."

"How do you know she was behind it? It could have been her partners."

"Well, Fletcher died in 1984, so it's only Maitland, who is older than dirt. Sure, he could have been in on it for all this time, but our Mariah is a clever girl.

If she wanted to keep the old fogey in the dark, I know she could."

"What provoked you—wait, let me amend that. What led you to investigate the products?"

"When I went to buy Dick a watch for his fifty-seventh birthday last year, I called her store and got their prices, which were whispered to me by a clerk who said they were available only to William Woods graduates. I don't believe that, but that's neither here nor there. Then I checked Tourneau in New York, and I called Keller and George. Had a lovely chat with Bill, then Howard, both of the store. They told me what to look for initially."

"Which is?"

"Weight. Most fakes are lighter than the genuine article. I had lunch with one of my friends who crowed about the great deal she got on a Schaffhausen two years ago, and I asked if I could try on her watch. She's one of our social leaders, and her signature, if you will, is to wear a man's Schaffhausen and a beautiful silk scarf. I tried it on and it was light. Also, the crystal isn't good on a fake. For instance, the crystal on a Rolex Submariner is thick but quite clear. Crystal isn't cheap, so you'll get more distortion in a fake."

"And have you informed the alumnae whose watches were appraised?"

"Bill, the appraiser, told each individual he would write up the resale value—high and low, since there's always a fluctuation—and mail them the results. He lied, as I told you, giving them a higher value than their true value. Nor did he identify which were fake. He will mail out the appraisals the Friday after our alumnae meeting. I'm sure most of them will arrive at their destinations once mail service resumes."

Jahnae was quiet for a moment, then switched gears. "And I assume she will be voted off the board at the summer meeting? You will make that motion?"

"Of course." Flo glowed inside.

"As I recall, one of the founding principles of our great nation is innocent until proven guilty. If you offer up your findings to the Kansas City police, that's one course of action. But someone will sue her. She will have her day in court.

You only know the products are inauthentic. You don't know that Mariah is behind it." Jahnae felt supremely uneasy. Flo's gloating made Mariah's absence all the more sinister.

"Jahnae, she had to know. If I can now spot a fake, so can she. She's made a fortune charging thousands and thousands for reasonably good fakes. Why else would she go on the lam?"

"I don't know, but I repeat," Jahnae's voice had a cool note, "innocent until proven guilty."

Flo, quick to hear the drop in vocal temperature, countered, "You're upset. You have every reason to be upset. A graduate is a crook. That won't reflect well upon the school we both love."

"Compared to Harvard and Yale, our criminal output is thankfully low. I don't think the bad apples that have graduated from those two universities or any other have dimmed admissions."

"Uh, yes."

"Thank you for informing me, Flo. This is deeply disturbing news. Good-bye."

What truly disturbed Jahnae was that Flo relentlessly worked to destroy

Mariah over what seemed to Jahnae a petty personality conflict that had started when they were freshmen. Then she remembered that both had been in love with Dick Langston. She sighed deeply. When sex and love entered the mix, brains flew right out the window.

She wasn't a drinking woman, but at that moment the slightly numbing effects of a cocktail held an allure. She quickly dismissed the thought and called Inez instead.

Inez was appalled and furious, because she'd spoken to Flo just before Flo's call to Jahnae. Not a word.

Inez then said, "I guess she wanted to start at the top."

"The problem is, Inez," Jahnae drew a deep breath, "who else is going to hear her crow?"

Liz Filmore, for one, and she hung up her phone, shaken.

17

The weather remained cold but clear on Wednesday, April 1. Even the sky was icy blue.

"Come on, Tomahawk, pick up your foot." Harry bent over and picked up the old Thoroughbred's hind hoof.

Inez, visiting Harry, chuckled at Tomahawk's intransigence then leaned over to look at the hoof. "Good."

"He's a tough boy. He can even be cooperative."

"Are you finished with my hoof?" Tomahawk was not feeling cooperative.

Tucker, sitting in the center aisle, advised, *"Just do what she wants. In the long run, it's easier."*

The two cats had chosen to remain in

the tack room/office, where it was warmer.

"Sure you don't want to go into the tack room?" Harry worried about Inez in the sharp cold.

"In a minute. I miss practicing. I never really wanted to retire, but there's a point where a horse leans over on you and you can't help but fall over." She smiled. "So now I check X rays if Blanca asks. Stuff like that."

She mentioned Blanca Drabek, D.V.M., who rented her clinic.

Harry put down Tomahawk's hind hoof and looked directly at Inez. "I don't know if I'll take it with as much good grace as you have when I have to take a backseat. Farming is hard physical labor."

"Harry, you'll do what you have to do, and you have too much sense to become bitter or bitchy."

"Thanks."

Inez's cell phone rang.

She fished it out of her front parka pocket. "Hello, Flo."

She wondered how she'd ever lived without caller ID.

"Inez, I apologize for not telling you about the scandal involving Mariah's business. I felt the president had to hear it first."

"Wait a minute. I'm in Harry's center aisle in the barn." Inez walked to the tack room, opened the door, and gratefully sank into the desk chair.

"I suppose she did, but it seemed a little shifty, Flo. I'm disappointed in you."

"I should think you'd be disappointed in Mariah." Flo's voice rose.

"I am. Desperately, desperately disappointed."

"Pete blames me. He swears he knows nothing. Of course he knew about the scam. He's been married to her for over twenty-five years!"

"Flo, how do you know that? You and Pete aren't on conversational, friendly terms any more than you were with Mariah."

"He called me to cuss me out." Flo flicked a cigarette ash into her large crystal ashtray on her desk. "He also says money is tight in her business, less in his, but they have huge expenses. Says I'm a nosy bitch."

Inez sighed, then added, "Flo, I'm staying with Tally, but I'm at Fair's a lot or in the truck, visiting cases. If it's an emergency, call on my cell. I'm not going home for a while." She paused. "You hated Mariah. I know that, but, Flo, your delight in uncovering her possible criminal behavior upsets me."

"Inez, you want someone on the board who cheats people? What's wrong with you? I did the right thing."

"You did the right thing for you." Inez pressed the end button on her cell.

Inez zipped up her parka, went back into the aisle, and noticed Simon, the opossum, peering over the side of the hayloft. "Harry—varmint." She pointed up.

"Oh, that's Simon. He's a little shy, but he wants his molasses and maple-syrup icicles. I make them for him."

Inez gave Harry the details of Flo's call.

"It's ugly no matter how you look at it." Harry shook her head. "I'm pretty much done. I'll carry you over to Tally's. First let me climb into the hayloft and give these treats to Simon."

Inez put her hand on her hip. "You spoil your animals."

"And you don't?"

Within fifteen minutes they all piled into the Volvo. While the three animals gossiped in the back, Harry carefully negotiated the treacherous roads. The intense cold meant that where there was runoff, there was also black ice, which could land you in a ditch faster than you could blink.

Rose Hill, as the crow flies, was maybe two miles away, but by road it was more like four.

Once at the lovely old house, Inez knocked, then opened the door.

Without greeting as she came down the hall, Aunt Tally simply said, "Now what?"

Inez repeated Flo's call as the three ladies settled in to the cozy den, where the fire was roaring. The animals played with Doodles, who had been right at the front door when they came in.

Hot tea and small sandwiches fueled their chat.

Inez sipped the delicious tea, warming from the inside out. "Tally, it's all so petty."

"Some people hold grudges all their lives. I figure that's the glue to hold together a weak, cracked personality. Although if Mariah did bilk her customers, which it appears she has, that's no laughing matter."

Harry grinned mischievously. "A sex scandal would be much more interesting than a watch scandal."

"Righto." Aunt Tally held up her tea, spiced with fresh lemon and a dot of gin. "And no one has heard a peep from Mariah. No one has seen her or thought they have. She could be dead."

"I hope not." Inez shook her head.

"If Mariah is as guilty as Flo swears she is, maybe Mariah committed suicide. It's the only honorable way out."

Mrs. Murphy and Pewter, tiring of the boisterous dogs, had joined the women.

"*Catnip,*" Pewter said rather loudly.

"*Aunt Tally doesn't have catnip. She just has her Gordon setter.*" Mrs. Murphy wished Pewter hadn't mentioned catnip, for now she wanted some.

"No. I mean this is about human cat-nip." Pewter expanded on her theme.

"Sex. Love or money. That's their cat-nip." Mrs. Murphy agreed with the gray cat.

Inez, meanwhile, bore down on Aunt Tally. "Do you read your investment reports?"

"No."

"Oh, Tally, I told you to take an interest in the money when we were students. You never listen."

"Why? It rolled in. That's Scott and Stringfellow's job, not mine. Anyway, why are you bringing this up? You know the answer."

"Women who inherit wealth are kept stupid by it, and kept from it, I might add. I've been telling you that for years. Just look at how Mariah's customers were robbed, so to speak. They didn't pay attention."

"Watches and stocks are not similar." Aunt Tally's face turned red. "Anyway, Mim has an interest in it. Bores me to tears. If anything is amiss, she'll tag it. You forget, Inez, that our generation usually had one member—male—of each generation who was to manage the family money. I didn't have a brother, so the job passed to my nephew, Mim's brother, who as you know died in 1942. Mim didn't exactly take over, but she browbeat Scott and Stringfellow into more participation. But women just didn't *do* money."

"You sure spent it." Inez couldn't resist.

"Not so much." Aunt Tally wasn't profligate.

"I'm being mean. Worry makes me . . . well, you know. I'm sorry."

"You take everything to heart. Look, Flo's investigation—if that is what it was; vendetta is more like it—is bad news, but don't dwell on it." Aunt Tally turned to Harry. "Put her in the truck with Fair tomorrow. Will keep her occupied." She then turned back to Inez. "Really, relax. All this fuss is halfway across the country. Nothing we can do."

"You're right." Inez nibbled another sandwich—egg salad, at the perfect consistency.

"I like egg salad." Pewter opened her nostrils wider.

"Me, too." Mrs. Murphy always liked eggs, any way she could get them.

The two cats sat on either side of Harry, faces turned upward, whiskers forward, the picture of concentration and concentrated affection.

Harry couldn't help but notice. She tried to ignore them.

Pewter put a paw on her leg.

"Damn," Harry muttered.

"Oh, break up a sandwich and give it to them. They won't leave crumbs, and if they do, the vacuum cleaner will suck them up. That's what it's for," Aunt Tally commanded.

"You're such a good woman," Pewter thanked Aunt Tally, as the much-desired sandwich piece came her way.

"Ditto," Mrs. Murphy agreed.

Inez looked at her watch, an old Bulova made just before World War II. "There's still some daylight left. Harry, will you drive me to where Ralston Peavey was found?"

"Why do you want to go there?" Aunt

Tally put her cup in the saucer with a *clink*.

"You've mentioned it. I think we drove by it years ago and you said something, but I don't have a mental picture of the place."

"You're just doing it to distract yourself. An old trouble is better than a new one."

"Well, maybe," Inez agreed halfheartedly.

Once down the driveway from Rose Hill, Harry headed east toward Crozet. She slowed down as she came to the spot. "Here. He was facedown, across the middle of the road. Run over forward and backward."

"You think once would have been enough."

"Maybe it's like pumping extra bullets into someone you've shot. Sometimes I think about that when I read the papers or see a TV report about a store owner or someone in their home. A robber comes in. The person has a gun. Shoots the intruder. Well and good. But then he or she empties more into the robber. When the whole sorry thing goes to

court, the defendant goes to jail. It
makes sense to me that when you're so
angry, so scared, maybe you do keep
firing. What do you think?"

"Same as you. I think any citizen has
a right to defend himself, even if he becomes brutal in so doing. Your property,
your person, are sacred. But these days
the sympathy seems to be toward the
criminal, not the victim."

"Insane, isn't it?"

"Yep." Inez looked at the road, as
Harry made a U-turn since there was no
traffic. "Lonely place to die."

"Yes. We come in alone and we go
out alone."

"That we do, but to die surrounded by
those who love you surely is better than
this."

That evening at around seven, Flo was
working late in her office, papers covering her desk, a small notebook in front
of her. She heard the front door open;
she hadn't thought to lock it. She looked
up with surprise.

"What are you doing here?" were her last words, pencil poised in hand.

The only evidence, which melted by the time she was found, was a large snowy rubber boot print.

18

Flo had been shot once through the forehead at close range. Any hope of tire track molds perished with the dwindling but still persistent snow. She often worked late at the office, but when she didn't answer Dick's calls, he drove over, found his wife, and immediately called the police.

A small puddle of water in front of her desk was all that remained of the boot print. Flo was slumped forward. When the police moved her, they found her body covering a notepad on which she had scribbled "NE." The pencil was still between her thumb, forefinger, and middle finger. No one had heard the shot because the other offices were empty.

The next morning, Thursday, April 2,

Kenda Shindler called Inez at Tally's, for she knew she was staying there. Inez told Aunt Tally, and they were both aghast. "It appears Mariah got her revenge. Who else would kill Flo?" Aunt Tally said.

Later that day, Liz Filmore called Aunt Tally to see if she and Terri Kincaid could come by to visit her and Inez. Tally told her that Inez would be at Harry's, helping to repair old tack. Inez might be ninety-eight, but her fingers were nimble. Liz said her husband was in San Diego, she was bored, business was slow, and the dreadful news about Flo gave her an excuse to visit Terri.

Before Liz and Terri came, Harry ran the vacuum cleaner, then warmed up shepherd's pie that she'd made the day before. When the two ladies arrived, the pleasing aroma pervaded the kitchen.

Terri, never one to eschew emotional display, hugged Inez. "Inez, you must be so distressed. I know I am, and I didn't even know Flo as you did."

"It's unfathomable," Inez replied.

Liz also hugged Inez. "What can I do to help?"

"Think," came the wise reply.

"Ladies, come sit. It's bitter cold. A little shepherd's pie ought to help. Here's some water crackers to get started."

Harry propelled them to the kitchen table, filled their glasses, then sat down to join them.

Pewter eagerly circled the table. Tucker and Mrs. Murphy sat on the floor but were less obvious in their intentions.

Tucker said, *"Fear."*

"Liz." Mrs. Murphy sniffed.

"Terri, too," Pewter added.

"Funny, Inez isn't afraid." Tucker thought the lamb in the pie smelled fabulous.

"Maybe because she's lived her life. The other two are young. Inez knows death can't be very far away," Mrs. Murphy wisely noted.

"Does anyone know how Dick is? It seemed to be a good marriage," Liz asked as she enjoyed the food.

Inez responded, "Kenda said his brother and sister-in-law are with him. According to Kenda, Dick is alternating between rage and tears."

"Poor man." Terri's hand shook slightly as she raised the fork to her mouth.

"Flo was very, very good to me." Liz misted up.

"She was good to everyone but Mariah." Inez found the crackers unusual and delicious.

"Any more tea? Water's boiling," Harry asked.

"I can always drink a second cup." Terri watched as Harry rose to fill the large teapot with a horse painted on it.

"Give it a minute or two." Harry put a small silver strainer on Terri's saucer, for the tea inside the pot was loose.

Terri, always one for dramatization, squeaked, "I'm scared. I don't mind admitting it. How do I know what's out there or who's out there?"

Liz said drily, "Terri, I'm sure you're quite safe."

Terri glared at Liz for a second, then softened her gaze. "You're probably right, but until this is resolved and Mariah is apprehended, I'm scared."

"How do you know Mariah killed Flo?" Inez didn't bother to ask why Terri came to that conclusion. It was obvious Liz had filled her in on the watch scam.

"Who else?" Terri's eyes widened. "If she were dead, you'd think someone would have found the body." Her voice rose. "I mean Flo threatened her. Mariah had to know an ugly arrest and court case would follow. She disappeared. Flo should never have opened her mouth. She should have gone directly to the police. For a smart woman, Flo was stupid."

"Emotions cloud judgment," Harry simply said.

"It does seem that Terri has hit on the most likely chain of events." Liz sighed, pushing back her saucer and cup.

Inez answered, "Things are rarely what they seem, Liz."

"Isn't that the truth?" Harry nodded grimly.

19

"I hate it when mud gets between my toes." Mrs. Murphy sidestepped a large slush puddle.

"Better than ice. Cuts my pads to ribbons," Tucker replied.

The tiger cat stopped and lifted her head. Overhead, the great horned owl flew back to the barn. She dipped her wing slightly in acknowledgment.

"Must have been a good night. She's happy," the cat noted. *"Between Flatface,"* she named the owl, *"Matilda,"* the blacksnake, *"Pewter, and myself, we keep the varmint population low."*

"What about the mice in the wall behind the tack trunk?" Tucker leapt over a log.

PG. - 169

"Doesn't count. We made a deal with them."

They reached the creek, which ran deep and strong between Harry's property and Blair Bainbridge's. Blair, having married Little Mim, now rented his land to Deputy Cynthia Cooper.

Pewter, loathing the cold and hating wet paws even more, refused to accompany her friends. She was sound asleep on the sofa in front of the fireplace.

"Know what? We aren't getting over this." Tucker, brave but not foolhardy, studied the rushing water.

"We could try the beaver dam," Mrs. Murphy, more nimble than the corgi, suggested.

"Worth a look." The mighty little dog trotted northward toward the large beaver complex.

When Harry's animals arrived, a slap of a tail on the churning water alerted the rest of the beavers, who dove under the water up into the huge lodge.

"The water's about at the top of the dam." Mrs. Murphy knew if she made one mistake, she'd fall into the flying

waters. *"If we get any more rain or snow, there will be flooding for sure."*

"So much for that idea. Let's head home." The dog, although a strong swimmer, didn't want to land in the drink, either. *"I really wanted to check up on Coop's."*

Cooper was in Atlanta. She'd be home tomorrow, Friday, April 3. Given her high performance, she'd been selected along with other law-enforcement officers for a special one-week training session focusing on community relations. One of the rewards was, during the weekend, the officers were given a special tour of the vibrant city. Officer Doak, a young fellow from the Albemarle sheriff's department, had accompanied her. He had been chosen to study cybersecurity. Albemarle, a county of about ninety thousand souls all told, happened to be quite rich—disgustingly rich, really. Still, Sheriff Rick Shaw had to fight for money for his force from the county. He did manage to get the funds to send Cooper and Doak off to Atlanta, though.

Apart from being a fine officer, Deputy

Cooper was a good friend to Harry, and vice versa. Harry's best friend, Susan Tucker, was in DeLand, Florida, tending to an ailing aunt. Harry felt alone without her two stalwarts. To make matters worse, Miranda Hogendobber, a surrogate mother to Harry, was in Greenville, South Carolina, because her sister was recuperating from surgery for breast cancer. This, too, was described as "ailing," to acquaintances. To close friends, only, the word "cancer" was used. The doctors said they got it all, but Miranda was taking no chances. Her sister, Didee, had told her to stay in Crozet, but Miranda would have none of it. Secretly, Didee was glad.

Harry depended on her friends for their insights. She wished they were home.

"Smell that perfume Terri was wearing?" Tucker asked.

"A heavy musk," Mrs. Murphy answered the dog.

"A distaste underlaid it. I'm not sure, but something's not right. Whether she didn't want to come out to us, doesn't

like Harry or Inez or Liz, I don't know, but it was noticeable."

"I halfway noticed, Tucker, but I didn't think too much about it." They approached the barn. *"There certainly seems to be a lot of drama among this group of women. Well, any group, I reckon."*

"Why is that?"

"I don't know. Men aren't as complicated, that's all I can figure. They might be devious, lie, or undermine others in a group, but it's about pecking order. At least, I think it is. The weaker the man, the more sneaky. But women—it's just too complicated for me." She laughed. *"PMS in concert."*

"Harry and her friends aren't like that." Tucker always defended her human.

"No, but think about it: With the exception of Coop, they've known one another from birth. Miranda used to babysit Harry. Susan and Harry shared a cradle. Different."

"Reckon so." Tucker pushed open the dog door into the barn. *"Everybody knows her place."*

Mrs. Murphy laughed. *"That's the*

great thing about being a cat. I'm not a pack animal. You and Harry are."

"You're part of the family. That's a pack."

"I'm part of the family, but I figure I'm always number one. No struggle for place."

"Oh, Murphy." Tucker couldn't understand this.

"Tucker, sweetie, dogs are so literal." Mrs. Murphy rubbed her head on the corgi's. Mrs. Murphy then pushed through the second dog door into the tack room. She hurried to the tack trunk, jumped on top, and peered behind it. A fairly large mouse entrance was there.

"Hey, you all. Crumbs in the aisleway. You know the deal. You can eat the scattered grain from the horse buckets, but you'd better clean it up or Harry will think I'm not doing my job."

A tiny set of whiskers appeared, a pair of bright eyes, then the whole mouse emerged. *"All right. Anything else?"*

"Nope."

The two friends left the barn, slipped through the dog door in the winter-porch door, cleaned their feet, then pushed through the dog door into the kitchen. Inez, like a teenage girl, was having a sleepover with the Haristeens. She was truly enjoying not having her own house to manage for a while. Aunt Tally's hundredth had been a good excuse to tarry, visit, talk about everything under the sun.

Harry and Inez were huddled around Inez's laptop. The envelope icon popped up. Harry fooled around and photos appeared: two photos of Flo slumped over her desk.

"Inez, this is sick."

"Sick or a warning?" Inez felt terrible seeing Flo like that.

The loss of Flo affected Inez, even though she was angry at Flo for not telling her up front about her investigation of Mariah. Sometimes you don't know how much someone means to you until they're gone. As to Mariah's vanishing, Inez didn't know what to think. She liked her well enough, but they'd never clicked the way she had with Flo.

"Before we call anyone—I mean the sheriff, who's a good guy—let's wait un-

til my friend Coop comes home tomorrow. I want her to look at this first."

"Are you sure we should wait a day?"
Inez couldn't look at the photos anymore.

"I think so. If I call the sheriff, you give
up your computer. I want to look at this
with Coop."

"If you think it's best." Inez breathed
deeply. "Whoever left this is part of it.
Well, I guess that's obvious."

"One day," Harry said soothingly.

"Harry, one day can be a lifetime."

Inez flipped her phone shut out of
nervousness, then opened it again.
"Well, I can at least tell Tally to be alert.
I don't know if she's in danger, but this
is much too close for comfort."

20

Cooper asked to keep Inez's laptop for a few hours. "We have a geek on the force now. Maybe he can retrieve information. I'll have it back by supper."

"Of course." Inez, back at Aunt Tally's, had packed her bags. She was returning home to shutter the place, collect some things. She thought it could be done in a day, but she wouldn't really know until she got into the middle of it. Hopefully, she'd return for good when Flo's killer was apprehended.

Once Aunt Tally had learned of the pictures and seen them, she'd insisted Inez not be alone. While the centenarian lived alone, too, Little Mim and Blair were on Rose Hill.

Inez, back with her old friend after her

sleepover, also wanted to make sure all was well back in Manakin–Sabot and to tell Blanca Drabek what she was doing. Liz Filmore, who had stayed over with Terri, was going to drive Inez home.

As Harry had driven Inez over to Rose Hill, she and Cooper drove back. Cooper wanted to talk to Aunt Tally, but it would wait until she returned later with Inez's laptop.

Inez, gazing out the window, never failed to be fascinated by the topographical changes as one left the Blue Ridge Mountains. Steep rolling hills and ridges that led up to the mountains gave way to land with a softer roll. The soil changed, too. The red clay and stone outcroppings yielded to Davis loam; in some spots, rich brown alluvial deposits beckoned. The red clay did not easily yield supremacy, though.

"Thinking?" Liz kept her eyes on the road.

"Nonstop," Inez, whose light feminine

voice had become a touch gravelly with the years, replied. "You?"

"Ditto."

"And?"

Liz's brow furrowed. "In a way, I still can't believe it. Flo was good to me; she shared her knowledge." Liz half-smiled. "Sometimes more out of irritation than affection."

Inez hadn't expected such an insight from Liz. "Well, dear, you can be persistent on your own behalf."

"I like to think it's on my clients' behalf, but," she paused, "I've benefited. Tim and I have been blessed."

"That means profit." Inez noticed the volume of trucks taking the exit to Zion Crossroads. "Dear God, how this place has changed. Zion Crossroads."

"Twenty years ago you couldn't give it away."

"Oh, you weren't sentient twenty years ago." Inez crossed her arms over her chest, pressed at her elbows, and released.

Made her tight back feel better.

"No, but I listen to those who were."

She accepted the teasing comment. "That's why I listened to Flo."

"I did, too. She piloted our board through smooth as well as treacherous financial waters. Always timely with her updates, always willing to listen, always had something interesting to say."

A tear rolled down Liz's cheek. "I guess I know it was Mariah who killed her."

"Innocent until proven guilty, yet she did have a clear motive. You know, Liz, I will never understand why people steal. It takes so much effort, planning, execution. Wouldn't it be easier to apply that to legitimate business?"

Liz slowed, because the car in front of her had swerved to the right. Its wheel caught the asphalt edge, and the driver overcorrected.

"Wonder what he's on?"

"Could be exhaustion."

"That's the truth. We're all working ourselves to death, and I really think part of the drug epidemic is to keep awake, keep alert."

"Or to escape. Wind down. But back to Mariah. It boggles the mind."

"It does, but you asked why people steal when they could put the effort into honest enterprise. One word, Inez, one word: taxes."

Inez's eyes widened; she turned toward Liz. "I never thought of that."

"I promise you. There will be more and more white-collar crime, drug cartels, more petty cheating. Taxes are out of control. You want to throttle initiative, growth? Raise taxes."

"History makes that point abundantly clear." For many reasons, Inez was glad she was at the end of her life, not the beginning; one was that she wouldn't be crushed during her most productive years by unjust taxation.

"Some days Tim and I swear we're going to chuck it all and move to Costa Rica."

"But you're okay."

"For now. Do you have any idea how many hours we waste filling out government forms or forms sent to us by Fast Grow," she named an agricultural giant, "which are generated ultimately to protect against lawsuits?"

"So you think Mariah's goal was to keep the fruits of her labors?"

"Of course. She'd make a much greater profit by selling the fakes. Sure, she'd pay taxes on that profit, but it wasn't as though she was taking the risk of selling OxyContin."

"I see." Inez viewed the flattening of the land, recalling when, as recently as in her eighties, she'd fly across it on the back of her beloved mare, Countess.

Where did the time go?

Liz pulled down the pea-gravel drive to Inez's house, passing the clinic and its attached stalls for horses needing intensive care. Behind the main clinic was a wire center-aisle barn with sixteen stalls for horses requiring other types of care. A covered arena containing a swimming pool for horses was screened by Leyland cypress.

"Business holding?" Liz asked.

"Blanca says it's fair. She gets serious cases, but people are trying to do their own doctoring on lesser ones. Blame the Internet for that. More lame and sick horses." Inez sighed. "An owner reads about symptoms that they think their horse has. They may be right, but even if they are, Liz, they don't understand what may surround the injury. They know nothing about the chemicals in the equine system, the proper amount of red cells in blood, synovial fluid—you name it. Oh, well, I'm bitching and moaning like an old lady."

"For Tim and me, we've seen all these reasonably bright people—lawyers, salespeople, you name it—crash and burn as day traders. Same difference."

"I can imagine."

Liz pulled up and parked. "Let me carry your bag."

"Thank you, dear, and thank you for driving me."

"My pleasure. I was glad to talk about everything. I mean, I still feel awful, but I know I'm not alone. When Tim gets off the plane tonight, that's when I'll burst into tears."

"I'm sorry." As Inez unlocked her front door, the faint odor of cinnamon tantalized her nostrils.

Cinnamon-scented pillar candles were in each room, and even unlit, they gave off their distinctive fragrance.

"You'll be okay?"

"I'll be fine." Inez smiled at Liz. "I keep forgetting to thank you for tending to my account over the years. I know Flo was your mentor, but I'm sure you'll go forward. Don't worry. I won't close my account."

"Thank you." Liz hugged her.

An hour later, Kenda Shindler saw the envelope icon flash on her computer screen at work. She'd been waiting for repair quotes for the water-heating system in an older classroom building. Anything like that went to the treasurer's office and to the president's as well.

She opened her electronic mail to read, "You'll never catch me. Mariah D'Angelo."

Inez and all the board members received the same message, except for Liz. Hers read, "You insufferable brown-nose. What are you going to do now? Mariah."

21

The next day Harry sat as a passenger for the first time in her new Volvo station wagon, with Fair driving. Old blankets filled the back so the animals could snuggle up. Eventually, someone would crawl over into the second-row seat. Mrs. Murphy, never one to miss action, bypassed the back and the second seat to sit in Harry's lap. She liked to watch the road, often commenting on what she observed—not that the humans got it, but it made her feel better.

"Boy, the roof is sagging on Mitch's hay shed," she noted as they passed a neighbor's house.

Fair commented, "How long do you give it?"

"Two more years." Harry laughed.

"Three." Mrs. Murphy knew they weren't responding to her observation, but she felt the process of communicating with humans might lead them in the correct direction.

"A roof that size, shingles, eight thousand," Fair figured.

"Given the Depression, I bet he could get it for six, if he shops around. People added a lot of fat to their labor over the years. Squeezed out now," she ruefully noted. "That's the nature of capitalism. I'm a believer that it's the best system, even when it's painful. If you shave off the valleys, then the peaks are shaved, too. Government intervention is destructive and antithetical to capitalism. Either you're a capitalist or you're not."

"People don't have the stomach for it anymore." Fair said this without malice.

"Honey, all people know is the nanny state. The point being, those in government think they know better than we do how to take care of ourselves. The arrogance is horrifying to me." Harry bit her lip slightly. "I guess to a lot of people, in government or out, things are black and white. Life really is shades of gray, isn't it?" Harry mused.

"I think maturity is the ability to tolerate ambiguity."

She turned to face him, stroking Mrs. Murphy, who purred like a Mercedes on full throttle. "You're a more philosophical person than I am. It's one of the things I love about you. I learn something from you every day. You know me, honey: I'm nuts and bolts, bread and butter."

"Nothing wrong with that. I learn something from you every day, too, you know."

"I can't imagine."

"The different types of sunflowers, the oil content in the seeds. What birds like to eat—some seeds, some bugs, and some fruit. You're a true farmer. I'm not. I mean, I can tell you the nutritional value of alfalfa versus endophyte-free fescue, but that's about it."

"That's okay. Your brain is crammed with scientific data: patients, their owners. You don't need to know the stuff I do. That's really why you picked me, isn't it? You needed someone to identify a thrush's call, tell you the 'hello' chirp from the true birdsong. And all this time I thought it was me."

"Your body. I worship and adore your body." He smiled broadly.

"Tell me again."

"For Christ's sake," Mrs. Murphy grumbled.

"I worship and adore your body." He laughed, and Mrs. Murphy had to laugh, too.

A silence followed this lovely interlude, then Fair said, "Dammit, I forgot to bring the orange-blossom honey. You know how Inez loves it."

"There's Trader Joe's at the Short Pump shopping center. We can get orange-blossom honey there."

He checked the time on the clock. "Okay."

"There are so many different honeys. The lavender one from France is divine." Harry respectfully paused following this delicious memory.

Fair, negotiating traffic, grumbled, "The shopping center takes up half of Short Pump." He hadn't been this far east in a year.

"Another five years and the sprawl will be all the way to Charlottesville."

He breathed in. "Where do the people come from?" Then he switched subjects. "Worries me. Inez being chair of the alumnae board."

"I know, honey, I know."

After the taunting emails last night, Inez had called Jahnae and learned that she, too, had received one. She also called Aunt Tally, who had not.

Liz, in a panic, had called Jahnae, then Inez.

Taking time to consider all the angles, Inez then called Harry and Fair. Fair, taking charge, told her he'd be at her door tomorrow at one in the afternoon. He was taking her and Erno back to his and Harry's farm, where Inez would be safe.

When she protested this all had nothing to do with her, he'd have none of it. Fair said she'd still be close to Aunt Tally and they could visit, but Inez was going to be under his roof and sometimes with him on calls.

Inez finally gave up. She was grateful for his concern.

Every now and then last night and then today, Fair would mutter, "Worries me."

Worried Harry, too.

"The world looks different when your parents are gone," he said out of nowhere.

She nodded. "Does."

"She's a remarkable woman. She really is a second mother to me. I'm glad Inez is still strong. I don't know what I'd do without her."

Fair's parents had lived much longer than Harry's, but his mother passed away five years ago, one year after his father had died.

"God sends us things in our life." Harry leaned closer to Mrs. Murphy. "Sent me you, too."

"The feeling is mutual." Mrs. Murphy put a paw on Harry's hand.

"Jesus, the traffic," Fair commented as they drove down the Short Pump exit, turning right on Route 250.

Within minutes, they pulled into Trader Joe's parking lot.

"Want to come in or you want me to do it?" Harry asked.

"I'll keep the animals company." As

she closed the door, he fiddled with the radio to get NPR.

Fair, a dedicated NPR listener, soaked up everything. He liked Terry Gross in particular. Harry, on the other hand, was bored stiff. She wanted her country-and-western music, which she used to disdain. If they got into an argument—which was infrequent—it was over who would control the radio. They settled it by the driver having the choice. If they didn't change positions for relief after three hours, the passenger handled the dial.

Pewter called out from her burrow in the blanket, *"Are we there yet?"*

"What do you want, Pewts?" Fair called back.

"Out of this car. I want to play," she responded.

"Ignore her. She probably has to go potty," Tucker teased.

"If I did, I'd poop on you," came the discourteous retort.

"We're at Trader Joe's." Mrs. Murphy stood on the passenger seat to face backward. *"That's a fancy food store. Good stuff. I've heard Harry talk about it."*

"Food! Why didn't you tell me?" Pewter leapt into the front seat to stand next to Mrs. Murphy.

Both cats, paws on the dash, faced forward.

"See?" Mrs. Murphy noted all the people emerging from the store, bags overflowing with edible treasures.

"I hope she remembers," the gray cat said wistfully.

"You're getting a little heiferous," Tucker called from the back, staying snuggled in the blanket. *"You need a kitty diet, not more food."*

Harry came out of the store with two full shopping bags.

"Cross your claws." Pewter was the soul of animation when Harry opened the door. *"Mom! Anything for me?"*

A muffled moan emanated from the back.

"Don't start, Tucker. I'll scratch your eyes out."

"Kitty babies. Treats." Harry moved both cats to the center console for a moment to take her seat after putting both bags on the backseat. She'd bought more than she intended.

She carried a small container in the shape of a cat. The top of the head and ears were yellow plastic.

"Me!" Pewter yowled.

Harry popped a treat in Pewter's open mouth, glad her fingers weren't chomped.

Mrs. Murphy, ever the lady, waited.

"Here." Harry gave her one of the multicolored treats.

"This is good." The tiger savored the flavor.

"More!"

"That's enough, Pewter. More when we get to Inez's."

"How far?" The gray cat was insistent. *"I could go into a coma from hunger."*

"Enough," Harry said. "Tucker, there's a rawhide chew for you later."

"Good."

Fair was still fiddling with the radio knob when Harry appeared. "Shall I assume that both those bags aren't full of honey?"

"You may." She leaned back in the comfortable seat. "Saw you hit the off button. NPR fix again?"

"Can't hide anything from you, can I?"

"Sure you can, but you have to get up early in the morning to do it."

He backed out. They headed west on Route 250. A half hour later, they turned down Inez's driveway. What should have been a fifteen-minute drive had taken twice as long, thanks to relentless traffic. The crushed pea rock crunched under the tires.

"Looks like her weather has been the same as ours," Harry said.

Tucker saw puddles of water in low spots.

"Yeah, it does," Mrs. Murphy agreed.

As both Harry and Fair were Virginians, there was no need to discuss that they lived in the Piedmont while Inez lived at the edge of the Tidewater, an expanse of plain with a slight roll to the land as one moved west. Technically, the Tidewater ended at the fall line—the waterfalls all up and down the state. The weather was hotter here than in Crozet; springs arrived earlier, winters later. Sometimes the rains pounding on the Blue Ridge never made it this far east.

The years Fair spent here were some of the happiest times of his life. He was actually practicing medicine, and the little guesthouse in which he lived was perfect for a bachelor. Harry, whom he had known since high school, would visit. He dated some Richmond girls, West End types, some of whom could be high maintenance. Inez was the one who told him he should have his head examined if he didn't marry "that good-looking country girl from back home."

He did. Years later, after he became restless in his marriage and had an affair, he and Harry separated. Inez tore him a new one. The divorce upset her terribly, but she loved Fair and endured what she called his "searching time." He learned, grew, worked hard to win back Harry, and did. He knew he was lucky to have had Inez's honesty and love throughout it all.

Now Fair knocked on the door of the simple taupe-colored clapboard house, the shutters a brighter green than the Charleston green Harry liked. Each shutter had a cutout of a trotting horse. The door matched the shutters and had a large pineapple brass knocker in the center.

"Come in," Inez called when Erno barked, announcing company.

Harry, who had been rummaging in the food bags, pulled out the honeys. The two cats and dog shot out onto the gravel the minute the hatchback was raised.

"Don't you go on the lawn. It's sodden. You'll make a mess of her rugs."

Too late: Tucker had already relieved herself on the lawn.

Fair opened the door and made his way down the short, wide hall to the living room on the right.

He embraced Inez, who had stood up. "How's my best girl?"

"Perfect now that you're here." She gave him a big kiss just as Pewter scuttled across the floor.

Inez's vizsla, ever attentive, remarked, *"Fatty's come to pay a call."*

"Hungarian asshole."

"Pewter, how you talk." Tucker came in and immediately touched noses with Erno.

Mrs. Murphy entered at a stately walk, Harry closing the door behind her against the bitter cold. Four honeys, two in each hand, didn't prevent her from kissing her hostess on the cheek.

"For you." She presented the prizes.

"Orange-blossom honey from Florida. Lovely. What's this?" Inez took a perfectly round glass bottle with a flattish bottom. "Italian. Chestnut honey. I've never had that. Look how amber the color is. Lavender honey from France, my second favorite, and, of course, good old clover honey. How can anyone live without honey? Thank you."

"I'll put them in the kitchen for you. Well, actually, I'll take them back out to the car and put them in the shopping bags," Harry offered.

"Later. I've made us a light lunch. Come on, Fair. Won't take but a minute, and I know you can eat."

"Now, Inez, you shouldn't be making lunch for us."

"Fair, I'd rather wear out than rust out." She had a lilt in her voice.

"Light lunch?" Harry exclaimed as a poached salmon was removed from the oven.

"What we need on a cold day."

Harry put out the plates as Inez sliced

the fish. The escaping aroma of hollandaise made her hungry. An endive salad and new potatoes with parsley completed the meal.

Fair fed the animals, putting chewies next to the dogs' dishes. He knew where everything was in this house. Better to have their noses in food bowls than have them bedeviling you for food while you ate.

The humans ate while reviewing the amazing events. Comments on the incredible weather inevitably crept into the conversation. Harry talked about her plans for her second-year Petit Manseng grapes, her sunflowers, and the corn Bubba Wickham had told her to plant this year.

"Ambrosia, a better corn than Silver Queen?" Inez was incredulous.

Bubba and Donna Wickham farmed right outside Montpelier—not Montpelier Station, which was up in Orange County and home of the Madisons, but Montpelier in Hanover County, not far from Richmond. Even Virginians not from Hanover County and counties close by could get confused. Everybody knew Bubba and Donna. The two were the local sitcom: funny, occasionally outrageous, and plain good people.

"You know his exact words when I told him I was going to plant Silver Queen?" Harry ate so much salmon she could feel her waist expanding. "'Don't dirty your mouth with Silver Queen. You put in Ambrosia. Now, you listen to Bubba, you hear?'"

She did, too. He was one of the best farmers around, and Harry admired a good farmer the way a suburban teenager admired the rock star of the moment.

Fair and Inez repaired to the living room while Harry stacked the dishwasher and turned it on. She entered the living room to find her husband and Inez smoking contraband Cuban cigars. Diplomaticos was the brand.

"Would you like one?" Inez offered.

"No thanks."

"Nothing like a good smoke after a meal. I so look forward to it," Inez confessed. "Didn't bring any to William Woods because I knew Big Mim would get her nose out of joint. As it was, Tally and I had to sneak cigarettes. Tally won't smoke a cigar, either. I tell her she's a wimp."

Fair tilted his head back and blew three consecutive smoke rings. "If I could blow five I'd have the Olympic symbol."

"Wouldn't you run out of wind?" Tucker inquired.

"He might, but Aunt Tally wouldn't if she smoked one." Mrs. Murphy laughed.

After the relaxing time in the deep-seated chairs, Fair checked his watch, the inexpensive Fossil brand. Few vets wore costly watches while on the job. "Time to throw your bags in the Volvo."

"I wouldn't mind a ride in the Volvo." Inez smiled. "Come on, Erno."

"A road trip!" Erno was joyous.

"With Bubble Butt." Pewter indicated Tucker, who pointedly ignored her.

Mrs. Murphy chastised her friend. *"Pewter, it's a long way home."*

"Cats are supposed to stick together, Murph."

It took fifteen minutes to pack up and lock up.

Erno gaily jumped into the back of the Volvo.

"Harry, you sit up front next to Fair." Inez opened the back door.

"Inez, I'm going to take a nap. I didn't sleep too well last night. Something was moving around outside and Tucker wouldn't shut up."

"It was a bear," Tucker defended herself.

On the way west on 250, Inez said to both of them, "Thank you for this."

"Ha. You think we're being nice. We're being selfish. You'll reorganize my house and barn for the better. I'm no fool."

Harry rolled up her coat for a pillow.

Inez enjoyed being teased. "Are you inferring that I'm an old version of Martha Stewart?"

"No. I'm saying it flat out." Harry giggled.

A Volvo full of happy people and animals rode back to Crozet. Despite all, they truly enjoyed one another.

"I told you about Liz's email?" Inez asked.

"Did." Fair responded.

"I hope she's not the next victim," Inez said.

22

On Sunday, April 5, the weather turned back toward winter. Sleet drove from the northwest, and the temperature hung near thirty-five degrees. Residents of central Virginia usually figured the last frost would be by April 15. Sometimes Mother Nature would fool you; a mid-April snowstorm was unusual but not rare. However, snow in April was often deep and very cold.

Harry, like most farmers, preferred snow to sleet. Although the mercury dipped lower for snow, it always felt warmer.

Cooper kept the fire going in the fireplace in her simple living room. Harry had filled in Cooper on everything that she knew to date, and Cooper, having seen the photos of Flo, was hooked on the case.

"Inez okay?"

Harry replied, "Horrified but okay. She's not one to embroider a disaster."

Cooper's hand found Mrs. Murphy's head as the cat squeezed between the two humans. "Hmm."

"Any ideas?"

"No. The Fulton police department was more helpful than St. Louis's. Big-city departments usually look down their nose at us country folks. I have no right to know facts from this case, as it doesn't involve anyone in our county. I explained my concern, but they waved me off, so to speak. I understand it, but it's damned frustrating."

"Thanks to her position, Inez has been able to check alumnae accounts. Nothing has been touched. I told you that Mariah's treasurer, right?"

"You did. Know anything about Flo's private account yet?"

"No. Given Dick's grief, no one connected to the board or college has inquired about Flo's finances or personal life."

Cooper stretched out her long legs, propping them up on the battle-scarred but sturdy coffee table. "This is like every other crime. Some are open-and-shut. Once you know the motive, things always make sense. You look at a person's finances, then business dealings, then sex life. Given Flo's intended exposé of Mariah, that provides a clear motive."

"It's a good thing Mariah's in hiding, because it's all over the news. The murder, I mean."

"I tapped in to the Kansas City news. Saw the shuttered doors at Fletcher, Maitland, and D'Angelo. Boy, what a mess."

"Gayle Lampe called Inez and said Mariah's business partner swears he's innocent and doesn't know where she is."

"You saw them a little. What'd you think?" Cooper inquired.

"Nothing really. Mariah and Flo both looked like two well-groomed, successful Midwestern ladies."

"As opposed to Southern ladies?" Cooper appreciated the purr coming from Mrs. Murphy.

"Cooper, we tend to be flamboyant in the South. Then you get to Texas and they're over the top. Fun, though."

"It's the hair." Cooper laughed. "Those Texas girls do big hair."

Pewter, on her side in front of the fire screen, was dead to the world. Tucker, also out cold, lay back to back with the gray cat.

"I've racked my brain; Fair has, too. I even wondered for a flash if the hostility between Flo and Mariah wasn't put on. Were they in on the scam together, and then Flo betrayed Mariah to cover her own butt? But Inez reinforced that they really had hated each other since 1970, when both were freshmen at William Woods."

"Harry, if Flo was a partner in crime, she wouldn't have betrayed Mariah to cover her butt, she would have killed her."

"Oh," Harry blinked. "Let's just suppose Mariah is dead. Who would kill her and Flo?"

Cooper looked out the window, the small handblown panes decorated with frost around the edges. "Whoever has the most to lose. The emails point to Mariah being alive or whoever is sending them is a convincing double. Mariah did have the most to lose."

"Right. Sometimes my mind just goes places, you know, like what if?" Harry propped her own legs up on the battered coffee table, something that would have drawn a sharp word from her very proper mother.

She changed the subject. "Isn't it strange? For the last ten years we've had some heavy snows, but not like when I was little. This year it's been like old times."

"Is Terri Kincaid a board member?" Cooper returned to the subject.

"No. She heads the Charlottesville alumnae chapter. Liz is grooming Terri. That's what Inez thinks. The fighting between Flo and Mariah dimmed Liz's desire to stay on the board. Then, too, given the economy, she probably wants to devote herself completely to business."

"Sensible."

"This thing is worldwide. It's scary."

"Yep, but it will be patched up and the

fundamental changes avoided. That's how I see it." Cooper paused.

"And you know, sooner or later, the day of true reckoning will come. Always does."

"Well, no one wants to know what a sheriff's deputy thinks about the world's confusion."

"I do. And I truly want to know what you think about the confusion in Missouri. Do you think Inez is in danger?"

"No. Well, let me amend that. It doesn't appear that Inez or any other board member is threatened by what looks like an old hate that finally ended in murder. But it wouldn't hurt to be a little cautious until Mariah surfaces."

Harry felt her feet growing warmer from proximity to the fire. "She could be out of the country."

"Yeah, but sooner or later, people do turn up. Get found."

"Never found Ralston Peavey's murderer. I told you about his granddaughter?" Harry thought she had.

"You did. Out of curiosity, I'll pull that old file," Cooper said.

"Not trying to be argumentative about murderers showing up."

"I know. But Ralston Peavey's killer didn't communicate. Mariah has. That means ego. I'm telling you, sooner or later, she'll make a misstep, and *wham!*"

"Her husband says he doesn't know where she is."

"Hey, Harry, maybe he's looking for her, too." Cooper smiled.

"Do you have milk, cereal, anything for breakfast?" Harry changed the subject. "You might not get out tomorrow."

"Let me check if the milk is still good. Bought it just before I left." Cooper walked into the kitchen.

Lifting her head, Pewter called out, *"Tuna."*

"I'm okay for breakfast." Cooper returned and sat next to Harry. "Can you keep Inez close?"

"Up to a point. I don't want her out in the weather when I do my chores. She can sit in the tack room if you think the house is too far away."

"Usually you hear a vehicle drive up. Tucker certainly does. I'm sure she's safe in the house. But keep her near. I'll call

Little Mim and Blair, too, to check regularly on Aunt Tally. This really will all clear up, but criminals who taunt are often imaginative. They crave publicity—not that there's much for her here. Still . . . From Aunt Tally's point of view, this certainly has made her hundredth-birthday celebration unique."

"You're terrible." Harry lightly punched her.

"I know." Cooper laughed.

23

"Good windshield wipers," Inez commented as the Volvo wipers cleared away tiny driving snowflakes.

Over the course of the day, the temperature had fluctuated between twenty-one and thirty-three degrees. The precipitation came down as tiny little snow bits. When the mercury dropped, the bits blossomed into slightly larger snowflakes. Harry replied, "You need only one worn-out pair of windshield wipers to realize you need good ones."

"Couldn't help but notice the double windshield wipers you have on the old Ford. Gold lamé," Inez teased her.

"Fair made me get silver for the dually. He said he's not driving around in a truck with gold windshield wipers. I said, 'But you wear pink.' He said he's man enough to wear pink but he can't do gold windshield wipers. Actually, I almost bought purple, but that would have sent him right over the edge."

"I look good in gold." Pewter curled in Inez's lap.

Mrs. Murphy, in the back on the old blanket, which she'd drawn up around her, said, *"Dream on."*

"Pay her no mind. She's jealous. Tigers are a dime a dozen, but I'm a perfect gray." Pewter's ego needed no enhancement. *"What's Tucker doing?"*

"Asleep. Low pressure makes her sleepy," Mrs. Murphy said. She was a little drowsy herself.

Inez's eyelids fluttered. She shook her head. "I could go back to bed."

"Me, too." Harry turned left into the parking lot on the north side of the Barracks Road Shopping Center.

"Not too many people here in this weather." Inez unbuckled her seat belt.

"Monday's usually a busy shopping day, at least at the supermarkets." Harry turned to Inez. "I'm going to run into Buchanan and Kiguel. Want to come in or stay? I'll keep the motor running so that it doesn't get cold."

"I'll stay. Hard to believe it's April sixth and only thirty-one degrees. I've never seen a spring like this, and you know how many I've seen."

Harry grinned. "You never know."

"You don't, which is why I'm in no hurry to exit earth."

Harry hopped out and made a dash for the framing shop. When she entered, she could see the top of Shirley Franklin's head as she was kneeling down beneath the counter.

"What are you doing?"

Shirley popped her head up. "Reorganizing these finished prints." She stood. "How are you, Harry?"

Harry gave her the story about Aunt Tally's hundredth, William Woods, the watch scam, the murder. Shirley had grown up in Missouri, so she could picture the scene.

"How awful. Is Tally all right?"

"I think so."

"Certainly turned into an unusual birthday."

"I turned forty last August seventh,

which you know. I don't know where those forty years went. Imagine how Aunt Tally feels reflecting on one hundred," Harry mused.

That was all it took. Harry and Shirley stood there gabbing for a half hour, neither realizing how much time had passed. Both women were independent thinkers, and they each egged the other on. Also, thanks to the weather, no one came in the store to interrupt the conversation.

Harry finally remembered that Inez was sitting in the station wagon. "Oh, my gosh." She checked her watch.

Shirley checked hers, too, and they burst out laughing. "Did you need anything?"

Harry thought a moment, then it came back to her. "Actually, I did. Well, it's a question. Larry and Enrique"—she named the late co-owner, then the very alive one—"used to get these wonderful old books with prints in them. Remember all the bug prints, each hand-colored? Well, if Enrique or you come across dog ones, I'd like to give Inez a framed print of a vizsla. She has a stunning vizsla."

"I'll start looking." Shirley glanced out the window. "Is it ever going to end?" The snow was falling faster, thicker. "It's snowed most of the last two weeks. The sun has peeped out, what, twice?"

"If that." Harry turned the collar up on her old Barbour coat. "You take care. Best to Dick." She named Shirley's husband, then stopped, her hand on the doorknob. "Enrique okay?"

"Enough time has passed, but you know those two were so close. It's so hard to lose your partner. I don't know what I'd do without Dick." She leaned over the counter, her lovely scarf touching the top of it. "Then I remind myself that we've been lucky to have had decades together. What about these poor kids whose husbands or wives never come back from Iraq or Afghanistan?"

"I think about that, too, Shirley. I guess I've reached the age where I realize how strong most people are, but I wish they didn't have to find out." She waved, opened the door, and made a dash for the car.

Inez woke up when Harry opened the door. "I must have nodded off."

"Good thing. I was in there forever." She started the motor, then drove sixty yards to pull into another parking place in front of Terri Kincaid's store. "You can stay here if you want."

"I want to see the guinea hens, after all you said about them."

Harry sheepishly replied, "I did go on. You know, Terri gives me hives, but she finds the best stuff. Expensive."

"The best usually is." Inez opened the door, carefully stepping out.

Tucker remained asleep, Erno at her side, but Pewter, braving the snow on her precious pate, ran out. Mrs. Murphy followed.

Harry hurried around to take Inez by her elbow. The distance to the sidewalk protected by the overhang was short, but it was slick. Healthy though Inez was, Harry assumed her bones were more brittle than her own. She didn't want her to risk a fall.

"I hate this stuff." Pewter shook her back paws, toes splayed out.

Terri looked up, saw the humans, and

hurried from behind the counter to open the door.

The cats skedaddled in.

Once certain Inez was through the door, Harry raised her voice. "You two come back here this instant."

"Come and get us," Pewter trilled.

Terri started after Pewter.

Harry called out, "You'll inflame her. I ignore her. She'll come round. I know, I know, Tucker broke a vase, but cats are nimble."

Terri shrugged. "Hey, it's one way to sell something."

Inez chuckled. "Hang in there, Terri, business will pick up. Came to see your guinea hens." Harry's eyes followed the cats, together now, tails straight up.

Terri, a true retailer, enthused, "You'll love them. Look at how accurate they are." She pointed to the display, which was clever—a tiny hay bale and small hand-carved cows within two-foot-high white fencing. The beautiful porcelain hens were in a little yard, real cracked corn scattered on the piece of green carpet, which actually did resemble grass.

"They really are delightful." Inez studied the almost life-size ceramic hens with a deep clear glaze.

The artist had correctly painted the black-and-white feathers; the head was a tad stylized but appealing. There were various sizes and color variations, for those desiring more decoration than accuracy.

Harry hated to admit it: She was in love with these guinea hens. However, Harry watched her money and was having a hard time justifying spending $75 on a small hen or $150 for a large one.

She tore herself away from the hens to look at the lovely plates, bowls, and mugs from Provence. The colors—some dark mustard, others cherry—set off the dinnerware. Each item was hand-painted and therefore individual, yet they were of a piece so all fit together.

Terri, secretly hoping the cats would break something, returned to the counter and cash register to check a price she'd forgotten to put on a large bowl, one with a painted background of white magnolias. When Inez walked toward the counter, Terri said, "Thank you for calling me. I should have said that when you walked in."

Inez had called Terri the evening when they'd received the vituperative emails from Mariah, after speaking to Liz.

"You know how Terri gets," Liz had said. "She'll hear this through the pipeline—probably tomorrow—pitch a fit, and fall in it."

"True," Inez had replied.

"I'll call her now. Give me twenty minutes, but then will you call, too? You're so good at calming people down." Liz paused. "Maybe because you calm animals."

"Well, we are just animals."

Inez had called Terri, who carried on as expected.

Now Inez said, "No need to thank me. I think we've gone over these bizarre and sad events enough." Inez really hoped Terri had gotten it out of her system. She didn't want to go over it one more time, nor did she have the patience for Terri's emotions. Maybe the cold was making her cranky. She didn't know and, at that exact moment, she didn't care.

Harry, trying to keep tabs on her two

bad cats, had noticed an unusual foot-high fat-bottomed glazed pot, with cork stopper and hardened wax around the stopper's edge.

She picked it up. "This weighs a ton."

"Oh." Dismay played on Terri's face. "That shouldn't be out here. I haven't cleaned it up yet. I'm a bit rattled with . . . well, you know. Here, let me take it to the back and clean it."

"Looks clean to me."

"No. If you're interested, you should see it at its best." Terri grabbed it.

The fat-bottomed vase slipped through her hands, smashing to the floor. It cracked in half but didn't split wide open.

The cats moved closer.

Inside was a plastic bag filled with something.

"*Sharp odor.*" Mrs. Murphy sneezed.

"You see," Terri explained nervously, "they're shipped from Mexico packed with sand, to make them more stable. Also, more of them would break in transit if they were hollow. And here I am, breaking one." She knelt down, squeezed the two thick crockery halves together, and walked the vase back into her storage area.

Harry, Inez, and the cats heard water running.

Inez plucked a mustard-colored cup off the shelf, whispering to Harry, "I'd better buy something."

When Terri returned, she brightened at the sight of a sale, no matter how small. "Good choice."

"*I don't trust her,*" Pewter remarked.

"*Me, neither,*" Mrs. Murphy agreed.

Back in the station wagon, Harry inserted her square key, put her foot on the brake, then hit the start button.

Inez laughed. "Can't they make cars with keys anymore?"

"Guess not." Harry smiled. "It's a great vehicle, truly, but I'm with you—keep it simple." She checked her rearview mirror after pressing the button for the wiper in the long window over the tailgate. "Think you got everything?"

"Yes. You were smart to hit the grocery store first."

"I usually wait until Wednesday or Thursday for that, but I haven't been as organized as I should."

"I haven't helped. You and Fair gave up half a day to pick me up, give up your bedroom, move some of your clothes and things around—time-consuming."

"Inez, don't give it a second thought. We love having you."

"You're a sweetheart." Inez petted Pewter, ignoring her wet paws.

Mrs. Murphy jumped in the rear to snuggle up to Tucker.

As they drove slowly through the snow, Harry remarked, "Sand."

"I know. Thought about that, too."

"Inez, are we jaded? Have we watched too many crime shows?"

"It was awfully white."

"You know, I'm not saying one word about it. None of my business."

"Well, if it is cocaine, you'd think she'd have more money." Inez breathed deeply. "This country's duplicity about drugs is really quite horrifying."

"That it is. Well, let's hope we have overactive imaginations." Harry let it go at that.

"Smelled terrible," Pewter told them.

Inez stroked her head. "You always have something to say."

24

An apple-wood fire crackled in the fireplace, the distinct fruitwood odor filling the large upstairs bedroom. Years ago, when Harry had upgraded her heating system, she divided the house into zones. She usually kept the upstairs at fifty degrees. Now that she and Fair had moved up there so Inez could have the master bedroom downstairs, she pushed the thermostat up to sixty-five. Because the original part of the old Federal-style house had been built in the 1830s, every room had a fireplace. With succeeding generations and more-modern technology, indoor bathrooms were created. The people who built the clapboard house—farmers, all—had a marvelous sense of proportion and function but making a huge bathroom with a fireplace had never occurred to those folks. Didn't occur to Harry, either, although she hated a cold bathroom—hence turning up the thermostat.

At nine-thirty that night, the mercury read thirty degrees and would surely dip into the twenties as the hours wore on.

Both husband and wife cut and split wood throughout the seasons. Splitting a log takes an eye for the grain and a sense of rhythm. Harry loved doing it, and Fair was pretty good at it, too. Little by little over the summer and early fall, they'd filled up the wood house, carefully stacking logs according to type and diameter. Harry's drive for symmetry often made her husband laugh, but he always appreciated the results. He even built a smaller wood house for the fruitwoods alone: apple, pear, cherry, peach.

Tonight, as they sat propped up against pillows, each reading a book and enjoying the view out the windows of an inky-black sky with silver dots of stars, they appreciated just why they swung those axes until they felt as if they weighed fifty pounds.

Pewter had made a nest on Fair's long legs. Mrs. Murphy preferred curling up in Harry's lap. Tucker sprawled in front of the fire, opening one eye when the wood occasionally hissed.

Pewter started to giggle, which sounded like a fluffy cough.

"You all right, kitty?" Fair stroked her.

"I'm fine." She giggled a bit more. *"You look funny in those reading glasses."*

"If you had to wear glasses, they'd be bifocals," Mrs. Murphy taunted her.

"You say," Pewter sniffed indignantly.

"Girls." Harry didn't know what they were saying, but the tone of the kitty conversation was not lost on her.

Neither cat replied. Mrs. Murphy pointedly made another circle on Harry's lap and dropped down again.

"Can't find a soft place?" Pewter raised up one long, long whisker.

"It's soft."

"Then why did you get up and circle again?" Pewter sounded so innocent.

"Felt like it," Mrs. Murphy said.

"Ha, you did it because you're getting old bones. Next thing you know, your fur

will fall out in patches." Pewter giggled louder. *"Then you'll be bald. Ha."*

Mrs. Murphy rose, stepped off Harry's lap, reached over, and gave the fat gray cat a swat.

"Violent, she's violent. She needs anger-management counseling." Pewter pupils enlarged, and her giggling was really loud.

"Hateful!" Mrs. Murphy raised her not inconsiderable voice.

Fair folded Lord Kinross's magisterial *The Ottoman Centuries* on his chest. "All right now."

"She started it," Mrs. Murphy grumbled, returning to Harry's lap.

Harry, reading Rowan Jacobsen's *Fruitless Fall,* looked up, folded the book, and gently patted Mrs. Murphy with it. "I can do this a lot harder if you don't settle down."

The tiger cat narrowed her eyes. *"Why are you reading that book? All it does is upset you. It's not bedtime reading, and furthermore, Fatso is the problem, not me."*

"Ha." Pewter turned her back on Mrs. Murphy.

The two humans looked at each other and laughed.

Fair picked up his book, then laid it down again. "I've been thinking about Terri dropping the expensive jar."

Harry had told him of the day's events, that being the strangest.

"Yes."

"Maybe that's why she's . . . what would you say, tightly wound?"

"Meaning she's a cokehead?"

"Yeah. Then again, it could just be sand. But she is jumpy and a trifle erratic."

"That's a lot of people," Harry ruefully replied.

"Got that right. But I think there have always been a lot of nervous people or gloomy ones—not that she's particularly gloomy. You know me, I've loved history since I was in grade school. Can't read enough, and what impresses me is how the same basic personalities occur over and over again. Including nervous types."

"I never thought about it." Harry was intrigued.

"Well, go back to your bee book." He laughed.

"To bee or not to bee."

He rolled his eyes. "Too easy."

"Then why didn't you think of it?" She reached over and put her palm on his cheek.

Inez, also in bed with a fire roaring, wasn't a bit sleepy. Instead of a book, she had her laptop. She liked being able to tap in to the latest veterinary advances. She always checked her email. Her great reputation meant that many equine vets asked her questions. Some of them were not about cases or injuries but about horses of the past. One equine vet in Kentucky asked who had the best mechanical motion, Man o' War or Citation.

"Neither," she replied. "It was John Henry."

Such questions were like asking a ballet choreographer who was the better athlete: Pavlova or Fonteyn.

Those questions always sparked debate, but Inez thoroughly enjoyed that because it meant people were passion- ate. What better to be passionate about than horses?

She hummed as she opened her "mail," then stopped abruptly.

A message from Mariah D'Angelo read, "Catch me if you can."

25

"You don't know from one minute to the next," Aunt Tally, arm linked through Inez's, remarked.

The two old ladies walked slowly to the stone stable not more than a quarter mile from the house. Tally's comment was about the weather. On Tuesday, April 7, the sun shone brightly and huge cumulus clouds, creamy white, filled a robin's-egg-blue sky. The forty-five-degree temperature, while nippy, was an improvement over the last few days.

Erno, Doodles, and Tucker tagged along. No little bunnies or fox cubs appeared, as it was too early in the season. Tucker thought the extended cold and snow might have delayed breeding. She had no desire to chase bunnies, but she did wish to herd them. If it had four legs, Tucker knew her job. When she was a puppy she'd tried to herd the two-legged creatures but learned how stubborn they were. Occasionally she'd be successful in getting Harry to the door, but that was it.

"Aha." Aunt Tally pointed the tip of her cane at a crocus not yet open. "There's hope."

"Blossom, there's always hope."

"I try to remember, but lately I've seen the shadow of the Grim Reaper fall across my path. I'm not ready to go."

"Are you sick? You'd better not be." Inez's voice thickened.

"I'm in rude good health." Tally shook her head. "Sometimes the swiftness of death shocks me, though. Flo at her desk. Or I pick up the paper and read about a young person killed crossing the street."

"I know what you mean." Inez inhaled the crisp air. "Funny, no one ever thinks it will happen to them."

"If people focused on it, they'd probably never get out of bed."

Inez sidestepped a puddle, dragging

Tally with her. "Look at all the businesses going under. People killing themselves over money. Money!" Inez watched Erno and Doodles romping. "If only we could be more like them."

"Ain't that the truth." Aunt Tally used "ain't" for effect, as her English was usually quite correct. "You haven't said anything about Mariah's latest message since you called me last night."

"'Catch me if you can'," Inez repeated Mariah's message on her computer. "What's to say? She's clearly enjoying herself. But I'm sure Liz isn't. She called me." Inez looked at Aunt Tally. "Liz certainly gets the vicious ones. Last night's read: 'I hope you die slowly of strangulation.' That's a bit much, but then, murder is a bit much." Inez sidestepped some remaining ice on the path.

"We still don't know if Mariah is Flo's murderer. The messages haven't confessed to it," Aunt Tally remarked.

"Well, no, but there seems little doubt," Inez responded.

They stopped in front of the elegant stone stable that Little Mim and Blair had rehabilitated at no small expense.

The mid-morning sun gave the stone a rosy, inviting warm glow. Each stall had both an outdoor and indoor Dutch door; the top halves remained closed as it was still nippy. The horses had come in to feed. Little Mim, like her mother, Big Mim, and Harry, had grown up caring for horses. She took excellent care of the four in the stable.

"Let's go inside." Inez, who had probably seen more stables than any three people together, never tired of studying them.

The dogs preceded them, and Erno let out a yelp. *"A mouse. I know where he is!"*

The gorgeous russet dog pounced at a tiny crack in the wood divider between stalls.

"Erno, all barns have mice, even if they have cats or Jack Russells." Doodles laughed. *"You should know that."*

"Of course I do," the young dog answered, *"but I am a hunter, you know. If I had to, I'd go after a boar."*

"Let's hope you don't have to," Doodles said drily.

Bred for bird hunting, Doodles wasn't

opposed to other forms of hunting but felt they were inferior to his task. He was good at it, too, and could stand stock-still for an hour.

Once inside, Inez whistled. The large brass knobs at the top of the scoop-necked stall openings had been polished until they gleamed. All the brass hardware shone.

"The last time I was in here, these were standing stalls," Inez remembered.

"Little Mim took out some of the dividers and made six big stalls. When this was built in . . . oh, 1822, that was the fashion, as you know. You tied them to the manger and kept water and feed there, but they couldn't run out. No stall doors. She kept the look but put up the stall doors." Aunt Tally pointed to the floor. "They worked on the laid-brick floor, too. Those two have such an eye," Aunt Tally bragged.

"They sure do."

"Inez, does it occur to you that there's more to Flo's murder? Do you really believe a woman as intelligent as Mariah would kill Flo, even though she despised her, to avoid being exposed?"

"Seems like enough motivation."

"Consider this. If Mariah confessed, groveled about her terrible mistake . . ." Aunt Tally paused. "Did she have a wretched childhood?"

"I don't think so." Inez looked into her old friend's lively eyes.

"Okay, she can't hide behind that." She took a deep breath. Eau de cheval, her favorite aroma, filled her lungs. "But if she acted contrite, how long would she serve? Three years? Five? And, being smart, she'd come up for parole. Apart from the public humiliation, it wouldn't be that awful."

"I never thought of that. But if Mariah is as intelligent as we think she is, she'd have never sold bogus watches."

"True, but greed infects even the intelligent. Maybe more so, because they think they can get away with it."

"You've got a point there," Inez agreed.

"Speaking of intelligence, Liz's lightbulb"—Tally tapped her temple—"is dimming."

Inez replied, "Every time Liz talks to Terri Kincaid, Terri carries on. Liz knows she's emotional. Actually, I'm not sure Terri is wrapped too tight."

"Maybe she has help." Aunt Tally had been told by Inez about the broken jar and the white sand in plastic inside. "Makes them jumpy. I remember some of Mother's big parties in the 1920s. I'd peep down the stairs. Some people were quite open about a snort here or there." Aunt Tally shrugged. "I don't know if it's right or wrong. All I know is these days everything is demonized: sugar, cigarettes, etc."

"Both Harry and I recognize that we don't really know, but can you imagine anyone not thinking cocaine?"

"Not these dogs." Aunt Tally turned to leave the beautiful stable. "Are you telling Cooper?"

"No. If we're wrong, what a horrible thing to do to Terri. If we're right, it will come out in the wash sooner or later."

"Right."

They retraced their steps, happy to be in the routine, as were the three dogs, who chased one another.

After a few quiet moments, Inez muttered, "It's the damned messages. Why take that risk?"

"Ego," Aunt Tally responded with conviction, tapping the paving stones with her cane.

"Then what else will she do?" Inez wondered.

"You mean to prove we're all too dumb to catch her, especially the police and, I shall assume, her husband? She's taunting everybody."

"Mariah will have to up the ante," Inez grimly predicted.

26

Yesterday's sunshine gave way to a low-pressure system with steady rain. Harry finished her chores, hung up her dripping Barbour coat, and stepped out of her work boots. The painted wooden floor of the screened-in porch felt cold to her feet. She stepped into the kitchen, where she peeled off her stockings. The work boots had sprung a leak.

After drying her feet with a towel, Harry knew she should clean out the broom closet—a chore she'd put off for two years. It's amazing how resourceful a human can be in avoiding an unwanted fox.

She opened the closet door, studied the mops, brooms, cleaning agents, and shelves with cans, jars, brushes.

Pewter, who'd opted to stay in the living room rather than help Harry with the chores, heard the door shut. *"So much for the broom closet."*

Mrs. Murphy and Tucker, coming in to the living room to join Pewter, laughed.

Harry found her moccasins with fleece lining, then called out, "Where are you?"

"We're hiding," Mrs. Murphy called back in a high register.

Harry walked into the living room, the fleece feeling so good on her cold feet. "Come here."

Tucker did. Mrs. Murphy didn't.

"Here." Tucker knew the drill.

Harry took the offered front paw, carefully wiping it dry. "You know to wait for me. I don't want tracks all over the house."

Finished with Tucker, Harry walked to the sofa. "Gimme."

Mrs. Murphy, already curled up on a needlepoint pillow, turned her head.

"I see wet paw prints on this sofa."

"They'll dry," the cat said.

Harry sat next to the beautiful tiger, who didn't move. She carefully wiped her paws.

"Think of it as a feline pedicure."

"Oh, Mom," Mrs. Murphy replied.

"Maybe she'll paint your toenails." Pewter giggled.

"All you do is giggle. What's with you?" Mrs. Murphy complained.

"I could dust these bookcases." Harry put one hand on her hip.

"Will you sit down and relax?" Pewter grumbled. *"Why do humans have to make work? I can't stand it."*

"That's why you're fat." Mrs. Murphy cast her green eyes at Pewter's rotund tummy.

"I have big bones. I'm not fat. Work has nothing to do with it."

Harry knelt down and slipped an early edition of *War and Peace* off the bookshelf. The edges of books on the bottom shelves displayed Tucker's teething marks from when she was a puppy.

The bookcase, which was floor to ceiling on either side of the fireplace, had been built by Harry's great-grandfather, a passionate reader, as was her mother. Many of the books they cherished remained exactly where Harry's kin had placed them. First editions of Faulkner,

Steinbeck, Fitzgerald, were recent compared to the first editions of Surtees, Tennyson, and Dickens. Harry knew these books would fetch a pretty penny in New York City, but there were some things with which one did not part.

Sandy McAdams and his wife, Donna, owned and operated Daedalus Bookshop at 123 Fourth Street NE, in the ever-expanding city of Charlottesville. Every now and then, Harry would wander in there, knowing she'd kill two hours browsing, dreaming. Sandy, who had a flaming beard with streaks of gray, could be relied upon for a bracing discussion. Once she'd asked him how people could part with such treasures, and he'd replied that so often the love of a good book didn't pass to the next generation. When the book lover died, the family sold all the books; hence Sandy's enormous inventory.

In his raspy voice, Sandy had said, "The Spanish have a saying, that when an old person dies, a library burns."

That had stuck with Harry. Although she carried a fear of poverty, she vowed that no matter what financial blows life might deal to her, she would never sell even one book. She had also vowed to read every volume in the cases. On that, she was making slow progress. She had read *War and Peace* in her twenties. It was time to read it again.

While Harry was giving in to the urge to read *War and Peace* instead of dusting the bookshelves or cleaning out the broom closet, Fair and Inez were driving up to Middleburg to see an injured mare who had been injected with her own stem cells. The tendon injury was healing rapidly, in only three weeks' time. It was a miracle.

The windshield wipers swept rhythmically left and right.

"What a counterpoint to the last three years of drought—light drought, but drought nevertheless." Inez liked that Fair's truck had a separate button for heat and air-conditioning for the passenger side.

"Certainly is." They passed Madison County's high school on the right. "For a small school, they sure can put together good football teams."

"Love high school football, baseball, track and field—you name it. I like seeing young people discipline their bodies."

"I figure if they're exhausted from practice, the number of teenage pregnancies will fall."

She laughed. "Don't count on it."

He laughed, too, then changed the tone. "You know, I've been thinking about Mariah sending people messages again."

"We all have."

"Didn't you mention to me that Mariah and Flo had a spat in the hallway? I mean at Aunt Tally's centennial celebration."

"I was too far down the hall to hear it myself. It was in the doorway to the ladies' room. There were a number of board members in the hallway who said they heard the whole thing."

"Hearsay."

"I didn't pay too much attention to it." She paused. "Why?"

"Thought there might be a clue."

"You're starting to get like your wife. Curious. That's a nice way to put it."

He laughed. "You're right."

"Well, what more than one of the board members repeated was that Flo set her—Mariah—up for a financial fall."

"Flo wasn't her broker. That would be crazy."

"No, but Mariah would occasionally ask Liz questions about stocks. Apparently Liz freely babbled her knowledge."

"Surely the D'Angelos had their own broker."

"His and hers, I believe." Inez crossed her arms over her chest. "Liz wants to avoid conflict. It could look like playing both ends against the middle." She sank down in the captain's chair, then sat up straight. "Forgive me. I'm going to make a call, and feel free to listen in."

She dialed Liz's office number. "Liz."

"Inez, how are you?"

"Fine. Any more messages?"

"No," Liz sarcastically replied. "No one has ever promised to barbecue my fingers before. Actually, the strangulation message that preceded the barbecue message was more imaginative."

"Jahnae and I were not treated to a bun. As you know, our message was

'Catch me if you can.' But I've been meaning to ask, how much financial advice did you give Mariah?"

A long pause followed. "Too much."

"Did she have an account with you?"

"Yes. Small."

"Liz, what do you call small?"

"About $150,000. For Tim and me, that's small. I'm surprised the St. Louis police haven't questioned us. Surely they've gone through her papers by now."

"No papers. The police have found nothing. Her husband says she never shared her business news or problems with him."

This got a reaction. "What?"

"Cooper, Harry's deputy friend, has been in contact with the St. Louis police. They aren't too willing to share, but the detective in charge of the murder investigation said they have been unable to find personal records. They have the business records. They've checked the recorded watch ID numbers with the various manufacturers, confirming that they are false."

"She destroyed her papers." Liz's

voice returned to a calmer tone. "She had to have planned this."

"So it would appear." Inez paused. "Aren't you somewhat concerned for your well-being?"

"Tim is. I'm watchful, but why would she want to kill me? I had nothing to do with the scam being exposed."

"She doesn't know that."

A long pause followed Inez's discomforting statement. "I guess she doesn't, but I had nothing to gain by it. I had something to lose: a client. Hers was a small account, her real money was with her Kansas City broker, but it still was an account. Why would I hurt her?"

"I don't know, but best not to assume she's a hundred percent rational."

27

On April 10, Good Friday, Fuji Wertland and his crew at William Woods reached the last big manure pile. Patches of snow still lay on the north side of the hills, but for the past two days they'd been moving the manure piles in dump trucks. The school had an arrangement with a local nursery. William Woods delivered the manure to acres owned by the nursery out of town. The manure was turned and monitored; long thermometer probes gauged core heat. Once the manure "cooked," it was ground up into a fine mixture. It could then be applied to small pastures or large gardens. If lime or calcium needed to be added, that was done at the small plant on the acres. It was quite a profitable operation.

While Fuji and his crew used the front-end loader to fill the dump truck, Trudy Sweetwater and Jahnae went over the sum raised by Aunt Tally's centennial. A few pledges had not come in yet, but they could make a fairly accurate accounting. Including Big Mim's large contribution, which pushed the sum way up, it came to $605,332.91.

"I can't believe it." Jahnae was ecstatic.

Trudy, thrilled herself, said, "God bless Tally Urquhart."

"This is just wonderful, wonderful. Does Tally know?"

"I thought I'd let you call her." Trudy wisely gave the credit to the president.

Jahnae, however, much as she might like that, demurred. "Trudy, you did the scut work. You call her. I'm not stealing your thunder."

"I'll remember every syllable."

"You'd better." Jahnae laughed. "Before she left, Tally asked me to remember how William Woods began. She requested that this money be used for scholarships for orphans, male or female. She also requested that we pay special attention to those children fathered by American servicemen but abandoned. You're too young to remember how many children were left in Vietnam, despised by their countrymen and with no way to come over here. You know, when the French left Vietnam in 1954, the French government arranged to bring over twenty-one thousand children and Vietnamese women, but we jettisoned our Ameriasians. It was one of the most shameful things we ever did, ever." Her face reddened. "Our government finally did try to make amends. Tally never forgot. She said to me, considering the dreadful treatment of women in Iraq and Afghanistan, surely there will be orphans. She's pulled us right back to our founding principle."

Trudy softly replied, "It's easy to forget, isn't it? How people can be left behind?"

"You don't mind if I share. Inez said if she makes it to one hundred, her request will be that any monies raised in her honor go to abandoned horses."

Jahnae paused. "You know, Trudy, this university really does turn out remarkable, responsible people."

The phone rang. Jahnae picked it up, because it wouldn't be coming straight through if it weren't important. "Hello." Within seconds, her face changed. "Good Lord! Did you call Deputy Sorenson?" She paused. "Good. Fuji, do what you can to keep everyone away and to keep things calm. You know the TV reporters listen in to the routing calls. I'll be there as fast as I can."

Jahnae, face ashen, hung up the phone. Trudy asked, "What?"

Jahnae exhaled. "When the maintenance staff broke up the last of the manure piles, Mariah's remains were at the bottom. Fuji said her jewelry had not been stolen and she was fairly well preserved."

"Oh, my God! But I thought she recently sent you a message!" Trudy felt queasy. "Did Fuji say how she was killed?"

"No."

Jahnae quickly pulled on her boots and a heavy coat. She blasted out of the building. She drove her car to the stables, cleverly blocking the stable road with it. That would keep the TV station's minivans back a bit. The reporters would walk around the car, but as far as she was concerned, every minute counted. She hoped the ambulance could remove the body, but she knew the sheriff wouldn't allow that until he felt his men had thoroughly investigated the site.

A bad wreck just west of Fulton on I-70 involving a pinned-down tractor trailer had occupied the only mobile news unit. This worked in Jahnae's favor. As the local TV station was small, they could afford only one unit. It would be some time before the reporters descended upon her. Even if the station pulled them off I-70, it would take a half hour to reach Fulton.

By the time the TV van did reach the stables, Mariah had been zipped up in a body bag and taken to the morgue.

Jahnae was pretty tough, but she didn't like seeing a corpse. She made a brief statement to a TV reporter, then walked back to her car.

Once back in the office, the first call she made was to Inez.

Inez, calm, collected, said, "Do you want me to call the alumnae board? You have a great deal to do."

"Inez, yes. Thank you." A pause followed. "Although campuses are safer than most environments, they still reflect our society, and we are a violent society. I never thought Mariah would turn up here."

"You can take comfort in the fact that this involves no students and that perhaps, in some way, Mariah brought it on herself."

"Oh, Inez. Selling bogus watches isn't worth murder. Surely not."

"You're right." Inez sighed deeply. "I'm so very sorry for what you are about to endure. I'll help in any way I can."

"I know you will, and I thank you in advance."

Inez first called Aunt Tally, who was stunned, then she informed Harry and Fair.

"What can we do for you?" Fair's deep voice and his tone brought the animals into the kitchen, where Inez had been using her computer on the kitchen table.

"Bring me hot tea. I've got to call the board members, and some of those calls will go on." She rubbed her temples. "I don't understand any of this."

"I told you!" Tucker sat right up.

"Tucker, you said you smelled blood in the manure pile, but how could it have been Mariah's? She's been emailing people. Don't jump to conclusions." Mrs. Murphy, rational as always, rubbed her head on the dog's chest.

"Missouri is a long way away. This has nothing to do with our people or Inez." Pewter, on her haunches, wrapped her tail around her body.

"Better stay a long way away," Erno growled. *"Anyone tries to hurt Mommy, and I'll rip their throat out."*

Inez now had Liz on the phone, who was gasping in shock. "Liz, Liz, are you there?"

"Sorry, I'm just . . . I don't know. It's unbelievable." She swallowed audibly, then spoke. "I'm both horrified and re-lieved."

"I can well understand," Inez sympa-thized.

"What next?" Tucker's pink tongue hung out.

"I don't know. I'm a cat, not a clair-voyant," Mrs. Murphy replied crossly, for she hated not knowing things.

The humans were upset. The animals, whose senses were much sharper, their minds not cluttered with ideologies that screened or blunted reality, often knew things before the humans did. But they knew nothing, except for Tucker, who did truly smell blood in the manure pile. Whose blood was it?

28

A velvet black sky, clear; the moon, close to total fullness, cast its silver spell at three in the morning on April 11. Mrs. Murphy paid careful attention to the moon phases. Full moons brought out many night animals. There was more activity than usual. This was true for humans, too—hence the word "lunacy," since "luna" meant moon in Latin. For thousands of years, sentient creatures understood that the full moon, the pull of the tides, affected minds.

Passover was this week. Mrs. Murphy knew about human benchmarks, mostly because she heard about them from her humans, but she thought cat holidays or major events should be on the calendar, as well. What about the cats that guarded grain supplies throughout history? Surely cats assisted in feeding the allied armies huddled before Waterloo, just to name one cataclysmic event. And what about the cats that kept Mark Twain, along with so many other great writers, thinkers, artists, and statesmen, company when they wrote? Then she considered the feline solace and advice given to kings and queens throughout history. It was true: Cats moved history.

She was having this discussion tonight with Simon the possum, up in the hayloft. A frost was already on the ground when Harry had put out molasses icicles before retiring at 10:00 P.M. Harry was usually in bed by then, but the terrible news about the discovery of Mariah had kept her restless.

Simon lived for sweets—molasses icicles in winter and fat white marshmallows in summer. Harry also put out Jolly Ranchers for him. He had to peel off the cellophane. Harry would watch him and giggle. Sometimes the possum would look up at her as if to say, *"Why don't you take the cellophane off?"*

Harry inspired confidence in animals;

she had the gift. That wasn't to say that wild ones would come up to her, but they didn't usually run right away. Foxes would stop to stare, perhaps exchange a few words, which Harry couldn't understand. Birds, especially hawks, shadowed her, and Flatface, the owl, would often call out a friendly "hoo hoo" on sight.

At this moment, Mrs. Murphy was telling Simon about the blood of the lamb and the Angel of Death and how the firstborn in the house without the mark died. She was trying to explain Passover.

"Oh, the poor lamb," Simon commented.

"Doesn't get much credit." Mrs. Murphy snuggled in the hay.

On a night like tonight, when the thermometer read twenty-nine degrees, it was cold, but with a little hay around her, Mrs. Murphy's thick fur and undercoat kept her warm enough.

Pewter, on the other hand, hated being cold. Currently the gray cat was sprawled full length on the sofa, the huge heavy logs Fair had put in the fireplace before going upstairs burning slowly. The fireplaces and the wood-burning stove in the basement went a long way toward reducing heating bills. They tried to keep the electric bills down by turning the lights on in only the room they were occupying. Harry's mother had drummed that into her head, and during her first year of marriage to Fair, Harry trailed behind him, switching off lights. When he saw the difference in the bill those eighteen years ago, he got the message. Today, the savings were much greater.

Mrs. Murphy, not born when Harry and Fair were first married, had heard about it nonetheless. Given the excellent state of her eyes, she didn't need much electric light, but that was when she realized that, while humans enjoyed good vision, their night vision was dreadful. No wonder they got scared, and no wonder their conception of evil always involved darkness. Didn't they call the devil "the Prince of Darkness"?

"Then what happened?" Simon gnawed on the molasses.

"Pharaoh set them free, and they

made it to the Red Sea. But Ramses re-
pented of his generosity, so he came af-
ter them with his army."

"Went back on his word. That's a bad
thing." Simon, a Southern possum, knew
that your word was your bond.

"Well, Moses arrived at the Red Sea,
so he had water in front of him and
Pharaoh barreling down on him from be-
hind. I guess Ramses would have killed
all of them or maybe just killed some and
enslaved the others again. Anyway, it was
not an appetizing prospect. So Moses
threw open his arms, and the Red Sea
parted."

"Huh?" Simon's jaw hung slack.

"The sea opened, and the Jews hur-
ried along the path. Well, Pharaoh rode
right in after them, and he was halfway
through the open path when the last of
the former slaves set foot on dry ground
and the sea closed."

Simon's eyes grew moist. *"Those*
poor horses." Then he whispered, *"I*
hope they didn't hear." He nodded to indicate the sleeping horses below.

Shortro, the gray Saddlebred who

had just turned four, flopped on his side, snoring at full throttle.

"How can you sleep with that racket?" Mrs. Murphy peered over the side to see the horses.

"You get used to it. He's good company, Shortro."

"I'm going home. I didn't hunt much this evening. Lost the impulse. Hunting's good when the moon waxes."

"Tomorrow night"—Simon meant the night of April 12—*"it will be one big party. Feels like rain, though. That will keep most everyone holed up."*

Mrs. Murphy backed down the ladder to the hayloft, then took a moment to hop on one of the large tack trunks containing extra horse blankets outside Shortro's stall. There he was, on his side, eyes closed, lips moving with each gargantuan snore. The young gelding had a clear conscience, for he could sleep at the drop of a hat.

The sleek cat slipped through the animal door into the tack room, where the mice were carrying sweet-feed grains behind the old small tack trunk there.

"Clean this up," she warned.

"Will" came the reply, and the fat fellow disappeared behind the trunk, his long tail staying in sight for an extra moment.

Just to be sure, Mrs. Murphy walked outside and checked the feed room. Harry rarely forgot to close the lid on the zinc-lined feed containers, which were big enough for a person to stand in. But, as always, some grain was scattered on the floor as well as under the buckets in the stalls. Sweet feed smelled delicious.

Satisfied, the cat exited through the animal door by the big sliding outside doors. The hayloft door was shut, or she would have waved to Simon. Flatface the owl flew directly into the cupola. In summer, she often swooped through the hayloft, which pleased the owl because it gave Simon a start.

With the trees denuded except for the conifers, Mrs. Murphy could see almost out to the mailbox. A rumble stopped her. A pair of headlights—close together, like those on a Jeep Wrangler—came into view. The vehicle, which she couldn't see very well, stopped. The headlights switched off. However, she heard the motor hum, then she saw the vehicle back out a ways and turn around. She barely saw the lights switch back on before the vehicle made the turn two hundred yards from the state road, a two-lane dirt road along this section. A mile north, the road became paved; a mile south, the old road intersected a crossroads, which was also paved. Harry was grateful that her part of the road remained gravel. It kept the traffic down, as people didn't use it much for shortcuts.

By now it was 3:45 A.M. The moon had moved along in the sky. Perhaps the driver had been coming home from a late night of partying or a late night at work and made a wrong turn. Still, Mrs. Murphy didn't like it. Her view was that if humans were up late, they were loaded on something. Or there was trouble in their personal life. Cats were nocturnal. Humans were not.

She pushed through the animals' opening in the outdoor porch door, which in summer was screened, then through the main door into the kitchen.

Inez, who couldn't sleep, was drinking more tea, sitting in front of her laptop.

Mrs. Murphy brushed against Inez's leg.

"Your fur is cold." Inez reached down to pet Mrs. Murphy's head, which displayed the "M" that some tiger cats had.

Cats and some humans believed an "M" on the top of a tiger cat's head meant the cat was descended from the cat who stayed with the Virgin Mary and Jesus. The cat slept in the manger in Bethlehem. So they were marked as Mary's cats.

Mrs. Murphy jumped onto a chair adjacent to Inez's. She did not get on the table. She kept company with Inez until Fair came down the steps from the bedroom at 5:30 A.M. She could hear water running in the pipes under the sink, so she knew Harry was up, as well.

"Are you all right?" Fair asked, as he tightened the tie on his robe around him.

"No. I can't sleep. I'm wasting time researching municipal bonds. Then I switched over to various theories about why people murder."

Fair pressed the red button on the

electric coffeepot. Harry had set up coffee the night before. She drank tea, but she made good coffee. He was grateful.

He sat down across from Inez. "You need to go to bed."

Ignoring this suggestion, Inez put down her mechanical pencil. She'd been filling up a red and black notebook with bits of information from her computer. "I know."

"Turn off the computer," he suggested gently.

She did. "I wonder how long it will be before the authorities tell us how Mariah died."

"And when." Fair got up as the coffeepot beeped.

"You know, this forensics stuff is not as easy as they make it look on TV."

"Won't be 'TV fast,' but I bet the forensics experts will get the information out fast enough. Otherwise, they look inadequate."

"You'd think they'd suppress it. You know, fears of a killer walking Fulton's streets."

He shook his head. "Better to keep people informed, ask for their help via tips, quell panic. As there's only one body, hopefully people haven't hit their panic button yet. And since the victim is a middle-aged woman, it would appear the students are safe."

"God knows, I hope so." Inez's eyes fluttered, her head dropped.

Fair put his filled mug back on the counter, gently woke her, and walked her back to the bedroom. She sat on the bed, her head bobbing again. He lifted her legs, laid her flat, and pulled a wool throw over her. He kissed her on the cheek and returned to the kitchen.

29

Aunt Tally's long mahogany dining-room table was covered with neat piles of papers. Inez sat across from Aunt Tally, while Liz Filmore sat at the head of the table.

Each woman had her year-to-date investments printed out, along with graphs. As a point of comparison, Liz included a month-by-month breakdown from last year, also with colored graphics. In front of her she had copies of each woman's portfolio plus a small lined notebook, a wafer-thin computer, and a pencil.

Harry was over at Little Mim's. She didn't wish to intrude. Aunt Tally probably wouldn't have cared, but Liz might have. As Aunt Tally and Inez rarely compared investment strategies and notes, Liz had suggested they go through everything together. They liked the idea, even though Aunt Tally had never been much for learning about how her money was invested. Of late, she was making a stab at it.

"Flip to page three." Liz waited until each woman turned to the correct page. "Look at the pie-shaped graphic and compare it with last year's." She leaned toward Aunt Tally, pointing with her pencil to the red wedges on the paper. "That's the proportion of your earnings differing from last year."

"Down," Aunt Tally said grimly.

"Yes." Liz tapped the eraser end of the pencil on the page. "But only twelve percent. The market lost thirty-five percent in value. You're way ahead of the game. You, too, Inez."

Inez, good at things like this, mentioned, "Liz, a twelve percent loss in value is still twelve percent. While I applaud you running a better race than the market, I do have some suggestions."

A frown crossed Liz's face but was quickly replaced by a neutral façade.

What could a ninety-eight-year-old vet teach her?

Plenty.

"Tell me." Liz tried to inject eagerness in her voice.

"I suggest you sell my Delta Petroleum stocks and, with the proceeds, buy the short-term notes offered by the state of California."

Aunt Tally exploded, "California can't even pay its state workers, and you want to buy municipal bonds?"

Inez held up her hands, palms toward Aunt Tally. "Debt issue makes sense, Blossom. I don't trust for a shining minute the stock-market rebound."

Liz piped up. "Money-market funds—"

Before she could finish, Inez crisply replied, "I don't trust that, either. California is an ungodly mess, but the tax advantages to shifting money to the notes remains attractive."

Aunt Tally rapped the floor with her cane. "You have no idea what you're talking about."

"Ordinary stock earnings—say, like those for Georgia-Pacific—are taxed at a higher rate than municipal bonds. Any form of government note carries tax advantages. It offers high earnings in other areas like stocks and real estate."

"But don't I want what will earn me the most income?" Aunt Tally, listening to Inez at this moment, wished she hadn't been so passive about her money.

"You have to mix it up," Inez explained patiently. "Or you'll lose most of your gains to taxes."

"That's unfair!"

"Indeed. That's why for years I've urged you to ride herd on your brokers. Liz has what you call your play money. Scott and Stringfellow has the real money."

Liz, clever, knew not to cast aspersions at Scott & Stringfellow. It would look as though she was trying to get all of Aunt Tally's money into her small firm.

"They are very good," Liz demurred.

The meeting wore on for another hour. Mostly it was productive.

As Liz gathered up her papers, she said, "This was better than wasting time on the murders. We've said all there is to say to one another about that. It's time to get back to business."

"It is," Inez agreed.

"It's still hard to put it out of one's mind." Aunt Tally leaned on her cane to rise.

"I wish we'd hear some results from the forensics lab," Liz grumbled. "Our state has such a great lab."

"I'm sure Missouri can't be far behind," Inez said. "It's April thirteenth. Mariah was only found on Friday, April tenth, and it *was* a holiday weekend."

"Why does it seem longer?" Liz sighed.

"Because it's so awful. You lose focus and track of time," Aunt Tally said, then spoke to Inez. "You don't need to tidy up my papers. I'll do it later."

"Okay."

Aunt Tally met up with Liz in the center hall and said, "I'm glad we had this time together."

"Me, too." Inez chimed in as she joined them.

"Are you sure I can't feed you something?" Aunt Tally offered.

"Oh, no, thank you. I've got to get down to Ivy." Liz named a small community just west of Charlottesville on

Route 250. "I promised Terri I'd go over her portfolio, too. Naturally she doesn't have the resources you two have, but given her age, she's been a steadfast saver and investor. She should wind up quite well off in her later years. Actually, I need to babysit her, sort of. She's rattled over Mariah and over the fact that she broke up with her boyfriend."

"Better you than me." Aunt Tally laughed.

30

Low-pressure systems made Harry sleepy. The baffling weather continued, with light drizzle and a temperature in the high forties. As Harry walked back from the barn, the rain picked up tempo and the water poured from the front of her oilskin outback hat. No one could "do" rain quite like the English or the Australians. With her hat, her old re-waxed Barbour coat, and her worn Wellies, she kept dry. The chill crept into her bones, though.

Inez was with Fair. Mondays were always busy, regardless of profession, so he'd asked her to help out after her meeting with Tally and Liz. She loved going on calls with him. Like many people who were successful in their careers, she hated being away from the action. She kept her knowledge up and she sometimes strayed to Blanca's clinic, but it wasn't the same as being a full-time vet.

Harry hoped that the day with Fair would take Inez's mind off things. Like all medical people, Inez was a problem-solver. Methodical, calm, with a touch of imagination, Inez, like Harry, was a good person to have on your team. Both were drawn into the two murders more than they cared to admit. Inez had a connection to both of the deceased, whereas Harry's drive came from curiosity and the desire for an answer.

Harry hung her coat up on one of the pegs on the porch. Better for it to drip there than in the kitchen, but the dampness and cold made her teeth chatter. She hung the hat up, too, pulled off her boots with the help of a bootjack, then opened the door into the kitchen and jumped in, skidding a little in her socks on the polished random-width pine.

The warmth felt glorious.

Near the door was a carved blanket chest in which household boots, sneakers, and slippers were kept. She pulled on an old pair of slippers. "Ah." Above this was a long bar of wood with pegs. More coats, an old shirt, and hats hung on these.

Harry put up tea, but she couldn't shake the cold, so she took an old L.L.Bean Buffalo plaid wool shirt off a peg and put it on.

Looking at the animals curled up in their fleece beds, she said, "You all are smarter than I am."

"You noticed," Pewter observed drily.

Once the tea had warmed her from the inside out a bit, Harry called Susan. She missed her friend. Once she caught up on the progress of Susan's aunt and the odds and ends of daily life, she told her best friend about the strange events and meeting Ralston Peavey's grand-daughter.

"Small world," Susan said.

"Isn't it funny how something that happened back when Christ lost His sandals still bugs you?" Harry used the old expression meaning a long, long time ago.

"Well, the reason you love your cats is that you're like them. Curious. Curious.

Curious." Susan laughed. "And you know what curiosity did to the cat."

"Yeah, I know." Harry laughed, too.

Susan then said, "You have a gift for getting in the middle of things."

"I know, and I don't have you to get me out of trouble." She hastened to add, "When are you coming home? I hate it when you're gone."

"Next week." Susan sucked in some air. "I have been gone too long. I'm beginning to forget what my husband looks like."

"Are you smoking a cigarette?"

A telling pause followed. "Well—"

"Susan, you said you would stop."

"I mean to, but you know how I get when I'm stressed. She's recovering, but the chemo is dreadful. I swear to you, if I get cancer, I'm not doing it, and I'm not doing radiation, either. Makes you sick as a dog. And I suppose most times it works, but then again, sometimes it doesn't, so instead of having three or five good months, the end of your life is hell."

"I can't disagree, but I can still chew you out for smoking."

"All right. All right." Susan stubbed out the cigarette, but she knew she'd light up another later.

"You know Didee has the same problem as your aunt. It's like there's a cancer epidemic." Harry wondered out loud.

"No wonder. Pollution. Hormones in our meats, milk. Plus stress. There *is* a cancer epidemic!" Susan then switched subjects. "Is Fair enjoying Inez's visit?"

One of the first things Harry had told Susan about was Inez's visit and her trying to hold her alumnae board together. "Loves it. He loves her." Harry paused. "You know, Inez is a second mother to him, and like most men, he loved his mother, and he loves Inez."

"We all love our mothers, but I swear the mother-son bond is extraordinary, just like the father-daughter one. I see it in my own children. I love them both, but it's different with Danny than with Brooks."

"I'll be at your door to greet you next week." Harry noticed Tucker, fast asleep on her back, legs straight in the air.

Before signing off, Susan jumped

back to the murders. "Is it possible these are some sort of revenge killings?"

"No one knows. Cooper has tried to glean some information from the St. Louis police and from the Fulton authorities. Not much help."

"There's probably not a compelling reason for them to include the Albemarle County deputy in their investigations."

"Cooper explained she has some concern for Inez and even Aunt Tally, but they paid little attention. Then again, they must be under a lot of pressure, especially the police in Fulton. It's a small town. There aren't a lot of murders. St. Louis must be full of them. Little shock value."

After returning the phone to its cradle, Harry looked outside at the rain, now steady and strong.

"Oh, what the hell." She took off her slippers, went out onto the porch, and put herself back together. As she did so, Tucker ambled out, along with the two cats.

She looked down at them, then out at the rain. The Volvo, though parked close, wasn't under cover. She didn't have a garage.

"All right, but all three of you are riding in the back, because your paws will be wet." She realized the minute she said it that the cats would be over the back seat and up to the front passenger seat in an instant. She went back into the house and grabbed an old towel.

Out they ran. The hatch lifted right up, and she put Tucker in, who weighed enough to make her grunt. She wiped the dog's feet. The cats, miraculously, stayed in the back so she could wipe theirs, too.

By the time she slipped behind the wheel though, both Mrs. Murphy and Pewter sat on the passenger seat.

"I'm ready for adventure," Pewter purred.

Two miles down the road, the rain became so heavy it looked like a silver-gray curtain. Harry pressed the flasher button on the Volvo. She was born here; she knew these roads. She knew Virginia weather. You could become disoriented in a hard rain or snow, especially with blowing winds and poor visibility. Many country roads had deep ditches alongside to funnel the runoff away so the road itself didn't flood. How easy it was to wind up in one of those ditches.

"I wish I hadn't done this," Harry said aloud. "I could have picked up the phone and called."

"You said it. I didn't." Pewter, like Mrs. Murphy, stood with hind feet on the leather seat, front feet on the dash.

"Tucker, come up into the backseat," Harry called to the corgi, who did as she was told.

"You'd be hamburger if we got rear-ended." Pewter appeared to relish the detail.

"Yeah, well, let's also hope no one crosses the center line," the dog called back.

Fortunately, no one else was on the road. When it got this bad, people pulled under the overpasses or to the side of the road. Harry usually didn't go to the roadside and park, because sometimes a car with a foolish driver would be tearing along and perceive the red flashing lights too late. Better to keep moving.

She rolled into Crozet at twenty miles per hour and hooked a right onto Route 240. A few miles later she turned left onto Route 250. The rain had slowed enough so she could see a little better, but in places where the road was banked, the water poured over it onto the other side and into the narrow ditches.

Twenty-five minutes later, she parked in front of Terri's store. While Harry usually kept some distance from Terri, this was a small community. You couldn't really avoid people. Remembering what Aunt Tally and Inez said that Liz had told them concerning Terri's distress, she thought she'd buy one of those damned birds. Then, too, she just needed to get out of the house.

"You all stay here. Let me make my manners."

"*Good.*" Pewter settled down for a snooze.

"*Take me. Take me,*" Tucker begged.

Harry twisted around in the driver's seat. "No. I'm not forking over another $261.41."

"*Two forty-nine,*" Tucker replied, not

figuring in the sales tax on the broken vase.

It really wasn't Tucker's fault.

None of the three animals understood why humans submitted to taxation. They thought it utterly insane.

Harry cut the motor, pocketed the keys, and slipped out. She'd slapped her oilskin cowboy hat on her head, for which she was grateful as the rain continued.

At the door, she took off her hat, shook it, shook herself to get some of the water off the Barbour coat, then stamped her Wellies, which weren't muddy. She opened the door. "Terri."

Terri looked up from the counter, where she was reading the newspaper.

"Hello." It was not a warm greeting.

"How are you feeling?"

"How do you think I'm feeling?" Terri folded the newspaper.

Harry ignored her attitude. "I'm sorry it's all so upsetting."

"What's it to you? You didn't really know them." Terri glared, then added spitefully, "You're just nosy."

Harry's restraint was thinning. "I'm out of here."

"You were at William Woods, and you didn't seem the least bit upset by Mariah's disappearance. That's what Liz said." Terri raised her voice.

"I met the woman once for all of two minutes."

Terri, sweating and restless, couldn't seem to focus. If anything, she seemed to be looking for a target for whatever was troubling her. "Wherever you are, there's a problem."

"I know how to remove the problem." Harry, realizing that Terri was irrational, strode for the door.

"You can get out of my store!"

Harry stopped at the door and turned, her hand on the long push handle. "Whatever you're on, get off it. Drink or drugs are a one-way ticket to hell."

Terri screamed, picked up a small porcelain guinea hen, and heaved it at the door Harry had closed behind her. It hit and shattered.

"See what you made me do!"

"That woman is certifiable." Harry shook her head, then got back in her

car. She drove west on Barracks Road,
which turned into Garth Road, all the
way to White Hall, where she turned left
toward Crozet. The rain came down
steady, but not as heavy. She could see,
although she stayed about ten miles under the speed limit. She passed the old
apple packing shed that Chuck Pinnell
had revamped into his house and work-
shop for making beautiful handbags,
belts, and chaps. She was still riding in
a pair of chaps he'd made twenty-five
years ago. They had been repaired, but
it proved her philosophy: Buy the best
you can afford, because in the long run,
it's cheaper.

She kept thinking about Terri Kincaid
going off the rails. She drove past the
old Crozet high school, the new elemen-
tary school on her left, and turned right
just before the railroad overpass.

Three miles later, she passed the spot
where Ralston Peavey had been found.
She pulled over and hit her flashers. The
Volvo could easily be seen now, but
Harry was a conservative driver for the
most part.

She was more upset than she cared

to admit. While she did wonder about this old murder, too, Harry was—perhaps without realizing it—trying to divert her mind from the smashed porcelain hen, the screaming.

"Bet Ralston was flat as a pancake," the ever-sarcastic Pewter giggled.

"He wasn't dead for very long when they found him." Tucker had heard about the murder, too.

"How do you know?" Pewter's tail tip waved slightly.

"Had his eyes. Wasn't dead long enough for the crows to eat his eyes. Birds consider eyes a great delicacy."

"Gross." Mrs. Murphy, fastidious, moved over to Harry's lap to look out the driver's window at the macadam road, which was unremarkable.

The road had been paved over five times since Ralston's body was discovered.

Pewter saucily remarked, *"What do you expect from a creature who eats decayed flesh, a garbage dog?"*

"Someone's got to do it." Tucker defended dogs. *"Do you know what the earth would be like without dogs and*

*buzzards? You wouldn't be able to move
for all the carcasses."*

"*People have gotten so fat, and there
are so many of them that you can hardly
move already,*" Pewter giggled.

"*You should talk.*"

That fast, Pewter shot over the center
console to fling herself on the corgi.
Hissing and growling filled the vehicle;
raindrops pattered on the roof for
counterpoint.

"What in God's name has gotten into
everybody?" Harry put Mrs. Murphy on
the passenger seat, got out, and opened
the back door to grab Pewter by the
scruff of the neck. "If there's blood in my
new car, there will be hell to pay."

Harry pushed Pewter over the console. The defiant cat, on her hind legs,
peered over the passenger seat back to
Tucker.

"You sit down, Missy, and I mean
now!" Harry felt some rain slip down behind her collar, as she hadn't flipped up
the Barbour collar.

"*Better do what you're told,*" Mrs.
Murphy calmly suggested. "*Or you
won't get supper.*"

Pewter immediately sat down, face forward.

Harry quickly checked over Tucker, who wasn't bleeding. She then got back behind the wheel and closed the door.

Taking a deep breath, Harry exhorted them, "Let's all calm down." She started the motor. "I would like to know who killed Ralston Peavey. Who wouldn't?" She started driving, then mumbled, "I probably shouldn't have told Terri to get off whatever she's on. If someone is loaded or high, I think it just makes the exchange worse. Bone stupid."

"Mom, you're burning more gas," Tucker called out, ignoring Harry's musing.

"She is not," Pewter happily contradicted the dog.

"Is, too. She'll never get the mileage this station wagon is supposed to get, because she's carrying so much weight. You!" The dog laughed triumphantly.

Pewter's pupils enlarged, and the fur rose up on her neck and spine. She was ready to fly back over the console.

Mrs. Murphy whispered, *"Supper. Don't forget supper."*

Pewter, seething, sat down. *"I'll get her. I'll get her if it's the last thing I do!"*

Harry knew the cat and dog were continuing to fuss at each other, but to what degree she didn't know.

She said to the three passengers, "I don't know if I will ever really understand people. Right now I'm having a hard enough time understanding you all."

31

Harry had no sooner walked into the house than the rain turned to sleet. She opened the door to the outside for a moment.

"Damn."

"Getting bigger." Mrs. Murphy noted that the sleet, which began as a small size, had now graduated to the size of rock salt.

Pewter slipped in to the kitchen through the animal door.

Tucker called after her, *"Don't you want to see? If it gets any bigger, it will tear up everything."*

"I've seen sleet before," Pewter called back, as she headed for the crunchy bowl.

"So jaded," Mrs. Murphy said sarcastically.

"Stay here," Harry commanded the cat and dog. She ran outside, fired up the Volvo, and drove a hundred yards away to park the car in the equipment shed.

There would be no dents in her brand-new station wagon. Might be dents in her, though. She covered her head and ran, slipping and sliding.

Once on the covered porch, she whipped off her coat, hung it up, and stepped inside the kitchen.

"Nasty." Tucker listened to what sounded like drumming on the roof.

Harry went into the living room, threw some logs on what was left of the fire, then flopped on the sofa.

She picked up *The Progressive Farmer,* leafed through. Put it down. Next she lifted *National Geographic.* It met the same fate. As a last resort, she grabbed the monthly magazine *Virginia Horse.* Slapping it down on the coffee table, she rose and strode into the kitchen. She turned on the stove, setting the stainless-steel teapot on the flame. By the time she poured the water into the Brown Betty and filled it with a lovely orange pekoe, she'd flipped through the newspaper on the counter and sorted her mail.

Finally, she couldn't stand it. She picked up the phone and dialed.

"Thompson and Watson," answered the light baritone voice.

"Garvey, I can't believe you pick up your own phone." Harry was surprised.

"Something to do on a rainy day. What can I do for you?"

"Two things. I noticed those light-weight V-neck sweaters—you know the ones, to the right of the front door when you walk in."

"Silk and cashmere. The hand is lovely."

"Will you wrap up an extra-large in the baby blue? I want to surprise Fair."

"Will do." He didn't mention payment, as Harry had an account, and he'd known her all his life.

"And one other thing. You're right next door to Terri. Have you noticed anything weird?"

"In what way?"

"Terri."

He cleared his throat. "She's highly strung."

"Highly strung? She's all over the map. I walked in there today, and she cussed me out and threw one of those porcelain guinea hens at me."

"Ah." A pause followed. "She's been touchy. On top of everything else, business is slow for all of us."

"She cussed you?"

"No, but she isn't sweetness, beauty, and light."

Harry chuckled. "Who is?"

"You, of course."

"Garvey, you're exercising that silver tongue."

Now it was his turn to chuckle. "You don't mind."

"I don't." She waited a beat. "Look, she's never been close to me, nor I to her. We don't really like each other, but we can be civil. She's never done anything for me to be ugly to her—until today, anyway."

"Let it pass," he advised.

"Have you ever noticed unlikely customers going into her shop?"

"What do you mean by unlikely?" He was intrigued.

"Not middle- to upper-middle-class ladies. Perhaps young men. Perhaps not well dressed."

"Come to think of it, yes. But not hordes. Why?"

"I'm not but so sure she isn't dealing drugs. To me, anyway, her behavior suggests she's on something, legal or illegal. I'm not trying to make her look bad. She *looks* bad. And I won't tell Cooper."

"I hope you're wrong. There's so much of that these days."

"And it's never going to end. Drugs are as American as apple pie, but there's a tax on the apples."

Garvey sighed. "I think about that, too. The tremendous loss of taxes, which could do so much good. Be the only positive thing to come out of drugs."

Next Harry called Liz Filmore, since she knew that Liz was close to Terri. She recounted the guinea-hen episode and her thoughts on the topic. She asked Liz if she knew what was up.

"She's got a lot of inventory sitting in

the shop, she broke up with her boy-friend, and she's worried about her position as head of alumnae in Char-lottesville. Why, I don't know." Liz took a breath. "But that's Terri. She lives to worry."

"Thought you liked her."

"I do" came the swift reply. "She has her immature moments—"

Harry interrupted, something she rarely did, as it was rude. "Immature, hell."

"Now, Harry. She's more emotional than you are, and you don't get it. But her fund-raising skills are good. She'll get even better over time. She's a busi-nesswoman. She knows how to ap-proach other businesswomen. She's raised five thousand-some dollars out of a small community of alumnae by her own hard work the year before Tally's celebration. That's impressive. She's al-ways eager to learn." Liz took a deep breath. "It's possible she's drinking too much or," her voice rose, "taking drugs. But I haven't seen anything to make me worry. I don't know."

"I'll take your word for it." Harry

hoped she didn't sound as sarcastic as she felt.

A note of anxiety crept into Liz's voice. "You aren't going to talk to a lot of people about this, are you?"

"Liz, what do you take me for?" Harry felt indignant.

"Sorry, but . . . well—"

"I'm not a gossip." Harry paused. "I reckon I'd best steer clear of her store."

"For a little while. I'll talk to her. We get along, and as I said, I like her but I see a side of her you don't."

"You okay?"

"Me? I'm worried, but I'm okay." Liz knew Harry was referring to the board murders.

"That was good of you to visit Aunt Tally and Inez this morning. I know you all had business to do, but given the alum murders, you needed to be with one another."

Harry felt much better after hanging up the phone. The sleet had passed, and the temperature was dropping rapidly now.

Grumbling, Harry figured she'd better

get the evening barn chores done right away, in case it worsened.

Later, when Fair and Inez returned, the aroma of roasting chicken filled the air. While she finished making supper, Harry filled them in on the day's events and her conversations.

Over the meal of roast chicken, crisp baby potatoes, and a light salad, they talked of her day and of their day, which was better than Harry's.

That night, the sleet stopped and the temperature was in the low thirties. The cats and dog awakened at 3:30 A.M. The sound of a car motor came right up to the house; a door opened.

"Intruder!" Tucker set up a ruckus.

The back porch door opened and shut, then the car door slammed and the vehicle drove off.

Mrs. Murphy jumped to the window over the kitchen sink. *"Same car I saw the other night, I'm pretty sure."*

Fearing for Inez, Fair, who had been awakened by Tucker, bounded down the stairs, his robe around him. Harry was right behind.

"Harry, stay back," he ordered.

He opened the door to the porch and turned on the lights. He'd forgotten the .38 in his haste, but Harry hadn't. She stood behind him. Inez, also wide awake, came into the kitchen.

Fair stopped to pick up a large porcelain guinea hen. He came back into the kitchen and placed it on the kitchen table.

A note was attached.

Harry opened it and read aloud: "Sorry."

32

"What should I do?" Harry asked her husband and Inez.

"Write a thank-you, and leave it at that." Inez raised her gray eyebrows.

None of them could go back to sleep, except Pewter. It was now 4:30 A.M. on Tuesday, April 14. The sleet had started up again, almost like a fine, sharp drizzle.

"And don't go into the shop," Inez advised. "She's not very stable and might lose it again."

"Right." Harry took a deep drink from her teacup. "I guess she was ashamed to see me. It sure is weird to drive out to someone's house in the middle of the night and leave a present."

"People on drugs are weird. Bet it

didn't seem weird to her." Fair figured at this point Terri was off her nut.

"Maybe I should tell Liz. She's a friend."

"That will just keep the ball rolling," Fair said.

"Well, I talked to her yesterday. Maybe she told Terri to apologize."

"Harry, why did you do that?" Fair leaned toward his wife.

"Well," Harry held her cup in both hands. "Liz knows Terri well. I thought she might know why Terri's acting so strange."

"What did she say?" Inez figured it was too late to chide Harry for calling.

"Just that Terri's the emotional sort and she recently broke up with her boyfriend. Anyway, she's worried about money. There's a lot of stuff sitting in the shop. Guess I set her off by not buying one of those hens."

"Honey, you're not obligated to buy anything."

"I know."

Fair leaned back in his chair. "For all we know, Liz is on drugs, too. It's like a forbidden club. Druggies protect one another."

Harry thought about that. "Liz was drunk at the William Woods party for Aunt Tally."

Inez pursed her lips. "No, she's stable. The only time I saw her tipsy was at Tally's do. I think she's okay."

Fair, knowing his wife well, asked, "Harry, who else did you speak to about Terri's behavior?"

Harry took a deep breath. "Garvey. He's right next door. I asked if unlikely customers came in to the store. Like young men."

"And?" Inez leaned forward.

"He said there had been a steady trickle of customers who he was surprised would be interested in imported French dinnerware. I didn't see the harm in it," she added defensively.

"Garvey can talk," Fair groaned.

"All right, I gossiped, but in the name of gathering information."

The corner of Inez's lip curled upward in a half smile. "Harry, you can put your nose in other people's business."

"I know, I know. Look, it was a big

scene, but by telling Garvey and Liz, I really was trying to find out if Terri is using or dealing. Best to steer clear of those people, especially if they won't go for help."

"Let's talk about something else besides Terri Kincaid. None of us is going back to sleep." Fair was getting irritated.

Little did Fair know that, within two hours, Terri Kincaid would be all anyone was talking about.

33

Garvey Watson kept it slow as he drove through the reluctant dawn to his store at six-thirty. At times, a swirl of fog surrounded him. The fine sleet had turned into a light, steady rain. Usually he took the back road from his house, which had been in the Watson family since before the War Between the States. The Watsons had been free blacks since the early 1700s. The dirt road that went past the farm looped around, and he could connect where Routes 240 and 250 converged. However, there were a lot of spots on that road that could fool you. Waters ran swiftly over it if the creek rose. Even when the creek subsided and the waters were calm, if one was foolish enough to drive through, the waters would be halfway up the car door before you knew it.

He peered over his steering wheel, keeping his lights low. All high beams did was bounce off the fog. As the rain commenced again, the windshield wipers stepped up tempo. Garvey loved cars, but he wasn't so much in love with driving by computer. He'd just bought a new Jaguar XFR, the first one to make the dealer's lot in Richmond. The 510-horsepower engine thrilled him, while the complicated touch-screen display drove him nuts. The wood and leather in the interior screamed Great Britain, and clearly that was where Garvey's taste rested, as evidenced by the high-quality merchandise carried at his store. He even included the classic Fred Perry shirts, not the Ralph Lauren Polo shirts derived from them. He also carried authentic cricket sweaters. Sold like hotcakes. Allied to his good taste was that he knew his market, plus he had received an excellent education at Howard University.

While trying to see ahead, he thought

he saw a large animal lying in the middle of the road, not twenty yards away. He slowed. The speedometer held steady at 30 mph. To go faster in this kind of weather was a death wish. He blinked. Again. The large animal was a human being. He slammed on the brakes, and shot out of that gorgeous machine. As he bent over the supine figure of a young woman, he realized it was Terri Kincaid.

"Oh, no, please, God, no." He checked for the pulse on her wrist.

None. He held his fingers to her carotid artery.

Nothing.

Then he noticed a trickle of blood on the road by her head. There wasn't a lot, as the increasing rain continued to wash it away.

All he could think to say was "Dear God, into Thy hands I commend this spirit."

He put his face in his hands and cried, then snapped out of it. Now dripping wet but hardly aware of it, he returned to his car to dial 911.

It wasn't until after he spoke to the dispatcher that he realized this was the

same spot where Ralston Peavey had
been found.

Cooper, on the early-morning shift, hit
the scene first. After ascertaining that
Terri was dead, she put up flares and
kept the lights flashing on her squad car.
    She listened to everything Garvey told
her. She put on thin latex gloves, turning
Terri's head just enough to see the entrance wound of a bullet. Slight powder
burns circled the wound. Since Terri had
lain with the wound side on the asphalt,
the rain hadn't washed away the powder burn. Looked like a .38 caliber to
Cooper. The exit wound—surprisingly
not messy—was above the right ear.
Terri's hair had fallen over the wound,
and a small piece of skull had exited
with the bullet. Using her flashlight,
Cooper searched for the bullet but realized that this would be like finding a
needle in a haystack. Locating it would
take a team in better weather than this.
    She returned to Garvey, who rolled
down his window—all electric, of course.

"Garvey, go home. Get dry. You're shaking like a leaf." She patted his back. "Want me to call Walter and tell him you're taking the day off?"

Walter was Walter Thompson, his business partner.

"I don't know if I should. I'll think about this more at home than at the store."

"Well, up to you, but do go change your clothes. Traffic will be one lane here for a good hour and a half. You're sure you don't want me to call Walter?"

"I'll do it. Thanks, Coop. She was a good woman. A little out there but good. Why?" He looked imploringly into Cooper's strong face.

"I don't know. All I know is, people have been killing one another since year one. But we'll do our best to find out who did it."

"Right." He nodded, closed the window, turned the car around, and headed for home.

At 7:45 A.M., Inez heard the news on the small radio in the heated tack room. She was cleaning the everyday tack, for she liked to be useful and her fingers remained nimble.

Forgetting to put on her coat, she hurried into the center aisle, Erno at her heels. She heard Harry in the last stall by the back doors.

"Harry, Harry, Terri Kincaid's dead!"

Harry stopped, pitchfork still in her hand. "What?"

"Shot. Her body was found near the same place where Ralston Peavey's was. Those are the only details, except that the murderer is at large."

"Damn." Harry slammed the tines of her fork into the deep wood shavings.

"I'm going to call Tally."

Mrs. Murphy and Pewter, who were up in the loft with Simon, heard Inez.

"Tucker," Mrs. Murphy called down to the dog, who rested outside the stall Harry was cleaning. *"Hear that?"*

"Of course I did." The corgi walked to beneath where the two cats looked down at her.

"It means the killer is here. Here!" Mrs. Murphy, cat intuition at the max, declared with certainty.

Pewter, unwilling to let Mrs. Murphy be the authority, said, *"I always said that. I said the killer would show up here."*

She had said no such thing.

In their excitement and worry, Mrs. Murphy and Tucker let it pass.

"It's no coincidence that Terri is dead." Mrs. Murphy's whiskers swept forward and back.

"She wasn't on the board." Pewter didn't disagree but wanted to point this out, as if the other two would have forgotten. *"And Harry graduated from Smith. She is safe."*

"Fat chance," Tucker replied with a vengeance. *"Inez is here. Harry is Harry. She needs to be watched."*

Erno's pupils enlarged. *"I'll kill anyone who tries to harm Mom."*

Mrs. Murphy mused sadly, *"If only humans would listen."*

Pewter laughed derisively. *"None of them does. They can't accept information from any species other than their own, and they don't even listen to one another."*

"Harry's good." Tucker always defended her mother.

"She's the best of a bad bunch." Pewter arched one silky eyebrow.

"You're being a hardboot," Tucker grumbled but then shut up.

She knew, as did Mrs. Murphy, that Pewter covered up her fear for Harry in this fashion. There was no doubt that the three would need to shadow her, as well as get Erno to stick with Inez non-stop.

"Tucker, if someone comes around with a hidden gun, do you think you can smell the oil in the barrel?" Mrs. Murphy asked.

Gun owners cleaned their rifles and handguns with special brushes dipped in light oil. They also wiped down the weapons with rags that often contained a hint of oil. Even a human could smell the distinctive odor if their nose was near the metal.

"Sure."

"Good."

Erno had gone to the office and now sat alertly by the chair as Inez spoke to Tally.

"Where Ralston Peavey lay." Aunt Tally was incredulous.

"Shot instead of run over. This is sick."

"You think a copycat murderer?" Aunt Tally thought it was sick, too.

"I don't know, but it's a distinct possibility. Look, Blossom, you have resources. Hire a twenty-four-hour guard until this is resolved."

"Oh, come on. I have Doodles, and Little Mim and Blair are close by."

"That's not good enough. Just do it. If you don't, I'm coming over there and I'm going to bust your provoking head." This was said with humor.

"Since you put it that way . . ." Aunt Tally needed an excuse. She didn't want to look chicken.

"I'm going to call Liz Filmore. Doubt this is in the news in Richmond. Henrico County endures far more murders than Albemarle."

"Okay, call me back when you're done."

"Actually, Erno and I will be visiting you. I want to make sure you've hired some kind of security."

"Oh, all right." Aunt Tally made it sound as though she was being forced into this, but she did want to see Inez.

After signing off, Inez dialed Liz's cell and got her driving to the office.

"Liz, I have terrible news. You might want to pull over."

"Hold on. I'm almost at the office." Liz pulled onto the road shoulder. "All right."

"Terri Kincaid has been found shot dead, lying in the middle of the road, near where Ralston Peavey was found, although I don't know if that name means much to you."

"Oh, no, no."

"No murderer has been found, and my worry is that any evidence like tire tracks will all be washed away in this rain."

"This is awful. I bet it was that worthless boyfriend. She said he tried to get a little rough with her. I'll kill him myself!"

"Liz, give me his name, anything you know about him. I'll pass it on."

"Better yet, have the officer in charge call me. I can tell him or her a lot, a whole lot."

"Good idea. You'll tell Tim, of course."

"He'll be devastated. He liked Terri.

This is awful, just so awful. Are you all right?"

"I am, but there's been so much death in a short compass of time."

"Yes, there has, Inez, yes, there has."

34

Spring finally decided to arrive in central Virginia on Friday, April 17. The redbuds opened, as did the native dogwoods. The imported dogwoods would take longer to open. The daffodils shone yellow, the tulips had yet to reveal their colors, but in another week, if the weather held, they, too, would be in full bloom.

The service for Terri Kincaid was held at the Lutheran church, with the Reverend Herbert Jones performing the Service for the Dead. Organizing the service had fallen to Inez and Liz Filmore, since Terri's parents, who were divorced, behaved with the immaturity so often associated with people who can't put anything above their own emotional response. Her mother, Alantra—a name she herself had chosen at age forty—did claim the body. Her father, Jason, cried, pouted, but attended the service. Alantra wouldn't come, because Jason was going to be there.

This unseemly arguing had swirled for three days after Terri's body was found. Finally, Inez lowered the boom, making arrangements without consent of either parent. Terri, a graduate of William Woods, then the Darden School of Business, had been part of the community for ten years.

The church, half full, lent a peacefulness to the proceedings.

Mrs. Murphy, Pewter, Elocution, Cazenovia, and Lucy Fur—the latter three being Herb's cats—sat in the balcony with the organist.

Terri's ex-boyfriend, Bob Ostler, seemed genuinely sad. At this point in her life, Coop trusted her instincts when it came to possible murderers. She didn't think Bob had killed Terri. That didn't mean Cooper wouldn't keep her eye on the young man.

Apart from Liz and Tim Filmore, the

person who seemed most genuinely distressed by Terri's passing was Garvey Watson. Sitting with his wife, he continued to wipe his eyes with a linen handkerchief. She held his hand throughout.

A small reception followed the service.

Pewter made a special point to sit under the table, where ham biscuits were piled on a plate above her.

Inez, Aunt Tally, Big Mim, Little Mim, and Blair paid their respects to Jason Kincaid.

Harry, having done so, sat with Garvey and Lila, his wife.

Fair was talking with Jim Sanburne, Big Mim's husband, the mayor of Crozet.

"Harry, thank you for being so kind," Garvey said.

"Garvey, I didn't do anything."

Lila, a bit plump but still quite attractive in her late sixties, said, "You called, then came by. He was so terribly upset. Just seeing friends helped him."

"It was an awful shock." Harry did what any friend or even an acquaintance would do. "I heard that Liz is the executrix. Terri didn't trust either of her parents."

"Small wonder," Lila replied curtly.

"Most people don't draw up a will in their thirties."

"Garvey pushed her on that." Lila never missed an opportunity to reveal her husband's foresight and involvement, because he never would himself.

"Now, now, Lila." His soft voice interrupted what would have become a torrent of praise. "She owned the store, and she had to consider things in a different light. She knew her parents would fight over anything, which is why she finally agreed. Running a business can make one grow up fast."

"Well, she would have dragged her heels without you." Lila looked at Harry. "He even helped her select some lines of earthenware, the wonderful stuff from Provence. They're—I mean, they were— her biggest sellers. No one has an eye like Garvey's."

"That's true. My husband loved the sweater, by the way."

"Ah." A small smile played over Garvey's lips.

"This is out of the blue, but maybe we should talk to Liz before she dismantles Terri's store." Harry thought out loud. "She did carry beautiful things. Surely there's someone who could step in. Seems terrible for her efforts to evaporate."

"That's a thought." Garvey's eyebrows twitched inward for a moment.

When Liz and Tim came over, Garvey brought up Harry's idea, and Liz liked it.

Harry had finally reached the little buffet by that time.

Pewter, refusing to be dislodged from under the table, knew, just knew, that some morsel would fall to her claws.

Tucker, not particularly hungry at this moment, wandered through the small gathering. She stopped by Garvey, Lila, and Liz, then moved back to Mrs. Murphy, who was seated on a bench along with the three Lutheran cats.

"Smelled that odor again," Tucker informed the four felines.

"What?" Mrs. Murphy didn't know which odor, since Tucker commented on so many.

"Remember when Liz and Terri came

to our kitchen? I thought I detected fear. Maybe it was underneath, but now I think this is something different. It's bitter. I smell it on Liz."

"Wonder what it means?" Lucy Fur rubbed her ear with her front paw.

"I don't know. I'm pretty good at identifying human scents. I've never smelled this. Fear has a kind of bitter, sharp tang, but this is really bitter." The dog, puzzled, sat down.

Aunt Tally, lingering over the water chestnuts wrapped in bacon, plucked one by the plastic-sword toothpick. "It's not a coincidence."

Big Mim and Inez also reached for the delicious little morsels.

"Are you listening to me?" The centenarian placed the toothpick on a tray used for that purpose.

"We are," Big Mim replied soothingly.

Liz came up, selecting some thin wedges of toast with asparagus spears and brie on top. "It's always good to see you all, even if the circumstances are sad."

"Thank you," Inez said with a nod.

Aunt Tally revved her engines again.

"Liz, it's no coincidence that Terri was found where Ralston Peavey was found. There has to be a connection. Maybe Terri was distantly related. Maybe she provoked the original killer."

"She's not related. Everybody knows everybody when it comes to that. There are no secrets." Big Mim sounded forceful.

"There's one now," Aunt Tally shot back.

"It could be possible." Liz sighed. "Anything is possible."

"Well, I am going to find out if it's the last thing I do."

"Oh, Miss Urquhart, don't say that." Liz's face showed concern.

"I'll outlive all of you." Aunt Tally thumped her cane on the floor, then moved off.

Big Mim, uncharacteristic for her, blurted out, "Sometimes I'm afraid she will, sometimes I'm afraid she won't."

35

On April 21, Tuesday, the weather remained mild. Harry was driving Inez down to Barracks Road at one in the afternoon after a morning of chores. Now that the weather cooperated, so much needed to be done—fields limed, seeds planted, grapevines checked, sunflowers planted after the soil was turned. The list made Harry dizzy. However, she couldn't allow Inez to drive by herself. The two cats and two dogs reposed in the back of the Volvo. Harry already wondered how she ever lived without the wagon.

"Are you sure you want to do this?"

Inez, resolute, said, "Yes. Tally said she'd drop by. A few of Terri's friends might come by, too. And Garvey's next door. I'm sure he'll help.

"All right." Harry changed the subject. "Did you sell your stocks? When was that—oh, April fifteenth. Black day when you mentioned selling them."

"I told Liz to sell them. Luckily, my taxes aren't too terrible. I need a new water heater at the house, so I might as well do it now."

"I don't know what's worse, renting or buying. Renting, you build no equity. Owning means it's one damned thing after another." She switched subjects again. "Inez, tell me how Cabinet officers get a slap on the wrist and can repay what they 'overlooked'? Had it been you or I, the IRS would have been down our throats."

"How it is, Harry, is how it has always been: politics as usual." Inez laughed. "I remember my father filling out his tax form. It was one sheet of paper." She touched the heavy links of the gold chain bracelet on her right wrist. "I used to care. Now I don't give a damn. One of the privileges of age. If the American public wants to be raped by Congress—

and, remember, Congress is the branch with the power to tax and therefore destroy—so be it."

"Leaves me in the lurch," Harry replied ruefully.

"Fight back." Inez's voice raised up.

"We need a leader."

"You need spine. Millions of you." Inez cleared her throat. "This will get me in a bad mood. It's good of Liz to come up; said it takes her only forty-five minutes from home. They're near the University of Richmond, so she hops on 64."

"Must have a lead foot."

"Well, yes. Makes me glad that Tally doesn't drive anymore. I swear her secret ambition was to be a Formula One driver. Scared the bejesus out of me many times. Maybe that's why my heart is so strong. I had consistent aerobic workouts just sitting still."

They both were laughing when Harry pulled into the north side of Barracks Road Shopping Center.

Harry knocked on the door of Terri's store.

Garvey, eager to help, opened it. "Come on in."

"What took you so long, Chickpea?" Aunt Tally barked.

"My fault. Not hers," Harry said.

Liz, who had been in the office, stepped out. "Thank you for coming. I've asked Tina Hotchkiss, a friend of mine, to run the store until I can figure something out. Rushing will only back-fire."

"When does she start?" Harry inquired.

"This Friday. So the store will be open for the weekend."

"What do you want us to do?" Inez asked.

"I came in last night and checked the inventory on Terri's computer. So we're up to date there. I think the only thing we need to do is dust and mop up a bit, and there were two deliveries today that we should go unpack."

"I can do that," Garvey volunteered.

Liz, taking charge again, said, "Inez and Tally, there should be an invoice slip inside those cartons. If Garvey gives them to you, you can check off the contents. If any items are damaged, there's bound to be some paper that tells us how to return the goods or make a claim. Okay?"

"Okay." Tally, with Doodles behind her, followed Garvey into the small storage room, which was quite neat.

Inez, Tucker, and Erno followed Doodles and Tally.

Mrs. Murphy and Pewter sat on the sales counter, enjoying watching Harry dust, while Liz, using a little Mop & Glo, brought up a shine on the floor.

"Aren't these beautiful?" Garvey had pulled out the shredded newsprint along with the plastic peanuts in one carton to reveal large outdoor ceramic pots in various subtle glazes.

Another carton contained smaller pots, mostly of a dark-blue glaze or a lighter green, with large round cork stoppers sealed with wax along the edges. Garvey set them on the floor, then Inez and Aunt Tally counted them. The jars, ranging from pint size to quart size, were heavy.

In the front part of the store, Liz chatted while mopping.

"Must have been a slap in the face when Terri's parents realized that, one, she'd made a will, and two, they weren't in it. I was overcome when I learned from her lawyer that she'd left the store to me. Twenty percent of the net profits must go to William Woods." Liz teared up. "I just can't believe it."

Harry, often a bit awkward when people became emotional, said sympathetically, "She knew you'd make a profit." Then she changed the subject. "You're doing a good job of mopping."

"Thank you."

As they chatted, Tucker, back in the storeroom, stuck her nose on one of the quart jars. Something in the wax drew her.

"What?" Erno was curious.

"I can just catch a hint of something. Not the wax. It's the smell I detected on Terri."

"Maybe we can break the jar." Erno's ears lifted up.

"I broke a big one once. Cost Mom a lot of money."

"Maybe my mom or Tally will open it."

"Good idea." Tucker whined, pushing the jar with her nose.

"That's enough," Inez said gently.

Erno started in, too. *"Come on, Mommy, open the jar."*

"Enough." Inez was still gentle.

"Hey, Mrs. Murphy and Pewter, come in here."

The cats responded.

"Better be good," Pewter said.

"Pat the jars with the cork sealed by wax," Tucker requested.

Mrs. Murphy and Pewter patted the jars. Pewter even unleashed her claws, sticking them in the cork.

"Would you look at those animals?" Aunt Tally was amused.

Inez, reading the invoice and checking off the jars, said, "According to this, there's nothing inside them."

Garvey picked one up. "Could be sand. You know, fill them so they won't break as readily."

"Liz," Inez called out.

Liz popped her head into the storage room.

"Do you know what's in these jars?"

Liz shook her head no, then said, "Let's finish up. Tina can open them on Friday. I need to get over to Merrill Lynch for a meeting."

"Okay."

Another half hour and all was done. The cardboard had been broken down and folded, and Harry had tied it up with twine, of which the store had plenty. She knew where the dump for businesses was, behind the center.

After everyone had left the store and she'd locked the door, Liz said with a shaky voice, "Thank you all. Thank you so much."

As Harry drove behind the supermarket with the cardboard, Tucker moaned, *"Erno was right. We should have broken one of those jars."*

"You'll get your chance. Mom will be down Friday to check on Tina. Her curiosity will get the better of her," Mrs. Murphy predicted.

36

On Friday, April 24, Harry and Inez marveled at the east side of the Blue Ridge, which was covered with white from the dogwoods, with flashes of pink in places. All it took was a few consistent days of fifty- to sixty-degree temperatures and the increasing light for the world to truly awaken. The apple groves gave off a wonderful fragrance, as they, too, were in bloom. The world shone white, pink, and magenta from the redbuds. Could there be anything as wondrous in the world as an Appalachian spring?

Harry organized her shopping trips to Charlottesville to one a week, but the last few weeks had upended that schedule. She was burning more gas than she wanted to.

The cats and dogs complained loudly when left in the wagon with the windows cracked open.

Inez walked into Terri's store, as Harry dashed into Thompson and Watson for a minute. After a quick visit with Garvey and a look at the wonderful colors of the Fred Perry polo shirts he had, she left. Good as all the other polo shirts were, they were all copies of the original Fred Perry. The French might argue that René Lacoste got there first, but no matter.

"Where's Inez?" Harry asked as she walked into the store. "Sorry. I'm Harry Haristeen. You must be Tina Hotchkiss."

The slender woman in her mid-forties smiled. "Inez is in the storage room."

Harry called out, "Inez, what are you doing in there?"

Inez came out. "I can't find the little pots—the pint-size and quart-size pots with the beautiful glazes. Tina says she never saw them."

"I have the large ones. Aren't they beautiful?"

"They certainly are," Inez agreed.

"Tina, these had some of the same glazes but were small; you could use them for flower arrangements. And they were heavy. Full of sand, I guess, with big round corks sealed with wax."

"Never saw them." Tina shrugged.

Harry changed the subject. "Much business?"

"Yes, I've been pleasantly surprised."

Harry asked, "May I?" as she reached for a small notepad on the counter.

"Of course."

She scribbled her home number and her cell. "If you need anything, I'm about a half hour away in Crozet—more when it's peak traffic time. But I can get here."

"Thank you so much. Garvey offered his services, too."

"Did you know Terri?" Inez inquired.

"Actually, I didn't. I know Liz from our days in Junior League. 'Course, we're too old now." She smiled. "But not that old. Anyway, I had an art gallery down on Cary Street in Richmond. Liz and Tim were regulars, and I got to know him a bit, too. I finally gave it up. I'd worked around the clock for ten years. That was enough, but now that I'm back here, I realize how much I miss retail. The challenge of it."

"I don't know how anyone does it." Harry smiled back at her. "We're sure glad you're here."

Once Harry was back in the wagon, up went the windows and she cranked the motor.

"Can you swing by BB&T?" Inez named a regional bank that had bought out many small local banks over the last ten years.

"Sure, Inez. Let me think a minute. Our best bet will be over by the university, by the giant clam. There's one down there on 250. Won't be too crowded."

"Isn't that clam the ugliest thing you've ever seen?" Inez mentioned the basketball arena.

"It is. If you want to make a list of hateful architecture, we could start with Madison Square Garden."

"Fortunately, I don't go to New York anymore, so I don't have to see it. To think that Penn Station, one of the most beautiful public buildings in America, was destroyed for that ugly mess."

"Was Penn Station a public building?" Harry wondered.

"You know, I'm not sure. Somewhere along the line it was owned by the railroad. Ah, here we are. That didn't take long."

"Want to go to the drive-in window?"

"No. I just want to check my account balance. Tally teases me. She says I'm obsessive about my money. I won't repeat what I tell her, but it rhymes with 'rich witch.'"

"Want me to come with you?"

"No, I'm fine. This way you can turn on the radio." Inez winked as she opened the door, grateful that the station wagon wasn't any lower to the ground.

Harry did turn on the radio, just in time to hear one of her favorite Kenny Chesney songs.

"When the sun goes down." Tucker and Erno sang along.

"Will you two shut up?" the cats instantly complained.

The dogs didn't.

Mrs. Murphy and Pewter hopped over onto the backseats.

"Send them to Nashville. I don't want

to hear it." Pewter's hackles rose to indicate further displeasure.

"Jealous, oh, so jealous," Tucker sang to the melody.

"That dog is mental. Seriously," Pewter intoned.

"Uh-oh." Harry looked at Inez's face as she exited the bank.

Inez got into the vehicle, fished into her purse, and plucked out her cell phone. "Something's not right. I told Liz to sell my Delta Petroleum stocks." She named a company in which she had a small number of stocks. "Seems she didn't do it, because the funds were to be transferred into my account. These things are so easy now. When I was young I had to go to my broker in person."

"Obviously, she forgot."

"Harry, if you're in financial services you don't forget things like that. Not if you want to stay in business."

She dialed the office.

The recording said, "You've reached Filmore Investment Services. This is Tim. I'm in Frankfurt this week, but Liz will get back to you. Thank you for calling."

"Rats." Inez next dialed Liz's cell.

Again, she heard a recording.

At the beep, Inez spoke in clear tone, "Liz, this is Inez. My funds aren't in my account at BB&T. Please call me. Also, the lovely little pots are not at the store. Thought you'd like to know. You can reach me on my cell. Good-bye." She pressed the end button. "I am furious. Flat-out furious." Then she dialed again. "Liz, sometimes my cell doesn't work near the mountains. It's eleven. I'll be at Tally's until two."

On the way to Rose Hill, Harry turned her eyes from the road for an instant. "Inez, why wouldn't the pots be there?"

"Dammed if I know."

"Because Liz came back and took them." Harry waited a beat, as Inez sharply turned her head. "Right. Who else has a key? Maybe Garvey. He's so close. It's possible Terri trusted him with a key. Worth a call."

"Call him. I'll call him. You're driving." Inez punched in the numbers. "Hello, is Garvey Watson there?" Pause. "Garvey, this is Inez. . . . Fine. How are you?" Pause. "Say, Garvey, you don't have a key to Terri's store, do you?" Another pause. "Just checking. Hope you sell a lot of good stuff this weekend." Pause. "You, too." She rested her chin in her palm.

The minute Harry and Inez got to Aunt Tally's, Inez used the landline to try Liz's cell again, getting the same result.

"Damn." She put down the phone, then explained everything to her old friend.

Harry told the two ladies, "I'm going over to Little Mim's. Said I'd help her put in her vegetable garden. If I dig in the dirt, it helps clean my mind. I'm a little jangled."

"Honey, we all are." Aunt Tally then suggested, "Want to leave your critters here? Just in case Tucker decides to dig."

"I'm not a terrier." Tucker was incensed.

"No, you're a bubble butt." Pewter giggled.

As Harry left, Inez counseled Aunt Tally, "Why don't you get the balance on your checking and savings accounts?"

"I didn't sell any stock," Aunt Tally responded. "Well, maybe I should."

"Does anyone have access to your account?"

"No. I keep my bank books in the drawer of my desk."

"What about Bev?" She named Aunt Tally's housekeeper, daughter of Big Mim's housekeeper. "Where is she, by the way?"

"Grocery shopping. Fridays are supermarket days. She goes out to the Harris Teeter on 250."

Doodles followed, along with Tucker and Erno, as the two women walked into the den.

Aunt Tally pulled out her bank books and dialed.

After giving her account number, she listened, then looked up at Inez. "I'm fine."

The two returned to the living room, where light poured in through the triple-sash windows.

"You know how I get about money. I'm probably being too fussy." Inez then said, "Let's take a walk. I'll feel better."

The two went out to enjoy the early

blooms in the garden, returning for a cup of tea in forty-five minutes. The air had invigorated them.

They had no sooner sat down, with Aunt Tally leaning her gold-headed cane against the table, than the three dogs barked.

"Intruder! Intruder!"

A knock on the door got them both up.

Inez reached the door first and opened it. "Liz."

"Come in," Aunt Tally said, as she rested her right hand on her cane.

"I am so sorry. I did sell the stock, but I forgot to transfer the money. I just called the office, but our secretary is out to lunch and Tim is in Frankfurt." Liz was wearing a lime-colored blazer, which she didn't take off.

"What's he doing there?" Inez's voice sounded cool.

"It's the finance capital of Germany. We do some business there. Tim calls it Mainhattan." She laughed at her joke—Frankfurt was on the Main River.

"That smell." Tucker sniffed Liz's ankles.

"Liz, what's going on? The little jars

aren't in Terri's shop. You were the only person who could have taken them. And you've certainly been in Charlottesville a lot."

Liz's face darkened. "I have business there, and Terri needed me."

"I'd like one of those jars." Aunt Tally acted as though nothing was amiss.

"I can get you one. Just let me clean them up."

"I don't mind doing that."

"Liz, I'm entertaining unhappy thoughts." Inez moved toward the living room.

The dogs followed, as did the cats, who promptly jumped up on the back of the sofa.

"Whatever about?" Liz's voice rose.

"Well." Inez didn't sit down, nor did Aunt Tally or Liz. "You were at the celebration in Fulton. After Mariah disappeared, we all assumed when the weather cleared you flew home to Richmond. Were you still in Missouri when Flo was killed? I wish I had called you when I got home but why would I? I never once thought to check up on you. You seemed so distressed when Flo was killed. And then these last days you've been with Terri. Now, I can't prove where you were at any given moment, but it's becoming peculiar. My bank account is also peculiar. You don't make mistakes like that, Liz. You don't sell stocks and forget to wire the money into an account."

"I was terribly upset by Terri's death. You've been overwrought at times in your life, Inez. People can make mistakes or be forgetful."

"I think not. Where's my money?"

Tucker edged over right behind Liz, sensing the younger woman tensing up.

"I'll get it put in before two-thirty." Liz's voice rose another notch.

"You did a lot of business with Flo and sometimes with Mariah. What's going on?"

"I know nothing." Liz's voice was angry now.

"It's occurring to me even as I stand here that if others could work a Ponzi scheme, so could you."

Liz stuttered, then rage took over. She shoved Inez, who fell backward, fortunately onto a chair.

Erno bit Liz's calf as Tucker bit her ankle. She shook the dogs off.

"Bite deeper," Tucker commanded the vizsla.

Liz pulled a snub-nosed .38 from inside her jacket. She hit Erno over the head, stunning him, then took aim at Tucker, who sank her fangs deep into Liz's ankle.

She struck down at the dog, missed. Tucker let go but circled to get her again.

Doodles, on Liz's left, grabbed her forearm. Liz clubbed the Gordon setter with the butt of her gun. As she was harried by Tucker she couldn't focus on Doodles, but she managed to hit the dog hard enough to stun the beautiful animal.

As Inez stood up, Aunt Tally moved toward Liz. The cats flew off the sofa to help Tucker, but Liz fired, hitting Inez in the leg. The old lady fell down on one knee.

"I'll kill you!" Aunt Tally screamed.

"You old bitch. You aren't killing anybody."

Liz aimed at Aunt Tally, who didn't flinch. Mrs. Murphy leapt straight at Liz, deflecting her aim just enough that the bullet lodged in the wall.

Inez, in pain but a fighter, crawled toward Liz.

Aunt Tally pulled her sword out of the cane. Before Liz could take another shot at Tally, Tucker sank her teeth deep into Liz's calf, throwing her off again.

The centenarian struck in that split second. Old but strong enough, she ran the sword right through Liz's throat.

Blood spurted straight out, showering Aunt Tally.

"Perfect!" Inez said through gritted teeth.

As another gusher shot forth, Liz's knees buckled, but she got off one more shot. The bullet narrowly missed Aunt Tally, who was preparing to ram the bloody sword through Liz's belly.

Liz dropped the gun and grabbed her throat, as blood flowed between her fingers. She died choking on her own blood.

Aunt Tally calmly placed her sword on the coffee table, then bent down to lift up Inez as best she could.

Doodles shook her head and took a

few wobbly steps to help Aunt Tally, but
had to sit back down to recover.

"Let me get you on the sofa."

"I'm all right, Blossom. Let me see to
my dog."

"You can't be all right with a bullet in
your leg."

"It's a long way from my heart." Inez
dragged her one leg as she reached
Erno, then knelt down. "Concussion.
Get me some ice. It will take the swelling
down."

Aunt Tally put the sword back in the
sheath and used her cane to hurry
toward the kitchen.

Tucker licked Erno. The cats sat by
the dog.

No one gave a thought to Liz or the
blood staining the carpet.

The front door burst open. Harry and
Little Mim, who'd heard the shots, ran
in, froze for a second, then flew to Inez.

Little Mim stared in horror at Liz. "My
God, what happened?"

"We'll explain later. Erno needs help."
Inez, in her element as a vet, took
charge.

Noticing the thin but steady stream of

blood from Inez's calf, Harry said, "Inez, you're hit."

"Came through the other side. It'll heal up fast enough. Help me with my dog, will you?"

"Is Liz dead?" Little Mim's teeth chattered from fear.

"If she isn't, I'll finish her off." Aunt Tally came back with a bag of ice in one hand, her cane in the other.

Harry hurried toward Tally, took the ice, and came back to Inez, who placed the ice on the dog. She lifted up Erno's eyelids, noticed some pupil movement. She checked his gums.

"Here, I can hold the ice," Harry volunteered.

"Well, don't just stand there as useless as tits on a boar hog. Call the sheriff!" Aunt Tally directed her shaken grand-niece.

Little Mim pulled out her cell phone and did just that.

Pewter walked over to sniff Liz. *"Notice the scratch on her right leg? I did that."*

"Mighty puss." Mrs. Murphy, half in jest, meant it.

"She must have been crazy." Having made the brief call, Little Mim knelt next to Harry by Erno.

"Greedy." Inez then turned again to her dog. "Erno, Erno, come on, sweet boy."

His eyelids fluttered and he opened his eyes.

Tucker licked the side of his face.

"What's that cold stuff on my head?" He staggered up, shook his head, and seemed none the worse for wear.

"Harry, go out and check her car, will you?" Aunt Tally, mind always clicking along, commanded.

Harry returned within minutes, carrying a jar. "They're in the trunk. Obviously the meeting with Merrill Lynch was a ruse, or if it wasn't, she came back for them."

"Let's just see what this is all about," Aunt Tally ordered. "Into the kitchen."

They walked into the kitchen. Inez limped in, keeping an eye on Erno.

Harry plucked a paring knife out of the drawer, ran it around the wax, then carefully lifted out the large cork.

"Oh, boy!"

The three other women peered in as

Harry plucked out bag after bag of cocaine.

"Smells awful." Little Mim crinkled up her nose.

"Sooner or later we'll figure this out." Inez leaned against the kitchen counter, because her calf stung.

"Let's get you to the ER," Harry said.

"Wait for the sheriff," Inez commanded.

Little Mim, not wanting to face the truth, said wishfully, "Could be sugar."

Sharply, Aunt Tally said, "Don't be a ninny. Who smuggles sugar in jars?"

A siren in the distance told them they wouldn't have to wait long.

37

When Tim Filmore disembarked from his transatlantic flight, the authorities were waiting for him. He remained silent until he was taken to the downtown Richmond police station, where he was informed that his wife was dead as well as the circumstances leading to her death. He collapsed, then spilled everything they needed to know. He and Liz had created a fairly sophisticated Ponzi scheme, which ran like a top for four years. Liz took special pride in fooling Flo Langston. Then again, when the profits roll in, folks tend not to be suspicious or ask too many questions.

As with so many things in life, a small event had begun the fall of the carefully constructed house of cards. Mariah

D'Angelo became nervous when a steady customer told her she had been contacted by a representative of Patek Philippe doing a survey. Mariah, in the business for years, had never heard of an elite chronography company doing satisfaction research. It was a grand watch, not a Frigidaire, was Mariah's response. Of course, in a sense, it was a Frigidaire.

Mariah sensed that Flo was behind this, but she didn't panic yet. Given that she had followed Flo's investments as best she could through gossip with Liz, she then checked her own investment portfolio against each stock's buy-and-sell amount with *The Wall Street Journal.* Every day, the stocks' highs and lows were recorded. She could see the exact time one of her stocks was traded.

She was the first to recognize that her portfolio had been falsified by Liz using accurate information. But when Mariah contacted the company, the trade had never been made. She found out that her bank, SunTrust, had no record of the purchase. Painstakingly, Mariah checked each of her trades without tipping off

Liz. This took two weeks. Still, she couldn't quite accept the horror of it.

Her first mistake was withdrawing money from the alumnae account. Her second was in loudly accusing Flo of setting her up for losses. The third and fatal mistake was confronting Liz after the classroom meeting. Flo had left. Mariah dogged Liz, who denied everything but recognized she had to silence Mariah.

Tim, who'd sold cocaine in college to pay his way, still had some of his old contacts left. They'd succeeded in their "profession," as had he. When the market crashed, he started selling again, but with much higher volume, to cover some of the payouts to clients. They shipped in cocaine through small boats that landed in the many coves of the Chesapeake Bay. He and Liz figured they could stay afloat for perhaps seven or eight months while they shifted their money to Costa Rica. Business was good—Tim repented of not sticking with it when he'd graduated from college.

Terri was paid five thousand dollars a month to allow the pots to be delivered

to her store. Although she was frightened of having drugs come through her
place, she was wildly happy with the
money. She didn't pay much attention
to Mariah's death, but when Flo died,
Terri began to get nervous. Ultimately,
she became unreliable, too scared, plus
she was taking too much toot herself.
What begins as a good thing—increased
concentration, feeling great—winds up
as a bad thing. This seems to be the
progress of any addiction.

As to Terri being laid out where
Ralston Peavey was killed, Liz thought it
would shunt people to the wrong track.
She'd heard stories about the old murder. Unsolved murders stay in people's
memories, providing curiosity. The Black
Dahlia murder certainly proved how potent a strange unsolved crime can be. It
was quite cunning of her to place Terri
on that road. She never figured on Inez
being so angry about her investments,
which she would have put into Inez's account as soon as she and Tim sold a
little of the cocaine. Selling cocaine in
a wealthy community is easy. Charlottesville was no exception. Tim's old

contacts had given him a few numbers. They in turn gave him more business through their friends, since the stuff was high quality.

Cooper relayed all this at the supper table at Harry's on Saturday night. Inez, released from the hospital, sat in the living room along with Aunt Tally, who was only too happy to get out of her house. She'd spent last night at Little Mim's. Liz's blood all over the living-room rug upset her, and she didn't want to stay there until the rug was carried out. She sent it to Rudy's Dry Cleaners with the instruction that, once cleaned, it was to be given to Goodwill. She couldn't bear to look at it, but it was too expensive to toss.

"I would have never figured it out," Harry admitted.

"We're not finance people. I guess you don't know something's wrong until you can't pay your bills," Fair replied quietly. He was horrified that Inez had been shot.

"You all know I don't know beans about money." Aunt Tally stroked Doodles's glossy head.

"We knew something was off with Liz. That nasty smell," Tucker said.

"It was sharp," Erno agreed.

"Is there any money left?" Inez asked Cooper.

"Tim had managed to get a lot of their money out of the country. It will take some time to get it back," the officer answered. "Of course, they blew a lot, too."

"How much?" Aunt Tally inquired.

"Tim says they took out twelve million. Whether one can believe him or not is another matter. He says—if you can stomach this—that Liz stole such a small amount compared to Madoff that he should receive a light sentence."

Fair drummed his fingers on the table. "If the Richmond police and whoever Tim hires for his lawyer think there's still a lot of money, some of them might be bought off. One doesn't like to consider such things, but Mafia dons can run their empires from prison. The corruption is within. Few people can resist a huge sum dangled under their noses. Why do you think drugs come into this country, and why do you think they don't get legalized? The nontaxable milk train

will dry up for a lot of people in law en-
forcement and government if drugs are
legalized. The louder a congressman
shouts about the evils of drugs, the
more you can bet he's on the take."

"Makes me sick." Cooper was an
honest person, an honest cop.

Harry put her feet up on the old coffee
table. "So there's probably more money
somewhere else."

"I expect so. He'll serve his time. After all, he didn't kill anyone—Liz did that.
When he's out, he'll go to the money
and live like a king." Cooper put her
drink down on the table.

"That's disgusting." Inez pursed her
lips.

"Doc, I'm afraid that's the world we
live in. Money sanctifies just about anything." Cooper sighed.

"So why do you remain a cop?" Aunt
Tally, forthright as always, asked.

"I don't rightly know. I keep hoping I
can do some good against the avalanche
of evil out there."

"Poor people." Erno came and rested
his head on Inez's knee.

"Their own fault, Erno. Don't waste a

minute feeling sorry for them." Pewter nonchalantly cleaned her tail, holding it in one paw.

Cooper asked Aunt Tally, "Were you scared?"

"No. In fact, I felt wonderful, energized. When Liz shot Inez, I suddenly felt forty again and I wanted to fight." She beamed.

"You weren't afraid to die?" Cooper put her own feet up on the coffee table. As a dear friend she could do that, but then, Harry didn't care much about the old furniture.

"Cooper, if you're afraid to die, you're afraid to live. You can't have one without the other." Aunt Tally smiled.

Inez giggled, then, as though Harry and Fair were her parents, asked, "Can Tally spend the night?"

Fair laughed and said, "Certainly, but I don't want you girls staying up all night talking."

They all laughed at this.

"No reading under the covers with flashlights," Harry added.

Aunt Tally roared with laughter, thrilled to be alive, thrilled that she won. Can there be a victory more clear than the death of an enemy?

Then she said wistfully, "We never will know about Ralston, will we?"

She was going to get her wish. It wasn't over yet.

38

On Monday, April 27, Inez received a call from the bank manager of the BB&T near Manakin–Sabot.

She hung up the phone and walked out to the barn, slowly, for the wounded leg still stung. She was using a cane. Aunt Tally had kidded her that if they held hands, they could prop themselves up with their canes and dance the can-can, kicking up their legs. Harry had just finished mucking all the stalls.

"Harry, my bank manager informs me there's little money. As my accounts are with Filmore Investments, God knows if I have any money at all there."

"Oh, Inez!"

"It's going to take time to find out." Inez took a deep breath. "I may have to sell the farm. It would be great if Blanca could buy it, but I don't think she and her husband can afford it. It's prime real estate. But as you know, the market is dreadful for expensive country properties."

"Inez, don't even think about it. Stay with us. Your farm is paid off, thank God. It will all sort out, and there's no point going back to Manakin–Sabot and being stressed. There's been enough of that." She checked the wall clock. "In an hour you'll be calling the president of William Woods and the other alumnae board members for a conference call on the next step for the board. Luckily, what happened has nothing to do with William Woods other than that Liz broke bad, Terri tagged along, and Mariah was a cheat. Harvard has produced far more rotters than that. Don't think about the money right now. Just concentrate on William Woods."

"I can't impose on you two like that, but thank you for offering. That's so very kind." Inez smiled.

"If you don't, Fair will be apoplectic. And you know, Inez, it's a joy to have you around." Harry took her by the hand and walked her into the tack room, seating her at the old school chair.

She then called Fair on his cell, explained everything, and handed the phone to Inez, who, upon listening, began to cry.

Harry put her hand on the old woman's shoulder. Although she couldn't hear it word for word, she knew the gist of what her husband was saying.

Inez handed Harry the phone. "Yes, honey?" Harry said to Fair.

"Thanks."

"Fair, I've learned to love her as much as you do."

This made Inez cry harder. Erno tried to lick her face.

Harry clicked off the phone. "I have a boon to ask, Inez."

Wiping away her tears, she said, "Anything."

"Ride with him when you can, and, Inez, please, please convince him he needs to take on a partner, or partners. He's going to have a heart attack before he's forty-five. Just like his father."

"I will. I most definitely will, and I don't know why he didn't do it long ago."

"He gets frustrated dealing with people. He's not a manager. If he takes on a partner, there will be some management in the beginning."

"Don't you worry about a thing. I can take care of management. And, Harry, I love you, too."

Harry leaned down and Inez kissed her on the cheek.

Tuesday at eleven, Harry and Fair drove Aunt Tally back to Rose Hill. Along with Inez, they walked her and Doodles into the house, just in case.

When Aunt Tally saw the new rug in her living room, she clapped her hands. "Beautiful. I know Mimsy did this."

As they left her, she was happily dialing her niece.

They stopped midway down the long drive because Garvey was driving in, the XFR gleaming.

"How are you?" Fair rolled down the window.

"Good. How's Tally?"

"She's a tough old bird." Fair smiled. "So's this one. Bullet passes through her leg and she wouldn't stay in the hospital for observation."

"You girls." Garvey smiled, then rolled on.

He had called ahead from his car, since he figured Aunt Tally might be wary of anyone knocking at her door.

She met him before he even put his hand on the large pineapple brass knocker, because Doodles told her someone was at the door.

"Come on in, Garvey. It's so good of you to call. I can offer tea. It's just about noon—a little sherry?"

"Sherry."

She poured him a fine old sherry, contenting herself with a stiff martini. They settled on the back patio, wearing light sweaters, for the temperature was only fifty-two degrees. The colors of the sunshine provided a beautiful background, as did the barn swallows, who had finally arrived. The birds darted everywhere, calling out as they did.

"Excellent sherry." He placed his glass

on the end table by his chair, where Aunt Tally had thoughtfully provided the decanter.

Her martini glass, jumbo-size, would hold her.

After some chitchat, Garvey turned to her. "Tally, I've come to grant your wish. Terri's death just reached down into my core."

Aunt Tally stared at him, uncomprehending. "What wish?"

"You always wanted to know who killed Ralston Peavey."

"You. You! Garvey, that can't be. You wouldn't hurt anyone."

"Let me explain." He drained his glass, raised the decanter. She waved a go-ahead, and he refilled it. "I was driving home. You might remember it was a foggy night, thick. I didn't see him until it was too late. He was standing in the middle of the road, taking a leak. He must have been loaded. I heard the sickening thump and then I didn't see him. I braked, backed up what I thought was a little bit so I could get out, but I ran over him again. I killed him. The only thing I could think to do was put my gloves on and zip him up. At least he'd be spared that indignity."

"Why didn't you go to the sheriff?"

"Ah, Tally, think. It was 1964. I was a young black man. There were already rumblings in the Deep South. I was scared. I thought I'd get railroaded."

"Dear God." She took a long draft herself. "I didn't think of that. White people don't, I guess. What did you do?"

"Daddy repaired all our tractors, so I woke him up and we worked all night, banging the big dent out of the fender. Put on touch-up paint and it looked pretty good. Then we pulled the tires off and Daddy buried them halfway up around Mama's garden. We painted the top of the tires white. He always had a pile of old tires; everybody did. He put them on my car."

"I see. Did anyone from the sheriff's department check your car?"

"They came by. Looked at Daddy's, looked at mine, those thin treads. That was that. Tally, I have carried this sin all my life. I liked Ralston. He could get loaded on the weekends, but it was a different time. Everybody drank. I guess

he thought the middle of the road was as good as the side of the road, if he even knew the difference."

"I'm sorry for both of you." She took another sip. "What now? I won't tell, if that's what you wish."

"I'll turn myself in tomorrow to the sheriff."

"Would you like me to be there?"

"Oh, Tally, thank you. Thank you, but, no, I have to do this myself. I've had since 1964 to think of this. I'm an old man. All passion spent, if you know what I mean, but I still carry guilt. It's time to be rid of it, confess, take my punishment."

"I see. I'll call Ralston's granddaughter after you've seen the sheriff. I admire you, Garvey. I truly do."

He nodded in thanks, finished his sherry, helped her carry the decanter and glasses back into the house.

As she opened the door for him to leave, she asked, "Does Lila know?"

"I'll tell her tonight."

•   •   •

Garvey did go to Sheriff Shaw. The sheriff allowed him to leave on his own recognizance. The papers that week blared with a headline as big as the one days earlier about Liz Filmore's attack on Aunt Tally and Inez.

The real miracle was that the case was hustled before the court, and Garvey hired an excellent lawyer from McGuire Woods. The Peavey family, all now in the Midwest, did not press charges.

The judge allowed that as so much time had passed, it was an accident, and Garvey had been an upstanding citizen all these decades, no jail time would be forthcoming. He did assign Garvey community service, which was right up his alley: Garvey was to mentor kids in the high school junior business program.

After it was all settled, Harry and Inez chatted in the barn, both thinking the judge's ruling was the only correct one.

In the loft, Mrs. Murphy and Pewter filled Simon in on all of it.

"No animal was run over with Ralston, was it?"

"No, Simon, just Ralston."

"Oh, I'm so glad. I'm still upset over Pharaoh's horses. I wish you'd never told me that story."

"I'll be sure not to tell any more Bible stories." Mrs. Murphy rubbed against the possum.

"Murphy, I don't know why you trouble him with that, anyway. You know the Great Spirit is a cat. A gray cat," Pewter announced with authority.

"Pewter," was all Mrs. Murphy could manage.

How I Came To Love William Woods University

Saddlebred shows, most of them taking place in the summer, bring together crowds of friendly people. I bring this up because it is not true of some of the other horse disciplines. Mercifully, I shall not name them and can only hope they repent their snottiness.

Mother knew her Thoroughbreds, Standardbreds, and some Saddlebreds (we saw the great Wing Commander together, when I was five, at his second show). I've sustained her interest in my life, which is how I met Gayle Lampe in 1984. I can't remember if it was at the Mercer County Fair or Shelbyville, two wonderful Kentucky shows. I remember it was hot and thunderstorms came up at night. They always do.

Gayle was and remains unforgettable. She mentioned William Woods University. I asked Larry Hodge and Joan Hamilton about the school. Larry and Joan own Kalarama Farm, which I explain to people is like old Calumet Farm was to Thoroughbreds, when Mrs. Gene Markey was at the helm. Kalarama's great rival, Callaway Hills Stable, was in the very county that is home to this university. I knew the late Mrs. Weldon in passing, for she lived in Charlottesville briefly. She, too, confirmed what Joan and Larry said, which is that WWU's graduates fill the Saddlebred world. They couldn't comment on dressage, hunt seat, or Western seat, which are also taught at WWU, as those are not their disciplines.

The next year I was at Shelbyville, a show I try to attend on the odd years; the even years I head to Saratoga, if I can. Sometimes the money is tight or there's too much to do on the farm. If you've never been to either Shelbyville or Saratoga, go.

Anyway, Joan and I were sitting in the bleachers at the warm-up ring, the night lights blazing, moths flying in squadrons, when from the west, heading toward us from the Ohio River, we heard thunder. Joan pointed out all those in the ring, the trainers, the assistant trainers, and many of the riders who had graduated from William Woods. Not only was the number impressive, but so was the skill.

Gayle and I would run into each other and exchange letters, and Joan and Larry would report on Gayle's progress and vice versa. You might say I was on the outermost ring of William Woods's Saturn.

Then out of the blue in the mid-nineties I received a letter inviting me to be the commencement speaker. I really adore giving commencement speeches, but this one was to stay with me forever, not because of anything I said but because of the magic of this community. First off, no one fussed over me in a sickening sweet way. Those whom I met were just who they are. How delightful.

The campus is pretty and I liked all the ducks who appear to have quite a high opinion of themselves whether walking down the middle of the road or swimming about.

Staying at Fairchild Alumni House felt like visiting your aunt. Gayle, knowing of my addiction, stocked the fridge with Classic Coke in cans, high test.

The faculty that I met were down-to-earth, yet very accomplished. The conversations, if only I could have chatted forever, were truly stimulating. My God, people who thought for themselves! Well, I was in the middle of Missouri; I should have expected that. It's not called the "Show Me" state for nothing.

Having dinner at the president's house, I felt as if I had known these people before I'd met them. Eddie—Jahnae's husband—played football for Ole Miss, and it's easy to see why they are together. The other guests—including a sophisticated couple from India—made this an evening I so often remember, realizing how lucky I was to be there. Then there was the standard poodle, who completed the gathering.

Before dinner the horses had welcomed me, too. I met the Saddlebreds, some Thoroughbreds, quarter horses, and I think some TB/QH crosses. So many of these horses were beautiful that I couldn't believe they had been donated. All of the horses' coats gleamed, all were happy. You can tell when a horse is not if you know horses. The barns were clean and smelled clean, too. And this was late spring.

Gayle indulged me while I checked feed—I'm always curious about that—and picked up a hoof here and there. A few William Woods horses evidenced a convivial streak so we got to know one another.

The graduation ceremony itself was dignified without being stiff. A moment I carry, a moment that seemed to me to distill this unusual institution, was when Melissa Smith and her Seeing Eye dog, Brinkley, came forward to receive her diploma. President Barnett gave Brinkley one, too, for he had attended all Miss Smith's classes. He carried his diploma off the stage.

And so I came to love this place far more than my own alma mater, Washington Square College at New York University. It's a great school and I studied under the incomparable Bluma Trell, who tried to teach me Greek. When she died on June 10, 1997, at age ninety-four, *The Economist* ran a full-page obituary on June 28, 1997.

But great as NYU is, it's no William Woods University. Apart from Professor Trell, I could have sunk like a stone. No one would have noticed or cared. Here in central Missouri exists an institution that puts the student first. I'm not saying they coddle the students nor do not demand intellectual rigor, but they actually care and the faculty knows those students. The president knows the students.

Lacking funds, most of my money goes toward abandoned animals, and my wardrobe proves it. I find the only gift I can give William Woods University is to introduce this institution to you. Perhaps you or one of your children will someday attend.

And there you have it, maybe more than you ever wanted to know. The cat will take credit for all of it but really setting this mystery in Fulton, Missouri, was my idea.

The one thing I can say though is I look older yet Dr. Barnett looks just like she did when I first met her. This is desperately unfair.

The Truth

She didn't think I'd read that. Thought she'd slide it right under my nose. It was my idea to set this mystery at William Woods University. All the horses, ducks, some dogs, and barn cats made me want to highlight a place where the animals mean as much to the community as the people.

Don't listen to her. She's an old windbag.

Sneaky Pie

About the Authors

RITA MAE BROWN is the bestselling author of several books. An Emmy-nominated screenwriter and poet, she lives in Afton, Virginia. Her website is www.rita-maebrown.com. She does not own a computer. God willing, she never will. Sometimes the website manager sends your queries. The safest way to reach her is in care of Bantam Books.

SNEAKY PIE BROWN, a tiger cat born somewhere in Albemarle County, Virginia, was discovered by Rita Mae Brown at her local SPCA. They have collaborated on eighteen Mrs. Murphy mysteries: *Wish You Were Here; Rest in Pieces; Murder at Monticello; Pay Dirt; Murder, She Meowed; Murder on the Prowl; Cat on the Scent; Pawing Through the Past; Claws and Effect; Catch as Cat Can; The Tail of the Tip-Off;*

Whisker of Evil; Cat's Eyewitness; Sour Puss; Puss 'n Cahoots; The Purrfect Murder; Santa Clawed; and *Cat of the Century,* in addition to *Sneaky Pie's Cookbook for Mystery Lovers.*